DECEPTIVE

AN ILLUSIVE NOVEL

DECEPTIVE

AN ILLUSIVE NOVEL

EMILY LLOYD-JONES

LITTLE, BROWN AND COMPANY
New York • Boston

Little, Brown and Company

Hachette Book Group
1290 Avenue of the Americas, New York, NY 10104
Visit our website at lb-teens.com

Little, Brown and Company is a division of Hachette Book Group, Inc. The Little, Brown name and logo are trademarks of Hachette Book Group, Inc.

The publisher is not responsible for websites (or their content) that are not owned by the publisher.

First Edition: July 2015

Library of Congress Cataloging-in-Publication Data

Lloyd-Jones, Emily, author.
    Deceptive : an Illusive novel / Emily Lloyd-Jones.—First edition.
        pages cm
    Summary: When immune Americans, those having acquired powers after receiving an experimental vaccine, begin to disappear in great numbers but seemingly at random, unrest spreads across the country and super-powered teens Ciere, Daniel, and Devon find themselves working together to find the truth.
    ISBN 978-0-316-25464-9 (hardcover)—ISBN 978-0-316-25460-1 (ebook)—ISBN 978-0-316-25462-5 (library edition ebook)   [1. Vaccines—Fiction.   2. Superheroes—Fiction.   3. Adventure and adventurers—Fiction.   4. Robbers and outlaws—Fiction.   5. Organized crime—Fiction.   6. Science fiction.]   I. Title.
    PZ7.L77877Dec 2015
    [Fic]—dc23

                                                                                    2014037473

10 9 8 7 6 5 4 3 2 1

RRD-C

Printed in the United States of America

PART ONE

The Cold War isn't thawing; it is burning with a deadly heat.

—President Richard M. Nixon, 1964

1

CIERE

Ciere Giba crouches beneath a sky threatening snowfall. Her heavy winter boots leave impressions in the slush and gravel, and her eyes are fixed on the highway. If a car were to pass, she'd be in danger of getting splattered with half-frozen water. But the only vehicle to drive by was a snowplow, and that was hours ago.

A gloved hand falls on Ciere's shoulder and she glances up. A teenage boy stands over her. He has smooth, coppery skin and his black hair is cut short. Dark eyes meet hers and quickly look away as he offers a small, encouraging smile.

Ciere reaches out and tugs on his leg. The young man obliges and kneels next to her.

"Still have all your toes?" Alan Fiacre asks, still smiling.

He doesn't look at her; all the while, his gaze roams over the nearby road.

Ciere grimaces. "Since I can't feel any of them, I have no idea."

He laughs. "If it makes you feel any better, the others look just as miserable. Conrad and Henry can only find one more hand warmer, and they're fighting over it."

"Really?" She peers over her shoulder, glancing at the four mobsters about twenty feet behind her. A woman, Jess, sits on the ground and feeds fresh rounds into a clip. Over her stands Pruitt, an eidos with curly black hair and scarred fingers. And sure enough, Conrad—that bear of a man—is holding out a fist toward Henry, a tall black woman who holds out her own hand with the index and middle fingers extended. Looks like Conrad wins.

"Wait," Ciere says, "are Henry and Conrad *rock-paper-scissoring* for the last hand warmer?" Somehow, she thought that mobsters would've had a more ruthless way of settling disputes.

When she looks at Alan, she sees that he's met her gaze. Alan has never been comfortable with eye contact, so it sends a shock through her. "What?" she says softly. He opens his mouth, but a loud crackle of static cuts him off. The screech and whirr of Conrad's two-way radio blaring to life.

"This is falcon one," a male voice says. "Repeat, this is falcon one. The target has been sighted. Over."

Conrad lifts the radio to his mouth. His words are heavy with a German accent. "This is falcon two," he says. "Message received. We'll get back to you once the job is complete." He clicks the radio off and stows it in his jacket pocket. He rubs gloved hands together. "All right, people. Showtime."

At once, the group is a flurry of action. Pruitt picks up one side of a chain laced with metal spikes and hefts it to the other side of the highway. Jess helps him, stretching out the line so it lies evenly across both lanes. Guns are checked and rechecked; extra magazines are passed between hands; soft, eager murmurs replace the annoyed mutterings. Sledgehammers and crowbars are hefted into gloved hands.

Conrad moves next to Ciere. Even when she stands, he still towers over her. "You ready, Kitty?" It's an old nickname a newspaper once gave her—the Kitty Burglar. If Conrad remembers her real name, he's never bothered to use it.

Ciere closes her eyes and inhales a long breath. A few months ago, she would've balked at the illusion requested of her.

"Don't let anyone see what you are, understand?"

The words come back to her, a whisper on the icy winds, but they don't inspire fear or caution. Rather, they spark life into her, and when she reopens her eyes, there is no hesitation. She stretches out a hand, a useless but familiar gesture, and it centers her.

Months ago, Ciere would have cast her illusion outward, like throwing a sheet over a table. It would cover everything, but the pain was debilitating. Now, after months of careful practice, Ciere reaches out and imagines the world the way she wants it. She visualizes the frozen white fields, the twist in the road around a clump of trees—the trees that make a perfect place to stash their getaway van—and the dirt-streaked snow covering the pavement. She gently pulls at the landscape, smudging over the lines of the spiked chain and the armed mobsters. The illusion settles into place, and anyone who walks into the scene will be affected by it—all they'll see are a few hazy flickers, like heat waves rippling across the snow.

It's a good illusion, and Ciere lets herself feel a moment of satisfaction. With a crime family as infamous as the Alberanis, one can never be too careful.

"I hate this part," comes Jess's voice somewhere to her left. "If any of you step on my feet, I'll choke you with your own scarf."

Henry laughs.

They hear it before they see it—a truck, huge and lumbering, taking up most of the road. The truck is painted white and has a covered bed—better to hide its cargo. Ciere sucks in a sharp breath. This is it. She takes hold over her illusion, pulling its edges around the truck. If its occupants found themselves invisible, she'd blow this operation in a matter of seconds.

Someone touches her arm. She doesn't have to see him to know it's Alan. "Steady," he whispers.

She finds his hand and squeezes tight.

"Three," Conrad says softly. The truck moves steadily toward them, leaving dark exhaust in its wake. "Two."

Alan's fingers tighten around hers.

"One," says Conrad's voice. The truck slows, as if its driver has seen something, but it's too late. The tires roll over the strip of spikes.

The sound is horrendous. A scream of tires being rent apart, metal grating on concrete, and a shriek of brakes. Sparks dance along the pavement and the truck tips to one side. It grinds to a smoky, screeching halt.

The mobsters are already moving. Ciere can't see them, but she hears the crunch of feet on gravel and sees the snow stirring around invisible legs. Someone swings an invisible sledgehammer at the back of the truck. A loud thud and the door wrenches free. It's yanked open and snow flutters into the air as invisible bodies climb up and into the truck bed. Ciere doesn't have to walk over to know what they'll find inside: crates and crates of automatic rifles.

The plan relies on invisibility and speed. It's worked before: disable the truck, open the doors, pull out the dazed driver and passenger, tie them up, locate and display the guns, and then call the police. The law takes care of the gunrunners, while Ciere and the crew make a quick getaway. It's quick, clean, and bloodless—exactly how the Gyr Syndicate likes to operate.

But this time, one of the gunrunners reacts with terrifying speed.

Ciere sees it in flashes. A dark object appears in the driver's hand. The windshield suddenly turns white as cracks begin to spider through the glass. Something small and powerful pierces her jacket and a curious numbness creeps down her left arm.

She finally recognizes the object in the driver's hand—a gun. *He must be carrying some of the cargo in the front*, Ciere thinks. It's her last coherent thought.

The world tilts sideways as she takes an involuntary step. Her foot hits a patch of ice and she begins sliding into a ditch. Gravel and snow cave beneath her and she stumbles, trying to stay upright and failing.

She instinctively reaches out to catch herself as she falls. Her palm hits the ground first and pain spikes up her arm, into her chest. It whites out her vision.

A hand clamps down on her left shoulder, tight enough to bring her back to the moment. Alan appears before her, his eyes bright with panic. "Ciere?"

That's when she realizes. She can *see* him.

They're visible. They're all visible.

"GIBA!" Conrad's roar echoes across the frozen landscape.

So he does know my name, she thinks, and then reality sets in.

An unfamiliar male voice begins screaming. More shots ring out and suddenly Alan is pushing her back across the frozen landscape, gripping her right arm, his body a solid barrier between her and the truck. "Put down the gun!" Henry shouts, and Ciere imagines a confrontation she can't see—the mobsters surrounding the truck, the truck's two occupants overwhelmed—

Then she hears it. The rip-roar of automatic weapons fire.

"GIBA!" Conrad yells again, and Ciere shoves Alan away, stepping free of him. The scene before her unfolds; her adrenaline-sharp sight makes it almost seem like slow motion.

Jess is on the ground, her arm wrapped around her chest. The snow beneath her is stained red.

Pruitt has thrown himself to the ground in front of Jess, bringing his gun around and firing wildly at the two Alberani gunrunners. The passenger-side window shatters, but it's all the damage Pruitt manages to do before he runs out of shots.

Ciere's gaze snaps to the truck. One of the gunrunners has taken refuge behind the truck bed. The other crouches near the front fender, a submachine gun tucked into his shoulder.

He has pale blond hair—almost white—and there's a calm to his features.

"GET JESS OUT OF HERE!" Conrad bellows. His shots are more methodical than Pruitt's panic fire. Conrad pulls the trigger once, twice, a third time, and then the gun clicks empty. He fumbles for a fresh clip, but Ciere can see it'll take too long.

"No," she whispers, and reaches out with her immunity.

Her touch is shakier than before. It's not quite right; there's blurring around the edges. But one moment, Conrad and the others are there—and then they aren't.

The pale-haired man rises from his crouch, plugs a fresh clip into the gun, raises it to his shoulder, and sweeps a wide arc. The rounds rip into the snow, kicking up a sheet of brown and white, pushing at the edges of Ciere's illusion.

A hand fumbles at her back, fingers clamping around her good arm. She can't see his expression, but Alan's voice is tight with fear. "Hurry up." They nearly stumble into the ditch and then they're running, aiming for the trees, blinded by adrenaline and snow. Her body is taut with fear, and she keeps expecting to feel a bullet rip into her. Her arm throbs in time with her racing heart.

Together, she and Alan crash through the underbrush. The van rests between two frozen trees, its white paint camouflaging it almost as well as an illusion.

Pain claws up her neck, into the back of her skull, the sharp throb a reminder that her illusion is still up. Releasing it is like letting go of clenched fists—immediate relief, followed by a hollow ache.

Alan flickers into sight. His hat is gone and his dark hair is damp with melting snow and sweat. He stares at something behind Ciere's back and she whirls, sees Conrad and the others rushing toward them. Jess is thrown over Conrad's shoulder in a fireman's carry. He eases her to the ground and the group converges on her.

Alan slides the van's door open, his other hand still gripping Ciere's jacket. He gently nudges her until she sits on the edge of the van. Her left arm feels numb, like when Daniel once snapped a rubber band across her skin. Only when she looks down does she see the bloody mess of her jacket sleeve.

This whole situation feels wrong, like a train that's jumped its tracks. Every other assignment went smoothly, effortlessly. Cleanly. This time, it's like that pale-haired man *knew*. She saw it in his face, certainty and calm. He'd known something was wrong before they sprang the trap.

A fist closes around her jacket and suddenly she's being shaken so hard, her back molars click together. Pruitt looms over her.

"What the fuck were you doing?" Pruitt says, and he drags

her away from the van. She stumbles, tries to step back, but he doesn't let go.

"Get off!" she snaps, her own hand closing around his wrist. For a second, they're locked together.

She's about to reach out with her immunity, ready to blind Pruitt, but Alan's fist collides with his jaw. Pruitt looks more startled than anything else, and his fingers yank free of Ciere's jacket. She takes two steps back and Alan slips into that open space.

"Back off," Alan snarls. For the first time, he really looks like the bodyguard he claims to be.

Pruitt's face hardens. "Jess is dead!"

"It wasn't Ciere's fault," says Alan.

"Her illusion fell and they saw us coming." Pruitt takes another step forward, trying to edge around Alan. "They saw us coming—that's how they managed to shoot Jess—" His arm draws back, his fingers clenching into a fist.

Conrad is the one to catch Pruitt's fist in midair.

"Don't do this," he says.

Pruitt shakes him off and Conrad lets him. "She—she—"

"Don't make me drop you," Conrad says, and there's nothing to his voice. No anger. Just a statement.

It is probably the only thing Conrad could have said to calm Pruitt. His mouth pulls tight and he turns away, half jogging back to the van. Conrad faces Alan and Ciere.

"Henry, help me get Jess into the back," he says heavily. "Pruitt, passenger seat. Kids in the back. Henry, sit between them—one fatality is enough for this mission."

"And what about the mission?" says Pruitt, still fuming.

Henry calls from the other side of the van. "I've already alerted the cops—they'll be here soon. And that truck isn't going anywhere."

Ciere allows Alan to lead her into the van. She liked Jess— the woman was friendly, for a mobster. And now she's dead, her blood staining the van's carpeted interior. Her body is covered by someone's jacket—the only dignity they can offer. Ciere scoots away until her back is pressed to one side of the van; she doesn't want to see.

She barely notices when Alan pulls at her sleeve. "Need to look," he's muttering, and it's probably not the first time he's said it. Ciere shrugs her shoulder, winces, and allows him to tug the fabric away. Alan's fingers are quick and surprisingly graceful; he gently pulls at the sodden material of her shirt until it comes free of the wound. Ciere forces herself to look.

The wound isn't bad; it's a graze. The bullet went through her jacket sleeve and carved a divot in her biceps. Blood drips down her arm and she finds herself fascinated with the bright color. Wordlessly, Alan presses a fresh bandage to the wound. He leans in, as if to steady her, and his voice is quiet in her ear. "We should leave."

Surprised, Ciere almost pulls away. "What?" She keeps her voice low.

"They'll blame you for Jess's death," says Alan. "Pruitt already does. We should leave now."

"We can't leave," Ciere says, running her fingers over the bracelet she wears. It's a silver bangle, tight around the bones of her wrist, its shiny exterior hiding the GPS tracker within. "Our time with the Syndicate isn't up yet. They'd find us. Or sic the feds on us." She doesn't continue with that train of thought: the feds would be even more deadly than the mobsters.

"So we're running from people who want us dead," Alan says, "by hiding with people who also want us dead."

Ciere lets her head fall back and closes her eyes. The ache of the wound settles into her bones. "Just another Monday."

2

CIERE

Five months ago, three criminals walked into a hotel.

There was one middle-aged man, with guns hidden under a custom-made suit jacket; one teenage girl who could conjure illusions with a mere thought; and one teenage boy who could remember things better off forgotten.

The clerk who checked them in was a young woman, probably working the graveyard shift in between college classes. When she viewed the middle-aged man's ID tags, her eyes went wide.

"Mr. Guntram," said the hotel clerk, looking both starry-eyed and nervous. "We thank you for your patronage." She handed over a set of keycards with trembling fingers and a flush across her cheeks.

Brandt Guntram gave her a polite smile.

"Come," he said to the two teenagers as he headed toward the elevators, and they hurried after him.

They got out of the elevator on the eighth floor. "I'm in the next room," said Guntram, holding out a room key. "If you need me, there's a door between our two rooms. Feel free to wander, but stay in the hotel, please."

Ciere accepted the keycard. "What," she said, not bothering to hide her sarcasm, "did you buy out this hotel or something?"

Guntram's mouth twitched. "Or something."

It was a mob hotel. Ciere knew that the moment they stepped inside. There were distinct signs, if one knew what to look for. Like the fact that every security camera's lights were turned off. Or the men who walked through the halls had barely hidden bulges around their shoulders and thighs. Or that everyone seemed wide-awake at midnight.

"The Gyr Syndicate helped the hotel owner out of a bad situation," Guntram said, untroubled by Ciere's flat stare. "His daughter is an eludere. The Alberanis tried to recruit her. We...discouraged them."

"And now they're letting you use this hotel as a base of operations," said Alan.

"I have to meet with some of my associates," said Guntram. "This is as good a place as any."

Ciere unlocked the hotel door and Alan went inside first,

flicking on a lamp. The room was clean and fresh, with two double beds and a view of the Manhattan skyline.

Alan dropped his backpack onto the bed nearer the door. "Only one chair," he murmured. He frowned slightly, then snatched up the chair and carried it to the hallway door.

"What are you doing?" said Ciere.

Alan wedged the chair beneath the doorknob. "Standard security. There are two doors—one to the hallway and one to Guntram's room. I'd rather have a chair for each, but since we only have the one…" He shrugged. "I suppose we just have to trust Guntram more than we trust the outside world."

Ciere stared at him. She didn't really know him—they'd been friends less than a week. In fact, she wasn't even sure they were friends. More like allies thrown together by chance.

"You don't have to do that," Ciere said. "Pretend to be my bodyguard." Calling him her bodyguard was a lie she'd come up with when she had no other way to explain his presence.

He shrugged. "How else would we explain why I'm here? It's not like we can tell them who I am."

True.

Alan was the last Fiacre—a remnant of the family that created the Praevenir vaccine. To conceal his identity, Alan spent most of his life on the run. Even now he used falsified ID tags—ones that Ciere's crew leader, Kit Copperfield, slipped into her hand as she was leaving the house that morning. The tags declared Alan to be "Mr. Alan Ashbottom." Ciere could just imagine Kit smirking as he decided on that alias.

Alan had spent most of his life in hiding. And not just because of his infamous family.

Alan was an eidos. He could remember anything and everything—including the Praevenir formula. The formula that people had killed and died for. The formula everyone thought was lost.

Everyone but Ciere and Alan.

Ciere sat on the other bed. It felt unreal to be in the same room with someone who shouldn't exist, with a mobster one door over. She still half expected to be at home in Philadelphia, to wake up in her own bed, to find Kit making breakfast in the morning. Some part of her couldn't grasp that her old life was gone and her new life had started— among a crime syndicate with a boy she barely knew.

Who was currently wedging a coffee table against Guntram's door.

"Would it disturb your security measures if I went downstairs? I saw a coffeemaker in the lobby." She wasn't exactly hungry, but she had a few of Kit's home-baked scones. They were all she had left of home. Eating them, drinking something hot, it might make her feel human again.

Alan's eyes darted to hers before settling somewhere on her shoulder. "Want me to come with you?"

She shook her head and grabbed the hotel keycard. She shifted the chair away from the door and stepped into the hallway. "I'll be right back."

The hallway itself wasn't remarkable—industrial carpet, a few framed pictures along the wall, and the soft shuffle of voices nearby. For a moment, Ciere simply stood there and breathed. Being a thief wasn't exactly a relaxing lifestyle, and she should have felt grateful for this moment of relaxation. She wasn't on the run, nobody wanted to kill her, and she was safe.

Safe among professional killers.

She released a shivery little breath, trying to shake off her unease.

Drinks, she repeated to herself, *focus on one task at a time.* She turned to the right, angling herself toward the elevators, and that's when she saw him.

A man sat in the hallway. Back to one wall, legs spread out before him, eyes unfocused—at first Ciere thought it was some drunk hotel patron unable to locate his own room. She started to turn around, when recognition froze her in place.

She knew this man. *She knew him.*

Kit Copperfield.

He looked just like he had earlier that day—thirty-something, with shoulder-length red hair and a waistcoat.

But his glassy eyes stared at nothing. Blood flecked his pale skin and Ciere suddenly realized that the carpet was soggy. Even in the dim light, she could see the huge crimson stain spreading out around her mentor.

She blinked hard several times, saw the scene in flashes. Splashes of red against bloodless skin, lips half-parted, fingers gone still. Ciere stared at the closest thing she had to a parent, gutted and splayed out like roadkill.

It was a nightmare.

It had to be a nightmare.

"Kit?" she said in a voice that sounded years too young. She sank to her knees beside him. *He's supposed to be in Philadelphia, supposed to be baking things and plotting out his next job—not here, not bleeding and pale and—*

Her trembling fingers reached for his collar, but just before she touched him, a flicker ran over his body. She recoiled when she felt it. A familiar vibration. A buzzing pressure that she'd never felt outside her own skull.

"No," she said, and squeezed her fists. Her immunity reached out—a tentative touch rather than a definitive shove. She lengthened her own shadow, used it to reach for Kit.

Her illusion encountered resistance. A shock of pain pulled through her temples and she pushed through it. Her illusion pressed against Kit, and there was a jolt like touching an open circuit.

The illusion shattered.

Kit disappeared. The carpet became white again. And Guntram lounged against the wall, his arms folded comfortably over his chest. He watched her, his expression remote.

Ciere swallowed, trying to force her thudding heart to slow. "You," she sputtered, her throat thick with shock. "You— you made me see—" She could still see Kit when she blinked.

Then she realized what she'd said and couldn't say another word. Because the only people who could conjure images were like her, and that meant—*that meant*—

"Took you too long to push back my illusion," said Guntram evenly. "And there's your first lesson working for the Gyr Syndicate: never let your emotions prevent you from recognizing reality."

3

DEVON

Devon Lyre stands in a frozen courtyard and listens to a fire alarm that he, for once, didn't pull.

"I hate drill days," moans a girl to Devon's left. She has her hands shoved under her armpits for warmth. "Seriously, who decided to schedule one in November?"

"Sadistic principals," says a guy to his right, earning a nasty look from one of their teachers. But even the staff looks pink-cheeked and miserable.

This is the problem with going to an elite boarding school. Angelien Prep actually cares whether its students live through an emergency... if only so their parents can keep paying the tuition.

The courtyard is usually a nice place to hang out; girls tend to sunbathe near a fountain, and a statue of some Greek god stands proudly near a pond. But now that pond is frozen, and the perfectly clipped grass is buried beneath a foot of snow.

This particular day consists of a fire drill (students shivering in the cold and pressing together in bundled masses), an earthquake drill (everyone trying to fit under their desks and then freezing in the courtyard), and the tsunami drill.

("No, students, there's no use running—you're all probably going to die in this case."

"We should be so lucky," Devon mutters, and someone laughs.)

When Devon and his classmates return to their classroom to thaw out, it's time for the last emergency procedure: instructions on how to protect yourself against adverse effects. The teacher sets down a stack of glossy government-sanctioned brochures. She picks one up, clears her throat, and begins to read to the class.

"'Nearly eighteen years ago,'" says the teacher, "'a new strain of meningitis caused a global pandemic. An effective vaccine was created by scientist Brenton Fiacre, but it was improperly tested prior to global distribution. The vaccine called Praevenir caused unexpected side effects in approximately 0.003 percent of its recipients.'"

Devon sits at his desk, chin cradled in one hand, eyelids drooping. He lets the words slip past him, catching only part of the lecture. He can recite it from memory, but that's not new. He can recite anything from memory—because that's what it means to be one of that 0.003 percent.

"'...The following symptoms—precognition, body manipulation, perfect recall—'"

Cheers, Devon thinks.

"'—levitation, telepathy, the ability to induce hallucinations—'"

That's what the government calls illusions. *Hallucinations.* Devon silently scoffs at the idea. Hallucinations make the process sound vague, blurry, and random. He knows firsthand what illusions can do.

"'—and mind control.'" The professor pauses a moment, letting the class absorb her words. Her eyes flick back to the brochure.

"'The names for adverse affects, in respective order from most to least common, are *eludere, dauthus, eidos, levitas, mentalist, illusionist,* and *dominus.* It's important to understand these dangers because we are currently in a state of tension with East Asia—'"

Come off it, Devon thinks angrily. *Just say that China hates us.*

"'—America has many territories to protect—'"

America invaded and is currently holding Korea hostage, Devon mentally corrects.

"'—other countries have chosen to ignore the global dangers—'"

The United Nations splintered. Japan closed its borders while the European Union told America to piss off.

"'Preparation and education are the best defense against adverse effects.'" The teacher clears her throat. "'In a situation involving adverse-effect terrorism, remember the three Cs. Cover. Conceal. Close. If you are confronted by someone you suspect has adverse effects, it is vital you do these three things. First, cover any exposed skin. Some effects only take hold when there is contact between bare skin—'"

Devon begins fidgeting with his pen, drawing its tip across his desk.

"'The second C is for concealment. Hide yourself, either in a crowd or a safe location. But do not run away from someone with adverse effects. Running draws attention. The third C is for close—close your eyes. Some adverse effects require eye contact.

"'Finally, it is your duty as citizens to remain observant and wary. Any and all suspicious behavior that you observe must be reported to the proper authorities.'" The teacher closes the brochure, picks up the stack on her desk, and distributes them to her pupils.

As he takes the leaflet, Devon's eyes sweep over the words.

Cover your vulnerabilities, conceal yourself in a crowd, and don't make eye contact.

It's how herd animals deal with predators.

When class is over, one of Devon's sort-of friends drifts over to him. "You coming to study group tonight?" she asks.

The thought of sitting down and trying to study like his classmates makes him feel ill. He pulls on a smirk. He's already earned his bad-boy reputation, so his words shouldn't come as a surprise. "I think I'm going to get a keg. Tell anyone who wants to party tonight that my dorm is the place to be."

She blinks at him. "Devon, if you get caught again with alcohol on campus—"

He waves off her concern. "What's the worst that could happen?"

For the second time in his life, Devon wakes up under a bed.

It's not his dorm bed—not that flimsy bunk—but a queen-size mattress. Beside his ear are a few dust bunnies that the maid must have missed.

He makes a soft noise of protest and presses his thumb into the bridge of his nose. His head feels hollow, like his brain has shriveled up. His skin is too tight and a dull ache sets up behind his eyes. Groaning, he wriggles out from under the bed. He begins to roll over, but there's a pair of leather-clad feet a few centimeters from his nose.

Devon's father stares down at him, wearing an appalled expression.

Devon blinks. "As my charming American classmates would say, 'WTF, dude?'"

"Former classmates." Mr. Lyre reaches down and hauls Devon upright.

Devon's bedroom has seen better days. There are beer bottles cluttered on nearly every surface. It feels odd being back here, like pulling on a shirt that clings a little too tightly. Devon doesn't spend much time at home, and when he stares into his father's glowering face, he remembers why.

"You will shower," Mr. Lyre says, iron in his voice. "You will come downstairs. And then we're going to look at some nice pamphlets about military academies."

Devon faces his father down without flinching. "Sure we will."

Mr. Lyre has always been intimidating. Maybe it's the man's sheer size—he's not exactly fat, but he takes up a lot of space. His voice is the deep rumble of a tank engine.

"We will," Mr. Lyre says quietly, "or else you're leaving this house and you won't come back."

Devon opens his mouth—probably to say something stupid like, *Good, that's what I've been trying to do for the last eighteen years*—but a knock at his bedroom door cuts him off.

A twentysomething girl stands frozen in the doorway. Darla Lyre is thin in the extreme, with sharp cheekbones and hair she must have spent hours straightening. "There's a man at the door. Says he's here for Devon." Unlike their father, both she and Devon were raised in London and their speech still carries the accent.

Mr. Lyre lumbers to the door. "I'll talk to him. Devon, I wasn't kidding about the shower." The sounds of his footsteps are heavy on the stairs and Devon finds himself staring at the floor rather than looking at Darla.

A moment of awkward silence stretches out between them. Devon feels even grubbier when standing next to his polished, Ivy League sister. When she speaks, the softness in her voice throws him.

"Didn't you like it there?" she says. "At school—were you miserable?"

"What? No," Devon says.

"Did the other students bully you?" she says. Her fingers tangle together, twisting and untwisting.

"No."

She takes another step forward. "Then why, Devon? Why would you pull this? Again."

He can't tell her the truth. Well, actually he could, but she wouldn't understand. Darla Lyre is normal.

"You don't belong with us." Ciere's voice hits him, and the memory makes him want to close his eyes, to crawl back under the bed and go to sleep amid the dust bunnies. He remembers every inflection in her voice, the way her eyes narrowed. It strikes him how true it is. He doesn't feel like he belongs anywhere.

"You really should shower," says Darla, angling herself toward the door. She's already trying to slip out, trying to remove herself from the conflict.

After he's showered and dressed, he ventures downstairs. He's almost ready to face whatever awaits him—he just needs one more thing. As usual, there's a pitcher of freshly squeezed orange juice on the counter in the kitchen. Devon pours himself a glass before ducking and reaching into the cupboard under the sink.

Mr. Lyre and Darla have no reason to look under here. Neither of them cleans, and the maid can be bought off. Tucked away in a bucket of cleaning supplies is a bottle of tequila. Devon uncaps it, pours a generous amount into the orange juice, and slips the bottle back into its hiding spot. He takes a sip of the spiked juice and a shudder of relief runs down his spine.

So far alcohol is the only sure way he's found to silence unwanted thoughts.

As far as Devon is concerned, drinking isn't optional. It's the only way he can be *bloody normal.*

His father's booming voice echoes through the hall, and a moment later, there's the sound of a stranger replying. Devon squares his shoulders. With a drink in hand, he's ready for anything.

Mr. Lyre stands in the dining room, talking to a young man in a suit.

The first thing Devon notices is how thin the stranger is—standing next to Mr. Lyre's bulk, he appears particularly reedy. He's maybe in his mid-twenties; his wire-rimmed glasses are pushed high on his nose, and he looks as if he hasn't slept in a day or two.

He looks like a fed.

"It's a pleasure to meet you in person, Mr. Lyre," he says.

"Devon, this is Mr. Macourek," Mr. Lyre says. "He would like to talk to you."

Mister. Not Agent.

"Alone, if you don't mind." Macourek gives Devon a welcoming smile.

Mr. Lyre flexes one hand—makes a fist and then relaxes it. "Are you sure that's necessary?"

"He's not in any trouble," says Macourek. Despite his youth, he isn't intimidated by Mr. Lyre's size or harsh voice. Either he's used to an air of authority or he's never been in a lot of fights, Devon thinks, eyeing Macourek's relaxed posture.

Mr. Lyre lets another moment drag past, his heavy gaze settled on Macourek. There's no threat in his face or posture, but he towers over the other man. "I'll be in my office," he says curtly, angling his gaze away from the fed and to Devon. His eyes narrow. "Okay?"

Devon forces a grin. "Fine."

Mr. Lyre nods once, and maybe it's reluctance that slows his steps into his office before he quietly shuts the door.

Devon eases into one of the dining room chairs. Macourek follows his lead, setting a briefcase on the table.

"Like your father said, I'm Aron Macourek," he says, opening his briefcase. "I work for the Affiliation of Intelligence. It's one of the subdivisions in Homeland Security."

Devon looks at him blankly.

"Homeland Security is huge," Macourek explains. "Even more so in recent years—it's been expanded due to increasing international tensions. Affiliation is a smaller division that analyzes data."

"Fascinating," Devon says, managing to keep a straight face. "What does this have to do with me?"

Macourek says, "My department has a partnership program with your school. Every semester we recruit an intern."

"I'm no longer a student at Angelien," says Devon.

"Yes, I heard about that. You were expelled last week for..." Macourek checks something on his phone. "Illegal possession of alcohol, distribution of that alcohol to minors, public lewdness, and"—his mouth stiffens like he's trying not to smile—"defacing an Angelien flag."

"I thought it would make a fantastic kilt." Devon raises his glass.

Macourek sets his phone down and knits his fingers. "Mr. Lyre, I'd like to offer you that internship."

Devon chokes and the tequila sets fire to the back of his throat.

"The internship is yours if you want it." Macourek draws a sheet of paper out of his briefcase and slides it over to Devon. "All you need to do is fill out the paperwork."

Silence.

"You're joking," Devon says.

Macourek gives him a level look. "I'm not, actually."

Devon tries to come up with a retort but only manages to say, "Why?"

Macourek smiles slightly. "I had lunch with Angelien's headmistress. I asked her about any interesting prospects among the students, but rather than discuss her bright young things, she began ranting about some idiotic hellion—her words, not mine. I was curious, so I did a bit of digging. Do you know what I found?"

"That the hellion also happened to be charming and good-looking?" quips Devon.

Macourek straightens his glasses. "You've been expelled many times. And not just for ordinary crimes, like plagiarism or sneaking into the girls' dorms. No—instead, you ran illegal poker tournaments, organized smuggling rings for things like alcohol and candy, sold standardized test answers, and even created a miniature version of an underground railroad to sneak students in and out of dormitories." He arches an eyebrow. "How did you manage that one?"

Devon glances down, sure that Macourek is mocking him. But Macourek's expression is mildly interested, so Devon answers. "I created several secret routes that could be used at varying times during the night."

Macourek looks impressed. "And security never caught you. Well, not for several months."

"The upkeep was a sodding nightmare," replies Devon. "The system had to constantly change. I set up a series of marks—just stupid little symbols so everyone knew which hallways to use. Then I'd erase the marks and redo them every week."

"Ingenious."

Devon's been called many things, but "ingenious" has never been one of them.

Macourek smiles. "Imagine if we focused that energy in a less destructive direction. I expect you'd be near unstoppable.

"I think you're an incredibly smart young man who, for whatever reason, has decided he needs to act out as much as possible. What I'm looking for is a motivated, intelligent intern who shows promise. I'll be honest with you. This job would be a lot of paperwork and data entry. The most exciting part of your day will probably be a coffee run."

"Then why would I join up?"

Macourek raises his eyebrows. "Because it would offer you a degree of autonomy." He taps the sheet of paper. "We arrange for our interns to live at the dorms of a nearby college."

Devon stares at the internship application. "Why would you want to help me?"

Macourek glances at the door to Mr. Lyre's office. "Because someone once made the same offer to me."

"Paying it forward?" Devon asks skeptically.

Macourek half shrugs. "Something like that." He rises to his feet and picks up the briefcase.

"And what if I say no?" Devon asks. For a moment, his memory drags up an image of Ciere. She's out in the world, doing her own thing. Of course she's with the mob, so that probably means she's in Atlantic City, sipping martinis and watching mobsters play poker. But if she can survive in the real world, so can he. "I'm technically an adult. I can go out, try to make a living on my own."

Macourek taps a finger to the glass of spiked orange juice, and there's a knowing look in his eyes. "Tell me, how well has being on your own been working out so far?"

4

CIERE

Ciere stomps into her boss's office and tosses a dead rat onto his desk.

"Look at that," she says.

Brandt Guntram doesn't flinch or look disgusted. He simply uses his pen to deftly sweep the dead animal off his paperwork and into the trash.

"Guess where I found it," Ciere says darkly.

Guntram puts his pen down, giving her his full attention. "Where?"

"My bed." Ciere points at the trash can. "I felt something moving around and I thought I was dreaming. Imagine my surprise when I woke up to Alan leaning over me, knife in hand. Then he stabbed the rat that *had snuggled up to me*."

That gets a reaction from Guntram. "Your bodyguard skewered a rat?"

"Third one this week."

Guntram looks offended on behalf of vermin everywhere. "Why haven't you set up traps?"

"Because Cole is using them! Since he runs the kitchen, everyone agrees he should have them. And it's not like we can buy more, since we're forbidden to leave the compound." She gestures at the walls—unpapered, unpainted affairs of twisted metal and the occasional pink fluff of insulation.

This building must have once been some kind of factory, but it's since been gutted and refurnished in what Ciere refers to as "postapocalyptic chic." Whoever built this factory never meant for anyone to live in it, never mind set up the headquarters of a crime syndicate. The walls barely keep the winter chill at bay, and the building's previous occupants—rats, mostly—refuse to vacate the premises. Add in the bits of broken machinery and wind whispering through the cracks in the ceiling, and the building is relentlessly creepy.

Guntram's quarters used to be the factory's security center. He fashioned a workspace out of a folding table and a rickety old chair, and his cot resides in the corner. A tiny portable heater rests along the wall, its coils burning orange in the dim light. The whole room is powered through a web of extension cords that Ciere has to remind herself not to trip over.

"Oh, yes," Guntram says vaguely, as if he's just remembered. "We're keeping a low profile thanks to someone's little slipup." He gives her a level look.

Ciere returns his stare. One would think a month would be long enough for people to let that go. "We cannot stay here. A deserted factory isn't meant for humans to live in. Rats, yes. Spiders, sure. Zombies, fine. But living, breathing people? We need things like beds—"

"We have cots," Guntram says.

"—electricity—" Ciere continues.

"We have generators," Guntram replies.

"—heating—"

"We have the portable heaters."

"—food—"

"We still have the canned goods."

"—showers," Ciere finishes.

That stumps Guntram. The lack of a water heater has meant that all fifteen occupants have been taking freezing-cold sponge baths and then bundling up in blankets. Personal hygiene is such an ordeal that some have decided in favor of using air fresheners and a few cans of dry shampoo.

"We're in hiding," Guntram explains, like this is a concept she's simply not grasping. "The Alberani family IDed an entire strike team—*your* strike team, I might add. They'll be out for blood." He picks up his pen, apparently ready to go back to his paperwork. The gesture is subtly dismissive, and Ciere chooses to ignore it.

"They can't kill us if we've already died of starvation. We need fresh food," she says, trying to wheedle a reaction out of him. He doesn't so much as blink. "Fresh coffee. We're running out, you know."

It's a low blow. If there's one thing Ciere knows, it's that nothing gets between Guntram and his morning coffee. There's a rumor an assassin once laced it with cyanide and Guntram's only response had been to complain about the almondy aftertaste. At least, Ciere hopes it's just a rumor.

She tries again. "We've been here for a month. Those gunrunners were arrested—"

"That hasn't been confirmed."

Ciere stutters to a halt. "What?"

"My contacts in the police department haven't confirmed the gunrunners' arrest," says Guntram. "The shipment was seized, but there's no word on the shooter you described."

A shiver goes through Ciere. The memory of the man who shot her, with his calm expression and pale hair, is too fresh in her mind. "Guntram, Alberani family or not, we need things. Like food and showers and living conditions that don't resemble Antarctic prison camps."

Before Guntram can reply, a knock comes from the open door. Henry stands there, fist rapping against the door frame.

Henrietta Williams is one of Guntram's most trusted friends within the Syndicate. Somewhere between forty and fifty, she is dark-skinned with lines around her eyes. Her mouth is constantly in motion—talking, smoking, and smirking. Whenever anyone tries to call her by her whole name, she'll glare and correct them—Henry. It's just Henry.

"Hey, Brandt," she says cheerfully, nodding to Ciere. "Ava arrived. She says a shipment was just dropped off at the train station. Oh, and Cole wanted to let you know that a raccoon's invaded the kitchen."

Guntram's grip on his pen tightens. Very carefully, he sets it down. "What is Cole doing?" he says warily.

"He put a hit out on it," Henry replies, unable to hide her wicked grin. "Whoever kills the raccoon wins the last can of baked beans. And if anyone can do it with a headshot, we get meat for dinner."

Guntram covers his mouth with a hand, but Ciere sees the way his mouth twitches—as if he's resisting the urge to grimace. "All right. I need to take care of a few things, so tell Ava we'll be leaving soon to pick up the supplies. As for Cole... well, tell him we're probably going to get food soon." He fixes Ciere with a look. "Not that it's any of your business, but I've been making arrangements. We'll be picking up new supplies this evening. As you can see, I'd never let things get too out of hand here."

At that moment, they hear the unmistakable crack of gunfire followed by a whoop of triumph.

When Ciere returns to her bedroom—she's sure it was once a storage closet—she finds Alan sitting on one of the two cots. He's bundled up in his usual puffy jacket, leaning over a dusty book.

"Training with Guntram?" he asks, not looking up from his book.

She shakes her head, and then realizes he won't see it. "Get up—we're leaving."

Alan smiles down at his book. "Ah. Your complaining finally got a reaction?"

"No," she says. Then adds, "Maybe."

"Guntram must value your opinion if he finally decided to leave the factory," says Alan, closing the book.

"Actually, I'm pretty sure Cole announcing he was serving raccoon burgers tonight was the deciding vote." She finds her heaviest jacket and pulls it on. "What're you reading?"

Alan begins lacing up his boots. "Book I borrowed from Conrad. He's got a small library." He glances up, peeking at her through overlong bangs. "Did you know they got the name of the Syndicate from a Yeats poem?"

She snorts. "Yeah. Because I had time to minor in the classics while learning to pickpocket rich tourists." She pulls on her coat, careful of the fresh scar along her arm. The gunshot wound has healed over the past month, but the new skin is still pink and tight. "How do you know that, anyway?"

"No friends," he says simply. "Never went to school. I spent most days hiding in whatever house Rich—" He trips over the name, and there's a flash of pain in his eyes. He forces himself to continue. "Anyway, my aunt would homeschool me. She liked poetry." He ducks his head, attention on his freshly calloused hands as he works on his boots.

Ciere lets herself watch him. She has watched him since their first night with the Syndicate, so she's seen the way he's changed over the last five months. He was always nimble and careful, able to pick up pieces of shattered glass in the dark with his bare hands. But now he appears capable of using those same shards to defend himself. He has always been observant, but there's a calculation behind his eyes. He no longer looks like a teenage boy whose only defense is to wedge a chair beneath a door.

And if Ciere is honest with herself, Alan looks...well, he looks good.

For just a moment, she entertains the thought of what it would feel like to sit down next to him on that bed, to lean into his warmth and know that she'd be welcome.

She wouldn't be. Welcome, that is. Alan cares about one thing and one thing alone—keeping the Praevenir formula safe. Grubby, freshly scarred thieves do not factor into his life plans. She tries to push her emotions away, to concentrate on the task ahead.

Ciere turns away from him, feeling every bit the thief who walks away from a lock she's not good enough to crack.

There's one upside to the harsh winter—the streets are all but deserted. Guntram guides his Honda away from the abandoned factory and onto an icy road. They're on the fringes of Newark, with tall buildings just visible through the clouds, but far enough that no one will stumble on their hideout.

The pickup team consists of Guntram, Conrad, Henry, and—much to Alan's annoyance—Pruitt. All fighters, all experienced—well, excluding Ciere and Alan. Ciere chooses a seat far away from Pruitt and stares out the window, determinedly not making eye contact.

Ciere has never really liked Pruitt, not even before Jess was killed. There's a sense of barely restrained violence around him, and it sets off all kinds of alarms in Ciere's brain. Not all members of the Gyr Syndicate are immune—in fact, they're a minority. There's Guntram, the illusionist, and Pruitt, the eidos. Ciere has always wondered if Conrad is a dauthus; it would explain so much. But he's never volunteered that information and Ciere isn't brave enough to ask.

The drive to the train station takes nearly an hour—for a

criminal, Guntram is surprisingly dedicated to traffic laws. He edges the car into an empty parking lot. Stacked crates and deserted cars indicate shipping trains, not passengers. It's a good place for a drop-off—the kind Ciere might choose herself if she were meeting with a fence.

"The tracks will be shut down due to the snow," says Guntram. He pushes his door open and fresh cold sweeps into the vehicle. Ciere's skin crawls. Grimacing, she opens her own door and takes a careful step onto the frozen ground. Alan follows, a silent shadow at her back.

Ciere sucks in a breath of air and holds it in her lungs. When she exhales, a stream of mist escapes her lips.

The van parks a few feet away. Pruitt is the first to emerge. He stares deliberately away from Guntram and makes no attempt to hide the gun shoved into his belt. Conrad and Henry are similarly armed. The Syndicate doesn't expect an attack, but they're always ready for one.

"The supplies will be there," says Guntram, pointing to a faraway loading dock. "However, since they're small and this place is huge, we're splitting up. The last thing I want is for someone to open a crate and find someone's replaced our coffee with live grenades."

"Or find a sniper waiting atop a train," says Conrad. Ciere sneaks a glance upward, unable to help herself.

"Exactly," says Guntram. "Henry, stay with the cars. Yell

if anyone shows up. Giba and I will scout the area first, make sure it's clear, and then we'll whistle when it's safe. Conrad, Ashbottom, Pruitt, you get the supplies."

"One thing," says Alan. "Where're our walkie-talkies?"

It's true, Ciere realizes as she glances at everyone's belts. Usually they're all carrying radios of some kind; Guntram always says staying in touch is the only sane way to operate.

Guntram frowns. "We ran out of batteries last week." He turns north, pushing his way through a snowbank. Ciere glances around. Alan's gaze briefly meets hers and a shiver passes through her bones. He nods once, a silent reassurance.

"Come on," calls Guntram, and she hurries after him, pushing her way through the snow and around an abandoned train car. "Cover us," he says, and Ciere sticks her tongue out at his turned back. Even so, she closes her eyes for a moment, lets her immunity take hold, and vanishes both herself and Guntram from sight. Guntram's hand closes around her arm and she links elbows with him. It's necessary when they can't see each other.

The air has a muffled quality and there's no sound from the nearby city—probably a result of so much snow. Together, they circle the train station. To Ciere's eyes, the place is deserted; there are no fresh tracks in the snow, no sounds or smells that would indicate people.

The landscape would appear deserted—almost untouched

by human hands—if not for the snow-covered trains and the stripes of paint left behind by taggers. Her eyes drift over the loops of color—gang symbols, a stylized word or two, and several lines of swears. One piece of graffiti is a star, drawn in brilliant yellow. It's pretty, and completely unlike the other pieces of graffiti. Ciere's eyes linger on it until she rounds a corner.

They remain silent for a good five minutes, until Guntram is sure the train station is empty. Then he whistles loud enough to make Ciere wince. She drops the illusion and he flickers into sight, two fingers still between his lips.

"We should circle around one more time," she says, nodding the way they came.

Guntram just looks at her. "Or maybe you're just avoiding someone?"

"Okay, fine. Pruitt," says Ciere. "He's still pissed off at me."

Guntram moves confidently through the snow. "Actually, I thought you were avoiding Alan. Things have seemed a little…iffy lately." He offers up a thin smile.

She scowls at him. "You're leading a crime syndicate into war and you have time to worry about my life?"

"I was always a good multitasker."

"Well, this is one task that doesn't need a multi," says Ciere, pushing past him. She strides ahead, kicking snow out of her path. "We're friends and we're fine."

Guntram sighs. "You're right about Pruitt, though. He isn't happy with you."

"When is he ever?" says Ciere.

"He has good reason. You let yourself be distracted and the illusion failed, thus killing his best friend."

Snow stings her face and she wipes at it irritably. "Getting shot will do that to you."

"You should've held on."

"Yeah. And when exactly am I supposed to let go?" Annoyance gives her words a bite.

Guntram looks pained, as if she's forcing him to state the obvious. "You hold on until your heart stops beating."

She tries to think of a sarcastic reply and fails. "The others don't hate me for it. I mean, Henry and Conrad aren't holding a grudge."

"Because no one they love was hurt," says Guntram. "Jess and Pruitt were old friends. Imagine if it had been your bodyguard who'd been killed."

Ciere crosses her arms. "I didn't screw up," she says, parsing her words carefully. "Well, I mean, I sort of did, but it wasn't my fault. That day when Jess died. The arms dealers knew something was wrong before I dropped my illusion. The driver—you know, the pale-haired guy I told you about— he slowed the truck just before he hit the spikes, almost like he knew something was up. And then he managed to shoot me. Out of all the people there, shooting blind, the driver managed to hit *me*. The one person he needed to take down to destroy the illusion." She forces herself to look Guntram in the eye and hold his gaze. "Almost like he could sense things that he shouldn't have been able to."

"You suspect he was immune," Guntram says after a moment's pause. "It's possible. The Alberanis are just like any other crime family—they'll press immune people into service, if it suits them."

"Like Pruitt," says Ciere dryly. "I heard you rescued his family from the Alkanovs?" A smile twists at her mouth. "And then there's me."

"You're paying off a debt, not being pressed into service," Guntram corrects, but then he switches back on topic. "You think the Alberani driver was an eludere."

"It would explain everything," says Ciere, adding hastily, "And it means I didn't totally screw up."

Guntram appears thoughtful, and he opens his mouth to reply. He never gets the words out.

Gunfire cracks the air.

Ciere ducks. It's instinctive—she drops to the ground, drawing on her immunity. She pulls the blankness of the snow around her until she's nearly invisible. Only after she's sure no one can spot her does she look around.

Guntram remains still. His jaw is tight and he appears to

be listening intently. Hollow echoes of the gunshot reverberate off the nearby train cars.

Sickening fear twists Ciere's stomach. Her arm aches, the memory of the bullet wound fresh in her mind. "Where?" She barely manages to choke out the word, but Guntram understands. His attention sharpens, his whole body gone tight.

"Not here," he says, and takes off at a dead sprint.

Ciere's knees are locked, numb with panic, until Guntram's words finally sink in. Not here. Someone else must be the target.

Alan.

She scrambles through the snow and slips on a patch of ice, her feet nearly falling out from under her. She catches herself on a train car, gloved fingers snagging on the rusty metal. Panic beats hard inside her chest.

She rounds the corner so quickly, she almost slams into Guntram. He's frozen in place, his gaze fixed on something ahead. Her heart races and she knows, she just knows, that something horrible has happened. The Alberanis have found them. They're under attack.

But when she peers around Guntram, what she sees is so much worse.

Pruitt is on the ground and Alan crouches over him.

A gun rests on the pavement.

5

DANIEL

Daniel Burkhart waits for Gervais to walk into his office before saying, "All right. Who did you kill?"

Special Agent Avery Gervais halts mid-step. He's carrying a folder in one hand and reaches for a cup of coffee with the other. "What?"

Daniel nods at the coffee. It's in a chipped mug and there's congealed milk collecting at the edges. "I wouldn't drink that."

It's not that the coffee is bad, per se. Daniel has tasted a lot of bad coffee over the years, from fast-food joints to reused coffee grounds. So it's not the coffee's quality that bothers him.

It's the extra DNA inside the cup.

"Don't drink it," Daniel repeats. "Contaminated. Which

leads back into my original question: Who did you murder? Because people don't spit in your coffee for nothing."

Gervais freezes, mug halfway to his lips. "Maybe people are just assholes," he says. He's a man whose job has worn itself into the lines of his face. A fed through and through. He looks at home in this office, which is cluttered with an old filing cabinet, a heavy desk, and several books stacked precariously on the floor.

At his age, Gervais should have a corner office. But then again, life isn't fair. Daniel knows that better than anyone.

Gervais and Daniel regard each other with what an outsider might have called camaraderie. *More like Stockholm syndrome*, Daniel reflects.

"Burkhart," says Gervais. He sounds more tired than angry. "When did you get here?"

"About an hour ago. Figured you wouldn't mind if I lurked in your office." Daniel offers up a sunny grin he knows will annoy the agent. He sits in the spare folding chair that Gervais keeps for visitors, few as they may be. "Someone said you were in a meeting."

No one walking by the office gave him a passing glance. He knows how he looks—dressed in a ratty T-shirt and jeans—like a delinquent high schooler. Daniel Burkhart may be the official liaison between the UAI and FBI, but he doesn't have to dress like it.

"How'd you know about the coffee?" Gervais settles into his own chair and gestures at the mug.

Daniel shrugs. A shrug is easier than explaining he sensed a whisper of intent from one of Gervais's coworkers. People shouldn't be able to sense intent.

"Why'd you tell me?" asks Gervais.

Another shrug. Daniel knows he should despise Gervais—after all, the government agent arrested him. If it weren't for Gervais, Daniel would probably be back in Philadelphia, pickpocketing wealthy tourists and planning jobs with Ciere and their mentor, Kit. He'd still have a life, a home, a semblance of a family.

But despite everything, Daniel can't hate Gervais. Not when everyone else does.

Instead of answering, he says, "You're really popular around here."

Gervais's mouth twitches. "If I were any more popular, I'd be you."

Touché.

Daniel reaches for his backpack and unzips it. He withdraws a paper bag, its sides gone transparent with grease. The logo of a donut company is emblazoned on one side. "Luckily, I still appreciate you," says Daniel, and hands the bag over.

Gervais reaches in and pulls out a bear claw. "What do you need?"

"I'm not asking you for anything," says Daniel, and there's real apology in his voice. "I'm just the messenger."

Gervais looks startled and then his face shuts down. "Aristeus sent you." He shakes his head, and then glances at one of the photos taped to his corkboard.

It is a portrait of a man in his thirties, with dark hair and clean-cut features. Beneath it is a newspaper clipping straight out of the obits. Daniel never liked Eduardo Carson, Gervais's last partner. The man was a hypocrite and an asshole. But the day the news came of Carson's body being dragged from the Schuylkill River, Daniel saw Gervais gather himself. He carried a box of personal effects out of the office, muttering something about visiting Carson's ex-wife and daughter.

It's a distinctly uncomfortable memory, if only because Daniel remembers how unsorry he was to hear that Carson was dead.

"The last time Aristeus pulled me into an investigation, my partner was killed," says Gervais. "If he thinks I'm going to work with him again—"

Daniel fumbles around in his backpack for a folder. "Not directly."

Gervais puts the bear claw down and takes the folder. The familiar overlapping circles of the UAI logo are stamped on the paper. Gervais opens it with the same respect most people reserve for loaded guns.

The UAI is the immune-only intelligence agency within the government. Commonly known as the United American Immunities, it is feared by criminals and normal people alike. Since the Adverse Effects Division of the FBI tracks down immune threats, the two agencies often find themselves working side by side. But it runs counter to the FBI's instincts; it's spent years hunting immune people, while the UAI consists of only immune.

So when the DC branch of the FBI is called to work with the UAI, they send the agent they dislike the most: Gervais.

There's mutual cooperation, and then there's being another agency's bitch.

Gervais is definitely the latter.

"This is that missing persons case," Gervais murmurs, still reading. "I heard about it, but it's small-time."

Daniel leans forward. "Not as small-time as you think." He reached over and points at one of the papers. "Check it out."

Gervais's eyes flick over the words and his face goes slack. Daniel understands.

"Over *twenty people*," says Gervais, aghast. "How has this gone unnoticed?"

"All adults," says Daniel, shrugging. "Some of them went unreported for a while. You know, coworkers thought they'd

gone on vacation or just skipped town. But all of their possessions are at home and there's no sign of a struggle. People are
just vanishing."

"Not exactly the UAI's typical case." Gervais leafs through
the papers, scanning each.

Daniel shrugs again. "So far all the missing are vaccinated
adults. It was kicked up to the UAI when someone proposed
that it might be a foreign agent trying to vanish some of the
immune population. You know, thin the herd. Aristeus has
several two-person recon teams from here to Boston. We're
just part of the crowd.

"We're not doing any of the heavy lifting," Daniel continues. "Aristeus just thought that an older dude and me wouldn't
look suspicious doing recon. We can pose as father and son if
you don't mind the fact I'll start claiming my fake mom was
overly attached to our gardener."

It feels weird being the person coaxing an FBI agent into
work. Daniel is—*was*—a criminal. He conned gullible rich
people and stole rare pieces of art.

But that life is gone. Even if his former allies would trust
him again (and they *won't*; they aren't *idiots*), Daniel can't
trust himself. Not with the voice of a dominus sitting in the
back of his mind. Aristeus hasn't used his power over Daniel
in months, but Daniel thinks he can still feel it, lurking somewhere in his skull.

"If I refuse this job," says Gervais quietly, "is Aristeus going to talk to my boss?"

Actually, Aristeus's exact words were: *Tell him to take this job or I'll make sure he ends up on the circuit as a mall cop.*

Daniel nods. It's the same threat, either way.

"I'll need to talk to my superiors," says Gervais, resignation in his voice. He heaves himself to his feet, takes the file, and walks into the hall. As he goes, his chin drops. Like a man bracing himself against a cold wind.

Daniel doesn't feel bad for him.

He *doesn't*.

Even so, he finds himself looking at Gervais's full cup of coffee. Grimacing, he picks up the mug and walks into the hall.

It's not kindness. It's professionalism. It's just getting Gervais a cup of drinkable coffee, so he can do his job.

There's a restroom near the coffee machine. Daniel empties the mug into a sink and scrubs out the inside with a paper towel and hand soap. As he works, two FBI agents stride into the men's room. They're both decades older than Daniel, and they don't give him a second glance. One of the men carries a newspaper in one hand and Daniel just catches the front-page headline.

ADITI SEN CONTINUES TO PROTEST TAG SYSTEM

"…idiots," the first agent is saying. "Calls herself an activist. She's just another anarchist."

"No argument here," says the second agent. "I mean, what do they expect? The moment the tags disappear is when we just give up and hand the country over to the immunes." He snorts, and there's the sound of a zipper being undone.

"Fucking privileged types," says the first agent. "Live in their pretty little elsecs and have no idea what's going on. I'd like to drag that Sen woman down here, show her how those immune people really operate."

The second agent makes a derisive sound. "We shouldn't be wasting resources on those freaks."

Daniel's hands go still. The voices of the men blur in his ears. He forces himself to dry the now-clean mug, and step outside without saying a word.

He's heard worse. "Freak" is one of the kinder terms applied to immune people. He shouldn't be rattled by two stupid FBI agents blowing off steam. He shouldn't—but he is.

Daniel closes his eyes.

Out of all of the immunities, an eludere's powers are the hardest to explain. It's part intuition, part precognition, and it manifests itself in one of the five normal senses. Daniel has heard of other eludere being able to smell threats, see things on spectrums no one else can. For Daniel, he can hear things—things that don't make a sound.

He closes his eyes and *listens* for the telltale hum of a camera. When his instincts whisper an all-clear, he slips an illegal lock pick from his pocket. It took him a few months to secure such tools, and Gervais pretends he doesn't know about them. Daniel eases the pick into the door's lock. It takes only a moment of prodding, a twist, and—

He locks the restroom from the outside.

It's petty and stupid. They'll be able to get a janitor in ten minutes. But for the moment, those two men are trapped and helpless.

See how you like it.

When Gervais returns, he finds Daniel in his office. "Fresh coffee," Daniel says, barely hiding a smile.

As they walk down the hall, he hears the sound of distant shouting.

6

CIERE

A t first Ciere thinks it's not real.

It has to be another test. That would fit; Guntram's teaching techniques tend to be blunt, frustrating, and sometimes nightmare inducing. Conjuring an illusion of Alan and Pruitt would play on all her new fears. She reaches outward, tries to sense that buzzing closeness that means she's been worked over by an illusion. She takes several shaky steps forward, trying to focus, to push against what must be an illusion.

There's the briefest hint of a hum, and for a moment she clings to it, holding to the hope that perhaps this isn't real. But then the sensation dies away, leaving her with nothing.

Guntram flies past her. "What did you do?"

Guntram shoves Alan back and he staggers. His usually coppery skin is as pale as the snow. "I—I didn't—"

Guntram pays him no attention. His hands are a blur, yanking a scarf away from Pruitt's neck, tearing at his collar. There's a harsh determination in Guntram's face, a look that Ciere has only ever seen when he was firing shots at an oncoming police car.

Heavy footsteps crunch across the snow and Ciere looks up to see Conrad running toward them. "What happened?"

Guntram tears Pruitt's jacket open. His voice is deeper, more guttural than Ciere has ever heard. "Check the perimeter, now!"

Conrad doesn't hesitate; he turns around and rushes into the shadows.

Guntram peels the shirt away from Pruitt's chest. Ciere tries not to look and fails. The man's chest has a gaping hole in it. He makes soft noises; his breath comes in soggy, heaving gasps. Guntram yanks at his own scarf and tosses it to Ciere. "Put pressure on the wound."

She kneels next to Pruitt, the gravel digging into her knees, and shoves the scarf down on the wound. So she feels it when Pruitt stops breathing.

"Guntram," she says shrilly. Guntram begins pressing down on Pruitt's heart, but it's close to the wound and his heavy hands collide with Ciere's. She tries to ignore the way the scarf dampens and soaks through.

Guntram continues compressions, and she doesn't know how much time has passed. Minutes, probably, although it feels like hours. "Pruitt," Guntram says, and there's a raw edge of desperation. "Pruitt, come on!"

Another minute crawls past. Guntram's face is shiny with sweat and his chest heaves. Exhaustion seeps into his face, and his movements slow. He checks Pruitt's pulse again, hesitates, then he goes still. His shoulders slacken and he sinks onto his haunches, eyes locked on Pruitt's unmoving form. Ciere's fingers feel warm and tacky.

Henry charges around a corner, weapon drawn. Her hands seem dwarfed by her huge pistol, but she carries it with ease. When she sees the others, alarm flashes across her face. "Alberanis?" she says.

Conrad appears from the opposite direction, his bulk materializing from the shadows. He moves with surprising stealth for his size. "Perimeter's clear," he says. "Brandt, it's just us. Pruitt?"

"He's dead," says Guntram.

Conrad makes a sound, as if he started to say something but it choked off. Henry lets out a volatile curse, moving as if to approach Alan.

The gun rests on the pavement amid the gravel and dirty patches of ice. Someone must have tried to clear this area of snow, Ciere thinks. For a moment, she clings to that thought, because it's easier to think about someone shoveling snow than to remember why her gloves are soaked through. "It's Pruitt's," says Guntram quietly, fingers sliding over the gun.

He ejects the magazine and Conrad says, "Was it fired?"

"It's cool, but it would be in this weather," says Guntram. "The clip's half-empty and I have no idea how many rounds he started with."

"But who would have..." Henry begins to say, then trails off.

Guntram turns hard eyes on Alan. "Henry, get the supplies," he says, never looking away. "Conrad, take Mr. Ashbottom to the van and keep him there."

"Guntram—" Henry starts to say, but he cuts her off.

"I'll help you in a moment." Guntram never looks away from Alan, not even when Conrad grabs the younger man by the arm and half drags him in the direction of the cars. Ciere finds herself drawn upward, out of her crouch, and she angles herself to follow them.

Guntram's hand clamps down on her shoulder. "Did you tell him to do this?"

Ciere shakes him off and wrenches her gaze away from

Alan. "He's never used a gun in his life—and you're asking me if I told him to assassinate Pruitt?"

Something in Guntram's eyes flickers. At once, Ciere knows she's let another bit of information slip; he's cataloging it away for later use. "What kind of bodyguard hasn't ever used a gun?" he says in a hard voice.

"What kind of mobster can be brought down by a teen-ager?" she snarls back.

That takes him back a little. He looks down at his own knees—stained with blood and dirt. He closes his eyes for a moment. "If he did this…"

She knows what it will mean. She knows Guntram too well by now, has watched him work for nearly six months. She can see the decision play out in his eyes.

"He didn't do this," she says.

Guntram doesn't answer.

"Please." The word slips out. Her anger drains away, leaves only terror in its wake.

"Alan isn't a murderer," she says. Her throat feels tight. "He wouldn't kill anyone."

The words are out before she has time to really consider them. Because the truth is, she doesn't really know Alan. She doesn't know the lengths he would go to. She remembers how coolly he once spoke of an FBI agent's death, how he rationalized it.

Could he rationalize something like this?

Guntram rests his gaze on her, studying with such intensity that Ciere feels goose bumps prick at her arms. "I'm not a mentalist," he finally says. "I don't know if you're lying."

She steps closer. "He wasn't the only person here—Conrad and Henry. Either of them could've done it."

Guntram's expression doesn't waver. "I trust them."

"I don't."

The worst part is, she likes Henry and Conrad. Henry is friendly, gives Ciere hot chocolate packets when there seem to be none left, and she carries enough weapons to supply a small army. Conrad has the smile of a great white and the muscles of a bear, and once described a shipment of guns as a "metric fuckton." He makes her laugh.

"Let me look around!" Her throat nearly closes up on the words. The adrenaline is draining away, leaving her shaking and dizzy. "Just—let me see—" She turns back to Pruitt. She forces herself to look at him, really look at him. The pavement is rusty red, ice and gravel churned beneath their feet. But without the thick snow, there's no way to tell who has come and gone from the scene. Ciere takes a step forward and begins walking around the body. Kit once explained how cops canvass crime scenes and now she dregs up the memory, hating herself a little for dozing off during that lecture.

"What are you doing?" Guntram's hard demeanor sloughs away, leaving exhaustion in its wake.

"A shell," says Ciere desperately. "If Pruitt was shot at close range, there should be a shell. If we can match it up to the kind of bullets in either Conrad's or Henry's gun..."

"Good try," says Guntram. "But do you have any idea how small those things are?"

She does, as a matter of fact. "We can't just walk away." She drags her eyes over the pavement. But the light is draining from the sky and she pulls out her cell phone, flicking it to the flashlight mode. As she aims the phone outward, a gleam of metal catches her attention.

Ciere darts forward, dropping to her knees about ten feet from Pruitt. She reaches down and touches the object.

"What is it?" asks Guntram.

Ciere frowns down at the object. "A money clip."

There are two fifties and a few twenties, carefully folded over one another. If the weather warms up, then the bills will be soaked through. But now, they're simply dusty with snow. Ciere brushes them off, feels something between the worn paper.

Tucked in amid the bills is a bright yellow card. It's a temporary key, one designed to slide into a hotel lock. ARATA SUITES, it reads, when she flips it over. WASHINGTON, DC.

"Was this Pruitt's?" she says, holding it up. Guntram crosses over to her quickly. His sharp eyes take it in.

"No," he says shortly.

"Yours?" she says. "Henry or Conrad?"

He hesitates a moment. "I don't know." He reaches out, ready to take the clip, but Ciere tucks it into her jacket. If it's Alan's only chance at redemption, she's not letting the clip out of her sight.

"Well," she says, voice hard, "I suggest we find out if anyone's gone to Washington, DC, lately."

7

DEVON

He stands on a frozen sidewalk in DC, staring up at a tall building. The marbled exterior resembles any other government office, but it makes Devon's stomach flip. Ice covers the ground, and the cold bites into his exposed skin. Passing cars crawl by, their windshield wipers making angry squeaking noises as they try to push back the falling snow.

He's not dressed for the weather. When Devon left home last night, he was only half thinking about what he'd need. And somehow, gloves or a winter jacket never crossed his mind. His numb fingers grip the handles of his luggage.

He picks his way up the marble stairs, mindful of the ice. When he pushes his way past the glass doors, the warm air sends a shudder of relief through his whole body. He stands there, just letting the melting snow drip off his shoes and sleeves, until he's steadier. The interior of the building looks standard—gleaming floors, high ceilings, and a security desk.

The guard winces when he takes Devon's tags. "Jeez," the man says, nearly dropping them onto the scanner.

"Bit cold out there, yeah," says Devon. "I'm here to see Macourek."

The guard scans something on his screen. He looks fit—nothing like the stereotypical fat blokes Devon always saw in movies. This man is well muscled, with sharp eyes and a grim little smile. He picks up a tablet and nods. "Ah, yes. Affiliation is on the fifth floor. Elevators are to your left."

When Devon steps out of the lift, he sees that there's industrial carpeting here rather than marble floors; the cubicles look scuffed and the receptionist's desk has a large dent in one side. Devon steps up to the desk, feeling suddenly more at home. Flaws he can deal with; it's perfection that makes him uneasy.

The desk is covered with the usual—a tin of business cards, a potted cactus, and a metal nameplate: SIA VILLAREAL. Devon says, "I'm looking for Mr. Macourek."

A young woman sits in a swivel chair, her hands darting over a keyboard. She has amber skin and sleek black hair. Her tags are worn on a silver choker, tiny gems embedded in the metal. At Devon's approach, she tilts her head and gazes somewhere past his shoulder. "Lyre?"

For a second, he's not sure if she's called him a liar or guessed his surname. "Yes," he says, because it's true either way. "I'm, uh, here for the internship."

"I figured. I'm Sia," she says. She rises to her feet and extends a hand for him to shake. His fingers are still stiff with cold and hers are almost unbearably warm. "Mr. Macourek told me you'd be arriving soon."

Which is a little creepy, considering Devon hasn't told anyone he planned on taking the job.

She reaches down and pulls a file from somewhere beneath her desk. She slides it to him. "Inside," says Sia, "you'll find a map of the building—please note the fire escapes, details about logging into the office networks, a list of duties you'll be performing, a contact list, and the temporary keycard that will let you into the building. We'll get you a permanent ID later." Devon attempts to shuffle his suitcase and backpack into one hand. Carrying the folder in his teeth wouldn't be a good first impression.

"I'll take you to Macourek," says Sia, coming around the desk. Devon shuffles after, still awkwardly carrying most of his possessions. As he passes by, he sees something resting against the corner of her desk.

It's a white cane.

And suddenly everything snaps together. The way Sia hasn't met his eyes, the lingering of her fingers on his, the careful way she ran her hand over the desk when she stood. As she walks, her fingertips skim the fabric walls of the cubicles, the way someone might absentmindedly stroke a familiar pet.

Devon tries to think of something to say, but all he comes up with is, "Um, thanks."

Sia strolls confidently through the maze of cubicles, pointing out the restrooms, copy room, and vending machines as they go. As they pass by, Devon sees a woman before an ancient coffee machine. She wears a pencil skirt and glares at a white foam cup. "This is dirty water," she says. "Sia, tell me why I'm drinking dirty water."

"Morgan, this is our new intern," Sia calls, not breaking stride. "Lyre, this is Morgan Clarke, the subdirector of our little office."

The woman, Morgan, glances at Devon, her gaze vaguely running over him before returning to her cup. "I need coffee."

"I put in the work order two weeks ago," says Sia. "Take it up with maintenance."

Morgan lets out a wordless snarl that doesn't sound human.

"She's nice once you get to know her," Sia confides, taking a sharp left. Devon hurries to keep up. His luggage nearly tips over and he wonders if there's someplace to store his things.

Aron Macourek has a corner office with his name emblazoned on a metal plaque. The office itself is dark and Sia flicks on the lights without hesitation. "He's in a meeting right now, but he'll be along soon," she says. "You can wait here." And then she's gone before he can open his mouth to thank her. He lets go of his luggage and lets out a groan of relief.

The office itself is rather sparse, with a heavy desk and expensive-looking chair. The only decoration is a row of bonsai edging the windowsill. When Devon takes a closer look, he realizes every single bonsai is made of twisted wire. Devon touches a "leaf" with his finger, the metal smooth and deftly looping into itself. Whoever created these did some fine work.

The door swings open and Macourek walks in, a briefcase in one hand and a phone pressed up against his ear.

Under normal circumstances, Devon wouldn't have been able to hear the voice on the other end of the line. But what comes out of the mini speaker is shouted so loudly that Macourek winces and pulls the phone away from his ear.

"*Someone just hacked the Customs and Border Protection website,*" a female voice screeches. "*They've replaced the entire thing with the TATE manifesto!*"

Macourek lets out a sigh and rolls up his right sleeve, glancing at an expensive watch. "What do they want us to do about it?"

"*No idea, but I'm sure we'll be blamed somehow.*"

"I'll see what I can do." Macourek gives Devon an apologetic shrug. "Just take a few deep breaths and if anyone tries to shift blame onto us, get Morgan to talk to them." He lets out a breath, says, "I'll be in touch," and snaps the phone shut.

"TATE?" Devon says, trying to sound clueless.

Macourek tucks his phone into his breast pocket. "A group of cyberterrorists."

Freedom fighters. Terrorists. Semantics, Devon thinks, and has to try hard to contain a twitching smile. "This the kind of thing I can expect from now on?"

Macourek sits down on the edge of his desk. He looks even thinner than Devon remembers—it looks like a good breeze could topple him. "Depends." The faintest smile creases his lips. "You planning on working here?"

Devon swallows, feeling the weight of the question settle on his shoulders. He glances to the window instead of answering. "Nice plants."

Macourek lets the subject slide; there's a knowing edge to his smile. "I like low-maintenance shrubbery. Coworkers kept giving me plants and Sia would be carrying out their corpses a few weeks later."

Devon blinks. "I hope you're referring to the plants."

Macourek laughs. He glances at the floor and his expression shifts from mirth to something thoughtful. "You packed a suitcase. And a backpack."

Devon tries to keep his expression impassive. "Yes."

Macourek runs a hand over his face. "Let me guess; your father doesn't know you're here."

"He will, once he finds the note," says Devon, trying to sound cheerful. "I'm eighteen. What's he going to do—disinherit me?"

A sigh escapes Macourek. "Sometimes it works out like that. Unfortunate but true." He fixes Devon with a look and all the amusement drains from his face. "Tell me, Mr. Lyre, what made you decide to come here?"

The question brings everything Devon hasn't been thinking about into sharp focus. For a moment, he tries to fumble for a lie—he thinks of everything he could possibly use to justify this decision.

"You don't belong with us."

What comes out of his mouth surprises him. It's the first honest thing he's said since he stopped trying to be a criminal.

"Because," says Devon, "I had no place else to go."

8

CIERE

When Ciere first began working for the Syndicate, she expected Guntram to make use of her immediately. Illusionists were too valuable to go to waste; she expected to find herself put on a bus to New Haven or Boston, or one of the cities the Syndicate was trying to conquer.

Instead, she found herself at a farmhouse outside of Gettysburg, Pennsylvania.

A genuine, chickens-in-the-backyard, red-painted-barn, porch-with-a-damn-rocking-chair *farmhouse*. It smelled like damp earth and cut grass.

"I bought it ten years ago," said Guntram. "Under a different name. It's the last place anyone would look for me."

"It's your bolt-hole," observed Ciere. She stood on the

gravel driveway, staring at the lawn with some trepidation. She wasn't sure if she wanted to step onto it, not with livestock running around. She'd lived in cities since her mother died. Kit always said cities were safer, more crowded, more anonymous. The idea of such isolation made her feel queasy, and it must have shown on her face.

"The chickens don't bite," said Guntram. Then added, "Often."

They went in through the back door and into the kitchen. The interior of the house was just as stereotypical as she'd expected. It had a harsh, rustic appeal and she found herself running her fingertips over the unpainted walls. Cupboards stretched along the opposite wall, and the sink was crowded with dirty dishes.

"Looks like Henry's back from Boston," said Guntram with a sigh. "Maybe cleanup will be part of your duties. Come on. I'll show you where you'll be sleeping." He walked around a corner and Ciere made to follow him, but Alan let out a surprised sound.

When she turned, she saw Conrad's bulk looming over Alan. The mobster was grinning.

"She goes with Brandt," said Conrad. "You come with me." In his rumble of a voice, the words couldn't have sounded more ominous.

Alan and Ciere exchanged a look.

"Why?" said Alan. Not exactly nervous, but with definite caution.

"You said you are her bodyguard." Conrad reached out and poked a finger into Alan's chest until he was forced to take a step back.

"You," said Conrad, "are not her bodyguard." He looked down his nose at Alan. He towered over the teenager by at least a foot. "Not yet," he added.

Alan gaped up at him.

"Come," Conrad said. "You want to protect her? I'll teach you how."

Before either Ciere or Alan could say a word, one of Conrad's massive fists was around Alan's upper arm. He all but dragged Alan away, cheerfully whistling as they went.

Alan glanced back at Ciere, his whole face scrunched together in an almost-comic expression of horror. *Help me*, he mouthed, and she felt a laugh rise in her chest. Alan was drawn through the door and out into the yard.

When Alan vanished from sight, Ciere shook her head in rueful amusement. So both Guntram and Conrad knew that Alan wasn't her bodyguard—and they'd chosen to ignore the lie. It didn't matter too much, not as long as they never guessed the real reason why Alan was here. She almost snorted at the thought. The truth about Alan was so unreal that only a conspiracy theorist might guess it.

She turned back to the kitchen, a faint smile still on her mouth.

Magnus lay in front of her.

A knife hilt protruded from between his ribs and he was still. Too still. His gaunt face gone slack. His fingers splayed on the hardwood floor.

A spike of pure terror went through her. Panic clouded out her thoughts, narrowed the world to a single point.

Her vision wobbled for a moment, because all she could think was, *We were supposed to be safe here.*

Then she got a grip on herself.

Felt that familiar buzz.

And pushed it back.

A slow clapping rang out from behind her. She whirled to see Guntram leaning against a counter, bringing his palms together in a parody of applause.

"Better," he said. "A little faster this time."

Her whole body trembled, her heart hovering somewhere in her throat. "You're sick," she said, when she could speak. Guntram must've seen Magnus when he picked her up from Kit's. Just a brief glance of the other man, but it was enough for Guntram to remember and use that image. "You're a sick bastard."

Guntram gazed at her coolly. "It may seem cruel, but emotions will wreck your ability to use illusions. If you want to master your skill, you need to master yourself first." The corner of his mouth twitched. "I know it sounds like Zen bullshit, but it's true."

"So this is your idea of training?" she snarled. "Torturing me with images of dead friends?"

Guntram smiled thinly. "Of course not."

She stared at him.

"You'll be expecting that now," Guntram added, and strode out of the kitchen.

Her initial training with Guntram didn't go well. Mostly because it was like living in a haunted house. There were spiders in the shower. A hooded figure standing over her bed. Hallways that shrank. A room without doors. Three Guntrams. A chicken that attacked her ankles when she walked out into the backyard—but it turned out that one wasn't an illusion.

One time, Guntram illusioned the bathroom door so that it appeared open. When it wasn't.

"Why is your head bleeding?" asked Alan, looking concerned.

"Don't ask," she snarled. Then paused. "Why is your face bleeding?"

Alan fingered his bottom lip. "Don't ask."

That seemed to sum up both their trainings.

Ciere and Alan slept in separate rooms in what would've been the attic, had this house been normal. Instead, it was set up in almost a militaristic fashion, with tiny barracks and bunks.

For his part, Conrad locked Alan in, so he had to get downstairs by going out a window and scaling a wall.

"I don't mind," he said. "All this training—it's miserable right now, but it could pay off in the long run."

Ciere forced a smile. "What? You thinking of being a professional bodyguard now?"

"No, but…" He tapped one finger to his temple. "I have things I need to protect. Knowing how to fight, how to defend myself…" His jaw went tight, resolve sharpening his usually mild face.

"It's good," he said, and left it at that.

It turned out Guntram wasn't kidding about the Zen stuff.

"I think, therefore I exist," said Guntram. "The same goes for illusions."

Ciere sat before a row of books, rolling her eyes. She was supposed to be vanishing a single dictionary, leaving the other books visible. It was impossible—when she tried, *all* of the books disappeared.

"Why am I doing this?" she ground out.

Guntram paced somewhere behind her. "Name the five most prominent United States crime families."

Ciere squinted at the dictionary and tried to concentrate. "The Alberanis, the Modicas, the Alkanovs, and the de Grandis. Oh, and you guys." The names came easily to her. If one wanted to thieve in certain areas, one had to know who controlled those places. She pushed harder on the illusion and all the books vanished.

"Wrong," said Guntram lightly. "Although I suppose the question itself was a bit misleading. Your information is outdated. As things stand right now, it's the Gyr Syndicate and the Alberanis."

The books winked into sight.

Guntram looked disapproving. Ciere ignored him. "Seriously?" she demanded. "Just you and the Alberanis?"

"Just us," agreed Guntram, "and the oldest, most deeply entrenched crime family to exist since the Pacific War." His gaze slid to the row of books. "That's why you're doing this. Because when we take them down, there will be no mistakes."

Ciere glared at the dictionary and stretched out her hand.

It took her two weeks to snap.

She was washing dishes, trying to scrub out the remnants

of a potato casserole. The soft sound of the faucet and the swish of the sponge distracted her, and she didn't notice the man until she saw his shadow.

A fire of fury kindled to life in her chest. She couldn't do it anymore. Couldn't bear to deal with another illusion, another nightmare, another damn shade meant to be pushed back.

The hilt of a knife protruded from the soapy water and Ciere seized it. She whirled to her left, lashing out, determined to break the illusion apart by force if she had to.

It was halfway through the strike before she realized there was no telltale buzz, no hint of an illusion. And it was Alan who stood beside her.

Time slowed and she had a fraction of a moment to think: *I'm going to kill him.*

But Conrad's training paid off.

Alan deflected the blow, his forearm smashing into hers. The knife was wrenched from her grip and clattered to the wooden floor.

Ciere leaned over the sink, gasping for breath. Alan rocked back.

"I—I'm sorry," said Ciere, rubbing furiously at her eyes.

Alan let out a startled little laugh. "And I thought my training had me paranoid. I've got Conrad jumping out of closets and practicing choke holds on me."

"I'm sorry," said Ciere again. Her heartbeat finally slowed

to something resembling normal. She still felt flushed, goose bumps prickling at her arms. "I thought—I don't know what I thought. That you weren't real, or something."

Alan's lips pressed together and he rocked on his heels, as if thinking hard. "Have you noticed that out of all the illusions Guntram's conjured to scare you, I haven't been one of them?"

It was true. Guntram had never created a dead Alan to scare her. "Wonder why," she muttered.

Alan frowned. "Isn't it obvious?"

She huffed out a frustrated breath.

"He's only created people he thinks you would care about dying," he said simply. "People he thinks you trust."

Ciere shook her head. "Guntram's a lunatic. He's probably picking people he's seen me with at random. Also, if you walked in while I was staring at your mangled corpse, that'd kill the illusion." Her mouth twitched. "Or traumatize the wrong person."

Alan looked unconvinced. "I wouldn't blame you if you didn't trust me. I am the last Fiacre." He said the words with a twisted smile, and she recognized the look. It was the same when Ciere said she was a thief or a coward—they were bitter little truths, but she'd learned that, by stating them first, she could prevent anyone from throwing them back at her.

Ciere wondered exactly how many times Alan had been introduced just like that: the last Fiacre. How many people looked at him and saw only a formula, saw only the potential of the vaccine reborn, of creating armies and building empires. How many times he looked at himself in the mirror and knew that he was the sum of his brain and little else. He'd grown up knowing that people didn't care about *him*. They cared about what he knew.

And Ciere might have been many things—a thief, a liar, and probably a coward—but at least she never treated a person like that.

Words caught in Ciere's throat and she tried to untangle them. "When I was thirteen," she said, "Kit taught me and Daniel advanced pickpocketing."

Alan blinked.

Ciere raised a hand and realized she was still shaking slightly. She slipped it behind her back. "I'm going somewhere with this, I promise. Back then, Kit brought me and Daniel to a park. He told us to pickpocket a rich man. It was an easy two-person job. Daniel was the distraction and I did the lift. But the mark realized something was wrong and grabbed Daniel."

When she hesitated, Alan inclined his head as if to encourage her.

Ciere sucked in a breath. "I had the wallet in my hand.

So I ran. I left Daniel to fend for himself." She clasped her hands behind her back, trying to steady herself. "I left him there. Daniel was hesitating, waiting to see if I'd come back or not, and he wasn't fighting back…and who knows what would've happened if Kit hadn't come strolling out of the bushes and smiled at the mark and declared the whole thing to be a test. The mark let Daniel go, and everything was fine."

Alan looked startled. "He was testing your pickpocketing abilities?"

"No." Ciere tried to smile and found she couldn't. "Kit said the only truly bad criminal was one who hesitated. He said that Daniel should've either tried to pin the blame on me or fought back. Either way, it would've meant he knew where his priorities were."

She could still hear Kit's familiar voice in her ear, murmuring a soft rebuke: *This wasn't a morality test. I don't need to know your morals, but you do. Before you can do this job, you have to know your own mind.*

"Kit said that Daniel failed that test," said Ciere. "And I passed."

"Because you took the money and ran." Alan didn't sound offended or surprised. "You didn't hesitate."

"I never do," said Ciere. "When it comes to danger, I've always done the smart thing, the criminal thing." She forced herself to look Alan in the eye, even if he didn't return her gaze. "I'm a survivor first, Alan. I've always run or hidden like a coward. It's how I'm still alive."

She said the words without any heat. She was used to having people look at her, frown lines between their eyes. She could still remember the betrayal on Devon's face when she left him behind.

Alan looked at her, and their eyes met. A spark went through her, a little jolt of surprise. "But when the feds were after me, you didn't run." He edged forward. "You didn't leave me behind."

He looked so bewildered that Ciere took pity on him. "Exactly. And I didn't do it because of your family or anything in your head. I did it because, well, I didn't want to see *you* dead," she said. She picked up a clean dish and handed it to him. "Dry this, please."

Alan took the plate and picked up a towel. They washed dishes for a few minutes, until Alan spoke.

"I don't think you're a coward for running," he said. "Living the life we had—being alive is a pretty significant accomplishment."

They still weren't quite friends, not yet. She didn't have a whole lot of experience with friendships—just Daniel, who treated her like a little sister—and Devon, who had been her best friend since she first became a thief. That was back when things were simple, when Devon hadn't seen anything wrong with giving her a bag full of cash, his e-mail address stuffed in the canvas bag.

But Devon and Daniel were both gone.

Alan dried another glass, working with the utmost concentration. As they worked in silence together, Ciere felt something unknot in her chest.

9

CIERE

It takes two days for Ciere to break into Guntram's office. She spends the first day sitting in her closet of a room letting Alan's keepers lull themselves into complacency. Then she goes hunting.

The office is the most heavily guarded place in the old warehouse, which is probably why they're keeping Alan there. It's deep in the building, with a single hallway leading to it. Easily defensible, single entrance, thick walls, and a door with many locks. It's not a bad place to keep someone hidden away.

If anyone else were holding Alan hostage, Ciere would simply illusion herself into nothing; by now it comes as easily as pulling on a shirt. She would yank her surroundings over her skin, let the gray concrete color her face and hair, until she's nothing more than a smudge against the wall. She would wait next to the office door until there's a guard change—and in the fraction of a second, she would slip through the open door.

The problem with this plan is that Guntram knows all the usual tricks.

Ciere finds a grate in a deserted corner of the building. She pries it free and wedges a small flashlight between her teeth. The heating vent smells like dust and the unmistakable odor of decaying animal. Her wobbly light bounces off the gray walls and she tries to concentrate on keeping her movements quiet. She goes on hands and knees, counting grates.

When she comes to what she thinks is the right room, she peers through each slotted grate. There isn't enough space to see through. She listens, instead, pressing her ear against the metal and closing her eyes. She doesn't hear Guntram's voice. Gritting her teeth around the flashlight, she feels for the vent's screws and digs out her lock picks.

Half a minute later, she all but tumbles into Guntram's office. Her knees and gloved hands are covered in dust—and who knows what else.

The office's interior is the same as ever: makeshift desk, chair, and a cot in the corner. A warm glow emanates from the heater's copper coils.

Alan sits on the floor, his arms wrapped around his legs. He glances up, eyes wide and dark. His mouth opens, as if to say something, but Ciere speaks first. "Come on," she says, hurrying across the room. "I've got a way out of here."

Alan gets to his feet and looks at her, the expression on his face torn.

"Hey," Ciere says. Her hand reaches out of its own volition; she wants to touch him, wants to reassure herself that he's okay. But she's not sure she has that right. "Listen, I'll get you out of this, okay?" She turns to go to the vent, but his hand is on her wrist.

His thumb traces a line down her palm and he pulls her around, his other hand on her hip. Ciere's breath catches, and she's not sure if it's the contact or the closeness. He's tugging her closer, until she can feel heat emanating from his chest. His hand comes up and he's cupping her jaw. Something quivers low in her stomach and she hesitates.

Then Alan looks at her, looks her right in the eye, and holds her gaze. And smiles.

A shock goes through her, then she finds herself drawing back. Ciere's hand falls to her side, clenches into a fist, and then she throws that fist at Alan's face.

The blow connects and a jolt of pain runs up her knuckles. Alan jerks back, a grunt of pain escaping his lips. The voice is wrong somehow, too gravelly and—

The illusion wobbles and sloughs away. Guntram stands before her.

Ciere's aching fist clenches again. "What the hell?" she shouts.

He touches the spot on his jaw. "Well, at least you're a fast learner."

"Alan doesn't try to feel me up," she says, livid. "And I thought you were married."

Guntram drops the smile and gives her a steady look. "Just testing a theory."

"Which is?" Ciere snarls the words.

"That there was motive for Pruitt's murder," says Guntram evenly.

Ciere scowls at him. Of course it wouldn't be so easy to rescue Alan; Guntram isn't an idiot.

"Anyway, he's not here," says Guntram, as if sensing her thoughts. "Come on, give me a little credit."

"Where is he?" she snaps.

Guntram dusts off his pants. "Not where we advertised, obviously."

"You knew I'd try to rescue him."

"I wanted to talk," says Guntram simply. "I didn't think you'd be open to it."

Ciere crosses her arms and waits. If he wants to talk, she's not going to help him.

"When I first saw you, I liked you," Guntram says. "An audacious thief with a rare talent. I thought you had promise, which is why I gave you a chance to repay me instead of just turning you over to the feds."

She can't resist saying, "Yeah, you're a saint."

"I've met only one other illusionist besides yourself," Guntram continues, ignoring her. "He was a bit older than me, and we met only briefly. I've never really had the chance to spend time with another one. Teaching you the finer points of our craft has been extremely gratifying."

"This is what you lured me here to say?" she asks. "That I'm a good student?"

"I'm saying you have promise." He pauses, and there's a weight between his words. "It would be a shame to waste that promise."

"Cut it with the veiled threats," Ciere says. "Just tell me what you mean." This is why she hates working with mobsters. Most of them revel in the theatrics of their trade; old phrases are bandied about, and traditions are held nearly sacred. No self-respecting freelancer wastes his or her time like that.

"I'm saying that when that boy is arrested, you should just let it happen." Guntram says it with surprising gentleness. "The others are angry—they want to turn him over and there's only so much I can do to prevent it."

"Alan didn't—"

"He saw Pruitt threaten you," says Guntram. "He made a choice."

Ciere fumbles for a reply.

"He killed Pruitt for the same reason that you crossed me," says Guntram before she can reply. His voice is careful and slow. "For the same reason you broke into this office. He cares what happens to you."

Frustration seethes through her. She wants to hit him again, wants to throw a fist at him again and again until at least one blow connects. Her hands ball without her realizing and she feels a tremor run through her arms. "You can't prove he fired that gun."

Guntram sighs. "The only people with any motive were you and the boy."

She says, "Why was Alan left alone with Pruitt? Where was Conrad?"

Guntram kneads the side of his head, as if trying to banish a headache. "Conrad said he heard a woman scream. He thought it was Henry, so he ran back to the cars."

"Was it her?"

Guntram shakes his head. "The gun went off before he reached her, but she says she didn't make a sound."

She feels her jaw clench. She's doing all she can and he just keeps tossing her arguments back. "Your friends—they're all thugs and mobsters and you're blaming the death on some teenager? Fine. How did Alan get Pruitt's gun? Pretty sure Pruitt didn't just hand it over."

Guntram watches her. "Conrad has been teaching Alan. I'm sure 'how to disarm an opponent' was lesson number one."

"What about the Alkanovs?" she says. "Pruitt used to work for them, right? Crime families like to make examples of traitors."

"Pruitt was a minor eidos in a large crime family," says Guntram, with that unflappable calm. "I can't imagine someone putting a hit out on him. And we broke that family a year ago. The last remnants were arrested sometime in late June."

Ciere represses a shiver. "You said it yourself, though. Pruitt was an eidos; he could've known stuff that someone didn't want getting out. Maybe he worked for some other crook that you don't know about. He had that look."

Guntram runs his thumb over the growing bruise on his jaw. "What look?"

"Professional," says Ciere shortly. "Hardened. You guys... you and Conrad and Henry—you weren't born into this. I can tell. You became criminals because of...well, I don't know why. But Pruitt grew up in the life."

Guntram's expression cools a degree. "So you know he was a professional criminal?"

91

Ciere twitches one shoulder in a shrug. "He was immune," she says. "We're either crooks or feds. Or on the run." She says the words without rancor; it's a fact of life.

Guntram doesn't reply. He leans against his desk and watches her with quiet intensity.

"Why do you think Alan's guilty?" Ciere says. "Why are you so sure it's him?" Her furious energy is already burning itself out. Cold prickles along her bare fingers.

Guntram looks at her calmly. "I'm a good judge of character. It was once part of my job. That boy, your bodyguard... whoever he is—he's got something I've only seen in a few people."

"What?"

"Utter resolve," he says quietly. "Complete and resolute faith in what he believes. He's fighting for someone and he'll kill or die before he gives up."

Her throat aches with all the things she can't tell him. She wants to say, *That might be true, but it's not about me. It's the formula. It's always been about the formula.* Alan has spent his whole life knowing he is the most valuable weapon in the world.

And if Guntram hands Alan over to the feds, they'll find out who he really is. Aristeus tried to kill Alan once before; she has no doubt he would try again. The thought makes her stomach clench.

But she can't tell Guntram any of this. Because who knows what a mobster would do with the Praevenir vaccine.

"Let me go to DC," she says. "Let me investigate—find proof that he didn't do it."

"Why should I risk that?" Guntram says the words slowly, as if he's talking to a child. And compared to him, she is a child. She feels powerless and it infuriates her.

"Because if Alan didn't kill Pruitt, someone else did." Ciere leans forward. "Someone's killing your people. And you protect your investments."

Guntram's mouth turns down. It's the first real blow she's struck, and she knows it.

"All right," he says.

Turns out, they've been keeping Alan in the kitchen.

"Here," says Ciere flatly. "You've been keeping him here?"

"There's near constant traffic," says Guntram. "Plenty of witnesses. Cole almost never leaves, and he's always armed with at least one knife." As if on cue, Cole tosses a paring knife into the air and catches it nimbly between two fingers.

Alan sits in plain view, handcuffed to a propane tank—the one feeding into the temporary stove. He sits on a folding chair, book in hand. Nearby, Cole hums to himself and chops a potato. The scent of fresh food would've tempted her on any other day, but she sees a familiar band of metal encircling Alan's wrist. It's identical to her own bracelet. They've tagged him with a tracker.

His head is bowed, sharpening the angle of his chin. His eyes are on the floor, lashes dark against his copper skin. But when he lifts those eyes, there's nothing like surrender in his face. His gaze is unfocused, but Ciere has the feeling he's watching everything. With his wrist cuffed, he looks like a trapped animal—all the more dangerous for being cornered.

"I'll give you a moment," says Guntram, nodding to Cole. The cook tosses a dish towel over his shoulder and strolls away. Guntram waits a moment, cool blue eyes on Ciere, then follows.

Ciere waits until they're both gone, then grabs a vacant chair and drags it over. The metal is frigid, but it's still better than standing. Her attention settles on Alan. "Nice digs," she says, going for light. "At least you've got first access to the coffee."

Alan doesn't quite smile, but some of the defiance leaves his face. "At least being a supposed killer has that perk."

"I know you didn't do it," says Ciere. "I mean, you didn't do it. Right?" Because there's still that niggling suspicion, even if she doesn't want to admit it to herself.

Alan hesitates, then shakes his head. "We were separated.

I heard the shot and ran over. I'd just gotten to Pruitt when you and Guntram rounded the corner. He'll never believe me, though. We're the outsiders. He wants me to take the fall, rather than blame one of his people."

"Have they told you anything?"

"No."

She quickly outlines what she knows. Alan blinks. "You think the hotel key belonged to Pruitt?"

"Guntram says he's never seen it before," says Ciere. "I'm hoping it belonged to the killer. If I can visit the hotel, and see if any of the Syndicate members—"

"You mean Conrad or Henry," says Alan.

"Yeah." Anxiety twists at her stomach and she rubs a hand through her hair, trying to distract herself. "I mean, I hate to think that one of them would try to frame us. I like them, but..."

"They were the only ones there besides us," says Alan. "And if we didn't do it, it had to be them."

"I'm thinking Henry," says Ciere, grimacing. "Conrad... well, I like Conrad and all, but he's not exactly an evil genius."

"You know who *is* an evil genius?" says Alan, eyes darting to the doors. "Guntram."

It's a thought that Ciere has tried to push away. It's lurked at the corner of her mind, but she hasn't allowed herself to fully examine it—because the implications are terrifying.

"Guntram was with me," says Ciere.

Concern settles into Alan's face, making him look older. "He's an illusionist. A better illusionist than you, no offense," he adds hastily.

Ciere shrugs. "But even if he could fool me into thinking he was there when he wasn't…why would Guntram kill one of his own men? You've heard him." She clenches her jaw and imitates Guntram's iron-hard pronunciation. "We protect our investments."

"Yes," says Alan gravely. "And what better investment is there than a young illusionist?"

The air freezes in Ciere's lungs. "You—you think…"

"I think," says Alan, "that our term of service is about to expire. And Guntram might not be willing to let a valuable immune soldier go. Even at the expense of holding me hostage."

"Shit," says Ciere, shaken. "I hadn't thought of that. But— but if it's Guntram, what can we do?"

She suddenly feels constricted by her jacket and scarf; she yanks at the latter irritably, tossing it onto the counter. "He can't do this." She gets to her feet, wanting to pace or run, or just move. "He made a deal, and if he's going to break it, he should just shove a gun in my face or something. Like a normal criminal."

"Ciere," says Alan, getting up and trying to take a step forward. His handcuff pulls tight and he winces, edging back.

"Kit won't stand for it," says Ciere. "He'll wonder why we aren't back. He'll come for us."

"Kit is an art fence," replies Alan, but he says it gently. "I'm not sure he can handle Guntram."

She exhales through her nose, eyes averted. She can feel his gaze. "I'll find proof that you're innocent," she says. "And if I can't... I'll come back and get you out myself."

His fingers go to the bracelet around her wrist. "What about these? They could track both of us. And Guntram...?"

"We'll break them," she says. "If Guntram wants to fight me, he's free to try. But by now I have enough info on the Gyr Syndicate that I could probably work out a cushy deal with the feds in exchange for my freedom. What's one illusionist compared with a crime syndicate?"

"Ciere," he begins to say, and she just knows he's going to protest. "It's too dangerous. You can't go to the feds."

"I don't care," she says shrilly, and she knows her voice is climbing, can feel it rising in pitch but can't seem to quiet herself. "They're not holding you here just so they can control me."

She's shaking. She hates this physical reaction—she wishes she could be as calm as Guntram, but she can't. She takes another step back, but he follows, and the chain binding him to the propane tank clinks in protest.

She isn't sure how it happens; his free arm comes up

around her waist and suddenly she's nestled against his shoulder, breathing hard into the cotton of his shirt. She only realizes how hard she's shaking when she feels his steady weight. "It'll be okay," he says. The words vibrate in his chest; she can feel him speak. But still, she doesn't step back. He feels warm and steady, and she can't bring herself to let go.

"I thought it wasn't real," she says. She's breathing hard into his shoulder, letting him take some of her weight. His arm presses around her, steady and familiar.

"What?" She feels the question rumble through his chest.

"When I saw you and Pruitt." The words shake themselves out of her. "I thought Guntram was testing me again. I thought it was just an illusion."

His arm tightens around her.

For the first time in weeks—months, really—her mind goes quiet. There are no feds, no Gyr Syndicate, no training sessions, no danger. For the briefest moment, she feels safe.

The second she realizes that, she's terrified.

"He cares what happens to you." Guntram's voice sounds smug, even in her memories.

But here's the thing—she knows he doesn't. They've been here before, teetering on the edge, and he was the one who stepped back. She can still feel the sting of his words, the explanation settling between them.

She manages to disentangle herself. This doesn't mean the same thing to him.

She takes a step back, further distancing herself.

"It's too dangerous," repeats Alan.

"I'll be back soon," Ciere says, looking away. She can't look at him, so she turns on her heel and walks through the door.

10

CIERE

Four months ago, Ciere went on her first assignment with the Gyr Syndicate.

When they left the Gettysburg farmhouse, Ciere didn't mourn. Having spent weeks being bombarded by illusions, she had learned how to detect and eliminate them without a second thought. It became habit to step into a room and send out her immunity, scanning for the telltale buzz of an illusion. She was also so inured to horror that she thought a haunted house or scary movie might never faze her again.

As she waited in the driveway, she glanced into one of the Honda's side mirrors. Her face looked different; hollows carved out beneath her cheekbones, darkened shadows around her eyes, and her lips looked thinner. Constant vigilance had a price. It whittled a person down until they were nothing but reflexes and sinew.

Alan had also changed. His coppery skin darkened a few shades, probably from sparring under the sun, and he'd filled out beneath his T-shirts. He looked healthier and less gaunt. He'd thrived under Conrad's tutelage. Ciere gave her sunken eyes one more glance before turning away. There were more important things than sleep.

The Syndicate's New Haven stronghold was part of a hollowed-out strip mall. Long abandoned by its owners, the mall was surprisingly clean and orderly, its debris swept to one side and replaced with temporary furniture. It still smelled of dust, and Ciere caught a glimpse of rat poison sitting in the corners.

Henry sat in a folding metal chair, her legs crossed. She looked at Ciere like she was a cute pet Guntram had brought home.

Alan hung back, a silent shadow at Ciere's shoulder.

Conrad emerged from a side door, a shoe box tucked under one arm. He set the box down on a plastic table and removed the lid with a flourish. He grinned and tipped the box toward her, revealing its contents.

"Oh, no," said Ciere flatly when she saw the silver bracelets. They were open, not yet hinged around some unsuspecting person's wrist.

The tracker bracelets were the Syndicate's ace in the hole. "They were developed for Alzheimer's patients," said Henry brightly. "They send out a medical alert to all local cops if they're broken."

Ciere knew exactly how they worked; a bracelet fit snugly around her own wrist.

"How do you keep track of them all?" she asked, unable to stop looking into the box. There must have been twenty of those trackers.

"We've got an online database," said Henry. "Jess set it up—she likes computers. Each bracelet has an individual number and we can monitor them with our phones. That way we can activate the bracelets from anywhere."

"Combine that alert with a tip to the cops about the tagged person being an assassin," said Conrad, "and the tagged person has little chance of escape."

It was a neat little plan. It meant the Syndicate could pawn off its dirty work on the feds. Bloodless and ruthlessly effective.

"I'm tagging an assassin?" she said.

Conrad blinked at her, all innocence. "Did I say that?"

Alan spoke for the first time. His gaze was settled on the bracelets, hands in his pockets. "Why doesn't anyone take them off?"

Conrad looked at him in surprise.

Alan didn't return his gaze. "I mean, there have to be people who are desperate enough to smash the bracelet and hope they can get away before the cops show up."

Conrad and Henry laughed. "We might tell a few people that the bracelet will explode," said Henry.

Ciere swallowed. "That's not true, right?"

Guntram strode into the room. "Why don't you try to take off your bracelet and find out?" He looked as calm as ever, but there was fresh energy to him. This was Guntram on the job—the days of training on the farm were over.

Ciere fidgeted with her own bracelet. "So if it's not an assassin, who *am* I tagging?"

"One of the Alberani higher-ups." Guntram's smile sharpened. "An old enemy, very dangerous. He knows what I am, so he'll be expecting me. But a young girl..." His gaze settled on Ciere and her stomach bottomed out.

"So you want me killed on my first mission?" she asked. "Seems like kind of a waste, after going to all the effort of training me."

Alan made a soft sound. "We're expendable," he said quietly. "And we have no way to be linked to the Syndicate if we're caught."

Henry and Conrad laughed again. "Two for two," said Henry. "He's pretty smart."

"Consider it initiation," said Guntram, idly twirling a

bracelet between his fingers. "Succeed in this job, and you'll truly be working for the Syndicate."

"And if you fail," said Conrad reasonably, "you probably won't be alive long enough to care."

Ciere sprinted onto the cement walkway of the New Haven metro. With Alan at her heels, she pushed her way through the crowd, trying to ignore the groan of subway doors. Heat rolled down the tunnel and she felt a gust of wind as one of the trains passed. It almost drowned out the sound of yelling— almost. The train behind her was still in chaos, its occupants blinking illusive darkness from their eyes.

The close press of bodies and sensation of the heavy ceiling above made her light-headed. Her eyes darted through the crowd, trying to find the emergency stairs. The blueprints had said they'd be here—they had to be here—

"There," said Alan, pointing. Tucked away into a dark corner was a side door. Ciere shoved through the crowd, her fingers closing on the hatch.

The door closed behind them and Ciere found herself leaning against a damp cement wall, hands on her knees, breath sawing in and out.

"Mission," said Ciere, barely able to gasp the words, "accomplished."

"Well, that was exhilarating," said Alan, still panting.

"That's one word for it," she rasped. For a moment, neither moved. Ciere let the seconds drag by, tried to grasp the fact that she'd actually just finished her first assignment for the Gyr Syndicate—and she was still alive. She let out a small, startled laugh and Alan looked at her.

"What?"

"It's just," she said, unable to hold her grin, "when you agreed to come with me—when I found you in that panic room—I'm pretty sure you had no idea it would lead to you cornering mobsters on subways."

Alan looked down, a smile breaking across his face. "There are worse places to be." He glanced up, and their eyes met. He looked brilliant, lit up with triumph.

She felt a sharp spike of want, the kind she'd only ever felt when looking at bank vaults or stolen paintings. She was a thief, and she was used to simply reaching out and taking things she wanted.

She was distantly aware that she'd stopped smiling, and he had, too.

"Guntram'll be waiting," he said, and reality came crashing down around her again. She felt unsteady, cold as the adrenaline drained away.

"Right," she said.

Alan held out a hand and she took it, letting him pull her upright.

The stairs spiraled upward, leading to a rusty emergency hatch. Alan yanked it open and they stepped into blinding sunlight. An alley rose up around them, buildings red-bricked and tall. Ciere blinked hard and tried to draw herself together.

"Let's find a cab," she said. "I want to get out of here before the Alberanis call for reinforcements." She strode onto the sidewalk, away from the metro, eyes scanning the crowded street. As she raised one hand to gesture for a cab, someone grabbed her.

"Hey," said a man.

It wasn't the man touching her that shocked Ciere. It was how Alan responded. He seized the man's arm and twisted. At the same moment, he lashed out with a leg, crumpling the man at the knee.

The man fell to the ground with a muffled cry and Alan retreated, his arm thrown out. Ciere suddenly found herself pushed a step backward, Alan squarely in front of her. "Come on," he said, herding her backward. "We need to—"

The man groaned and rose to his feet. "If you run, I am going to tell Guntram that I tried and failed to get you back to base."

Ciere froze. "What?"

"I'm working with Guntram, you idiot," the man snapped. "I'm your ride. He told me you'd need a lift after a job."

Ciere pushed her way around Alan so she could get a

better look at the man. He had curly black hair and scarred knuckles. "Who are you?"

The man was giving her the same once-over. He reached down and touched his knee, his face gone tight with pain. "My name's Pruitt."

11

CIERE

Guntram is waiting for her outside of the warehouse. Ten minutes ago that fact might have been comforting, but now it's creepy.

Ciere steps through a side door, her Hello Kitty backpack over her shoulders. Her boots crunch through the gravel and snow.

"Washington, DC," says Ciere, her words clipped. "None of your team have been there recently, right?"

A shake of his head. "People have gone missing there recently, though" he says. "It doesn't look like any of the crime families are responsible, but you should still be careful."

"You're really going to just let me go investigate?" she says.

He doesn't answer for a long moment. He merely watches her. "If I said no, what would you do?"

Her heartbeat picks up. "Probably wouldn't go."

Guntram's scrutiny seems to intensify. Ciere feels herself shrink under his gaze. "Really."

"You sound like you want me to argue," she says, frustrated by his lack of emotion. "But it's not like I could."

"Really."

She bristles, and her frustration simmers to the surface. "I can't fight like a dauthus or run like an eludere. No levitating away from danger." She gestures at herself. "I cast shadows, that's all. And shadows never hurt anyone."

Guntram backhands her.

The blow rattles her teeth. Pain flashes through her skull. Stumbling backward, Ciere presses a hand to her mouth and forces herself to steady, to meet Guntram's eyes. She works her jaw, running her tongue over her teeth to make sure everything is there. When she wipes at her nose, she sees blood. "You gave me a bloody nose," she chokes out. "You insane bastard—what the hell—"

And then Guntram *vanishes*.

For a long second, Ciere stares at nothing. The air in front of her is utterly empty.

"Sorry about that," comes Guntram's voice, and she whirls. Sure enough, Guntram stands behind her. He lounges against the warehouse's wall, his arms crossed and a slight smile on his lips. "Had to prove a point."

"Was that—" The words freeze in her mouth, she can't speak them—they're too big. "Did you—"

"Hurt you," says Guntram, "with an illusion. Yes. Again, sorry about that."

It's all she can do to stare at him. If he's telling the truth, then the implications are staggering.

Guntram pushes away from the brick wall, striding slowly through the snow. "The strongest illusionists can affect more than sight or smell. We hadn't gotten to that part of your training yet, I'm afraid."

"I'm bleeding," she sputters. "You can't—an illusion can't make someone bleed!"

He taps the side of his head. "Scientists are still discovering how much power the brain has over the body. Placebos can make real illnesses recede. Men can have sympathy pregnancies. Stress can cause any number of illnesses, from migraines to digestive problems." He stands before her, his gloved fingers reaching out to touch her chin. He wipes away a dribble of blood. He tilts her head back so that she has to meet his eyes.

She forces herself to concentrate on his words. "I believed I was hurt, so I felt it." She can still feel echoes of the blow. "I bled because of it." She studies the red on her hand. "I burst a blood vessel?"

"Capillaries," says Guntram dismissively. "If that had been a blood vessel, we wouldn't be having this lively discussion."

"Wait." A thought occurs to her. "How do I know that it wasn't real? How do I know that you weren't really standing in front of me, hit me, and then vanished yourself before projecting an illusion to make me think the real you was the illusion?"

Guntram outright grins. "Now you're asking the right questions."

"But how do I know—"

"You don't. That's the beauty of a truly good illusionist." He reaches down and taps a finger against Ciere's collarbone. "Illusion is powerful," he continues, and his voice turns deadly serious. "It's taking control of another person's senses. It's making them believe exactly what you want them to. It is, in my opinion, the most dangerous of all the immunities. Not even a dominus can make a person doubt herself."

What he's suggesting is insane. Ciere can barely wrap her mind around it—illusion has always been something of a trick to her. A dangerous, deadly trick, sure, but it's never been what Guntram is suggesting: a weapon.

"Could you kill someone?" she says. Pruitt's name rests heavily in her mind and the taste of copper is still fresh in her mouth. A memory pulls insistently at her—a warm summer night, rough pavement beneath her knees and two Taser barbs lodged in her skin. She remembers conjuring the image of a gun, desperate to frighten away her attackers. It hadn't occurred to her what might have happened if she'd pulled the trigger.

If what Guntram says is true, then he's far more dangerous than she ever suspected.

Guntram appears to consider her question. "I don't think blunt trauma could be delivered through an illusion. That takes actual physical cause."

"But this"—Ciere points at her bloody nose—"you did this."

"Yes," he says. "There are other ways besides force to injure someone. Make them believe something until it kills them—that could work."

She stares at him for a long while. None of this makes sense. If he did kill Pruitt, why would he show her this power? "Why are you telling me this now?"

"Because," says Guntram, "you need a weapon."

She rubs at her nose, still startled by the phantom pain that shoots through her. *It's not real*, she thinks. *I'm making it real just by believing it.* She tries to push the sensation away. She doesn't try to disguise the disgust in her voice when she says, "Of course you'd think that way."

She can almost feel the unsaid implications settle between them, like a fissure opening up in the ground.

"What is that supposed to mean?" Guntram's eyes narrow by a fraction.

Ciere faces him head-on. "It would never have occurred to me to use an illusion like that. It's the same reason I think either Conrad or Henry killed Pruitt. Killing people and taking over—it's just what you mobsters do." She throws the words out before she has time to think about them. She sucks in a sharp breath, lungs suddenly rigid. Part of her can't believe she uttered those words aloud; she's seen what Guntram does to his enemies. Her shoulders stiffen, and she realizes she's unconsciously bracing herself.

Guntram hesitates, and something almost like regret passes over his face. It vanishes a moment later. "Yes," he says, "it's exactly what I do."

PART TWO

The United States stands at this time at the pinnacle of world power. It is a solemn moment for the American Democracy. For with primacy in power is also joined an awe-inspiring accountability to the future.

—Winston Churchill, March 5, 1946

12

DEVON

Working for the government doesn't come easily to Devon. Walking in is always the hardest part; stepping through the front doors reminds him of all the illegal things he's done—and there have been a lot. He runs his tags through a scanner, nods to the now-familiar security guard, and strides into the lift.

His desk is just beyond Sia's. It's a small cubicle, with felted walls and a plastic desk. Its previous occupant left behind pens and a pencil sharpener shaped like a bulldog. Devon always takes a moment to sit in his chair, to reacquaint himself with the office.

It's just like putting on another mask is what he tells himself. It's just like going to school or being with Ciere's friends.

He's pretending to be something he's not. He's done it for most of his life.

But there's one thing he can't fake: the mandatory drug test.

"Congrats," says Morgan Clarke cheerily. She's petite and pretty and scares Devon half to death. There is just something too confident about her, something about the way she holds herself. She looks a few years older than Macourek, probably in her early thirties.

"For what?" he asks hopefully. "I passed?"

Clarke traces a finger down the paper. "No. It's just, we've never had anyone test positive for *everything*."

Disappointment settles heavy in his stomach. "Right. So am I fired then?"

"Nope," says Clarke, snapping his file shut. "But Macourek did say that if you ever show up to the office inebriated, you'll be fired on the spot." Her smile makes Devon go cold. "Got it?"

Macourek himself is a bit of an enigma. He isn't intimidating or commanding, and Devon tries to figure out how someone like that ended up head of a small government department. Macourek is smart, but he doesn't come off like a reclusive genius; he's thin; he doesn't seem to have any secret ninja skills that Devon is aware of. What he is—he's *nice*. He says hello to everyone in the halls, always speaks politely, always looks happy to see everyone in the office.

Devon's day begins with waking up around six, shower-ing, putting on a nice shirt and slacks, and taking a bus to work. Since the coffeemaker remains broken, it's his job to brave the ice and foot traffic and bring back drinks from the shop around the corner. Most mornings Devon feels like an overdressed waiter, carrying a pad of paper and taking down drink orders. (The pad is just another prop; he could remem-ber the orders easily.) Sia's orders are the most difficult—she orders triple soy lattes with syrups he's never even heard of.

Devon's other duties include calling people, delivering papers to other buildings, and then grabbing a second round of coffee after lunch. But Macourek was right—this job consists mostly of data entry. There are hundreds of folders contain-ing personal information about individuals—ages, genders, jobs, education, and the like. The names are blotted out, but Devon doesn't mind; it's one less bit of information lodged in his memory. He types and types, listens to the soft electronic voice of Sia's computer, and then types more.

It's all simple work and Devon sometimes finds himself staring at his own coffee cup, wishing he has something to spike it with. He yearns for the dulled senses, for the gentle buzz of the alcohol, but he forces himself to abstain.

He can't be fired from this job. If they fire him, he'll have to go back to Boston. And as boring and tedious as this job is, it's still better than his father's house. Devon's home now is a dorm room, where he's blissfully alone. No one looking over his shoulder, no one hassling him about his future.

His dad calls once. Devon sees the caller ID and smashes his expensive mobile against a wall. The next day, he goes out and buys a burner phone with a new number.

It's three weeks before the monotony breaks.

Devon is completing his morning coffee run when the lift doors open with a soft ding, and two men and a woman stride into the hallway. The dry, crisp scent of winter hangs around them. Devon's eyes sweep over them, his brain taking notes in case he needs to remember them later. The woman is in her mid-forties, with carefully brushed hair. The men flank her, bodyguard-style.

They try to walk past Devon, one of the men knocking him aside with his shoulder. "Hey!" Devon cries out as Sia's coffee goes flying. The hot liquid soaks into his white shirt, scalding him.

The second man gives him a narrow-eyed look, but before he can say anything, Macourek strides around a corner. Sia is at his shoulder, her fingers trailing along the cubicle's felted wall.

"Gentlemen," says Macourek. "Madam." His voice is heavy and hard as bedrock. "I'd appreciate it if you didn't manhandle my employees."

The man sneers openly at Devon, eyes flicking to the stain on his shirt. "You call that manhandling?"

Macourek takes a step forward, insinuating himself into the man's personal space. Devon can't put a finger on Macourek's expression—it's not quite angry. *Hungry*, Devon thinks. Like a cat staring at a bird through a window—all twitching tail and bunched muscles, unable to strike at its prey.

"You are going to leave," Macourek says softly. "Tell your boss that if she wants greater control over my department, she's welcome to set up a meeting and arrange it."

The woman speaks up. "She sent us—"

"Yes, and you're such good little employees." Macourek's mouth creases into a thin smile. "Now run along." His voice never loses its pleasant tone.

As if the movement has been choreographed, all three turn on their heels and speed toward the lift. The doors slide shut behind them and Macourek lets out an audible breath.

"I thought we scared them away months ago," says Sia. She reaches out and puts a hand on Devon's arm. "You okay?" Her fingers brush his sodden shirt and she frowns. "Why are you wet?"

"I'm wearing your coffee, courtesy of our visitors," Devon says. "Who were they?"

Macourek's gaze remains distant. "Rival department."

Sia adds, "They think we're insignificant and we think they're assholes. It's a good relationship."

Macourek seems to shake himself, coming back to the moment. His eyes sweep over Devon and rest on the coffee stain. "You'll need a new shirt," he says distractedly. "Sia—take an early lunch break and go with him."

Devon barely has time to protest before Sia reaches for her coat and takes him by the arm. When he glances over his shoulder, Devon sees Macourek reaching for the fallen coffee cup.

The good thing about having an office in downtown DC is that a department store is never too far away. Devon buys a new shirt, tosses the old one, and glances at his watch. They still have an hour left before they're due back at work. "Coffee?" he says. "Since you never got yours?"

"Please."

The streets are crowded; there was fresh snowfall last night and the roads aren't entirely clear yet. Traffic crawls by and everyone on the sidewalk looks harried. Sia takes Devon's arm. Her fingertips touch the skin under his sleeve and he shivers. "You're freezing," he says. "Don't you ever wear gloves?"

She lets out a laugh. "I wasn't planning on an impromptu shopping trip."

Devon steps off the curb. Sia stumbles, then jabs him with an elbow. "Warning next time, please."

"Sorry," he says, contrite.

They walk to a nearby coffee shop, and Devon has to push his way through the door. The shop is thronged with the lunch hour crowd. With the heaters on high and the snow melting off clothes, the air feels muggy. The windows are smudged with fog and fingerprints. Devon and Sia take a two-person table near the restrooms.

"So how are you liking work?" asks Sia, taking a drink of her latte.

Devon tries to think of an answer that won't get him into too much trouble. "It's...uh, different."

"You're bored."

"No!" Devon grimaces. "Maybe. It's just—I'm not really an office guy."

Sia knits her fingers around the coffee cup. "Well, when I started this job, I wasn't exactly an office girl."

That brings up an interesting question. Devon weighs his words, tries to think of a polite way to ask, and then decides to plow right in. "How'd a person like you end up with this job?"

She frowns. "What do you mean?"

What he means is how did a young, pretty, blind girl end up as Macourek's assistant. Not that he can say any of that aloud.

"I mean," he says, "aren't you a little young to be head secretary?"

She raises her eyebrows. "You make it sound like I'm twelve. I'm nineteen. Also, I'm a PA, not a secretary."

"Whatever. You're only a year older than me. Macourek's head of a government department—even if it is small. How'd you end up working for him?"

Sia takes a sip of her coffee. "I used to go to a boarding school, like you. But I had some...issues fitting in. Like you did. Macourek recruited me and I worked my way up."

Devon tries not to sound skeptical. "Macourek always goes after the loner types like us?"

Sia's face smooths out, as if contemplating a happy memory. "He's a good man. He looks for kids who otherwise wouldn't receive second chances and he offers them one." Her mouth twitches. "Or sixth chance, in your case."

Devon takes a drink of his own coffee; it's too hot and he swallows it quickly. It burns down to his stomach, settling there like a lump of hot coal.

Sia's phone beeps and she presses it to her ear. It's a welcome distraction. Devon fidgets with his cup holder, shredding the cardboard between his fingers.

After a minute, Sia sets her phone down on the table. "And here's yet another joy of being a smaller division," she mutters. She tosses the last of her coffee back. "Sometimes the other agencies think we should run errands for them. We get called in to do some pretty odd jobs."

Devon glances at her phone. "You're running an errand for someone?"

"No," she says brightly. "*I'm* delegating. *You're* running the errand. There's a surveillance car that hasn't had any backup in six hours and apparently the occupants are getting hungry. Usually the FBI or local police would handle this, but there was an accident a few blocks down and that takes priority."

He stares at her. "You want me to deliver food?"

"That's the general idea of a food drop, yes."

"Can you get back to the office by yourself?"

She reaches into her purse and withdraws a small white stick. She snaps it open and it extends, folding over itself, until it becomes a long cane. "Please," she snorts, looking highly unimpressed. "You worry about yourself, all right? Just don't get caught in a shootout or anything."

He flashes a flirtatious grin. "Because you'd miss me if I died?"

"Because," she says, "as an intern, you don't qualify for our health insurance."

13

DANIEL

Daniel begins to doubt himself when he doesn't take the last donut.

For one thing, he's sitting in an unmarked car with a sleeping FBI agent and he's not doing anything about it.

Then there's the fact that they're down to the last donut. He spends a good fifteen minutes contemplating the white bag sitting on the dashboard. He's hungry and he really should just take it, but something in him nags. The donut technically belongs to Gervais.

Which means that they've run out of food. In any other situation, they could've just gotten out of the car and traipsed to a nearby street vendor. But the cold weather has kept most of the food trucks off the streets, and since this is a *stakeout*, they can't leave and find a restaurant.

This job, this *life*, is twisting his instincts. In the old days, he would've handcuffed Gervais to the car and then strolled out to get a lunch of sushi.

But he isn't that guy anymore. And that scares him.

Gervais's temple rests against the driver's-side door, a newspaper spread across his chest. Daniel scans the headlines: a new law about how many mentalists are allowed to work for the TSA, something about Aditi Sen's latest speech, and a feel-good story about a three-legged puppy. Daniel almost breathes a sigh of relief. He keeps half expecting to see a news article about one of his former friends—an art heist gone wrong or an illusionist caught in the act.

Daniel resists the urge to sigh and turns his attention back to the office building. They've been staking out this street for the better part of a week. Which wouldn't be so bad if they had concrete evidence that their perp would show. But all they have is rumor and hearsay.

The word comes back to Daniel: "perp," not "colleague." It's official. He's gone native.

Gervais comes awake with a start. His hand twitches toward his shoulder holster; he touches the gun, as if to reassure himself that it's still there. He shakes his head, like a dog trying to rid its ears of water.

"Good nap?" says Daniel, turning to stare out the windshield again.

"Not really." Gervais sinks back into his seat. "Have you seen her?"

"Nope."

According to the UAI files, over twenty people have gone missing in the last four months from the DC area. It wouldn't seem so ominous if there weren't similar disappearances as far away as Boston and Tampa. Those missing all have one thing in common: testing positive for Praevenir.

The only real clue in the case of the DC disappearances is a woman who was seen with five of the missing persons. This should make her an easy person to bring in and question. That is, if anyone could find her. If she's a crook, Maya Cooper is a good one. ("Age thirty-four, Caucasian, red hair, high school educated, bounced between temp jobs for several years," went the file.) Her apartment is empty, her PO box unused, her car unregistered, and her friends nonexistent.

A street camera caught a glimpse of Maya Cooper here two weeks ago. It's a weak lead, but it's better than nothing.

"I just don't get the motive," Daniel says. He doesn't have to explain. "There's no ransom demands. None of them have connections to crime families. The missing people weren't even rich. I don't see a pattern."

Gervais makes a thoughtful sound. He doesn't seem frustrated or annoyed by the case—but then again, he's used to this kind of thing. "Motive isn't always obvious," he murmurs.

"There must be a link." He straightens. "Or Maya Cooper could just be kidnapping and killing people at random. The psychotic ones are the most difficult to track."

"If they're all dead, where are the bodies?" says Daniel, frowning.

Discussing the disappearances, morbid as they are, is reassuring. The friendly debate is almost reminiscent of home with Kit and Ciere.

Gervais doesn't answer. His eyes go to the donut bag and he reaches for it, shakes it. "You left one?"

"Technically, the last donut is yours."

Gervais appears nonplussed. "Well, thank you." He contemplates the pastry for a moment before setting it back on the dashboard. "This is kind of humiliating. Usually, we'd have three people so two could stay in the car and one could get supplies, but ... well ..." He trails off and Daniel gets it.

"If it makes you feel any better," says Daniel, "the scanner reported an accident nearby, so the fact that we've been ignored might not mean that everyone hates us." He opens his mouth to say more, but a whisper passes by his right ear.

He hears a quick heartbeat and a sharp inhalation. Daniel shifts his gaze to his right without moving his head. Looking at a threat is a sure tip-off.

Gervais isn't an idiot; his whole body tenses. "What is it?" he says, barely moving his lips.

Daniel's fingers close around the door handle. "Someone's watching us."

Gervais shifts slightly, angling his body so that he can reach for the Glock under his left arm. "Man or woman?"

"Don't know." Daniel feels the muscles in his neck strain; he wants to look, but he knows he shouldn't.

"Recline your seat," says Gervais slowly.

"Nap time?"

Gervais's mouth twitches. "I want you out of the line of fire."

Oh. The word forms on Daniel's lips, but he doesn't say it. There's a swooping sensation in his gut—he feels painfully exposed, fear crawls up his throat—

And someone raps on his window.

Daniel jerks in surprise and he looks before he can stop himself.

A young man stands just outside of the car. He's tall, black, with closely cropped brown hair. His pants are pressed and he wears a heavy wool coat. There's a coffee tray cradled on one arm and a bag dangling from one hand.

"I can't believe this," the man says, his British accent slightly muffled through the window. "If Sia was having me on...ah, well." There's something familiar in his voice and it sets Daniel on edge. The young man raps on the window again. Daniel looks to Gervais. The older man nods slowly. Daniel rolls the window down an inch.

"What?"

The young man makes a disgusted face. "The pigeon flies over the bench."

It's the code phrase—one that means, *Hey, I'm on your side; please don't shoot me.*

Daniel worms his arm behind his seat and yanks the car's back door open. "Get in."

The stranger blinks. "What?"

"Get in before you attract attention," Gervais snaps, seemingly restraining his urge to add, *Obviously.* The stranger blinks again, nods, and folds himself into the backseat, pulling the door shut behind him. "Who are you? What are you doing here?"

The young man hands over the tray of coffees and a brown paper bag. "Food delivery."

"Oh, thank god," says Daniel, and all but rips the bag in his haste. There are sandwiches—several of them, and he doesn't even bother to glance at the labels. So long as it isn't a donut, he doesn't care. He rips the plastic wrap with his teeth.

"Who are you?" Gervais gives the intruder a narrow-eyed look.

The stranger watches Daniel tear into a sandwich, looking both fascinated and vaguely horrified. "I'm with Homeland Security. Everyone else was busy, so they asked me to bring lunch over."

"Tags," says Gervais, holding out a hand expectantly. The stranger fumbles around his neck for a moment and then hands them over. Gervais presses one to the car's dashboard—like all fed cars, it comes with its own tag scanner. The windshield flickers and its transparency shifts into a screen only visible from the inside. An image appears—the young man facing a camera, a smug smile on his face. Words blink beneath the portrait. *DEVON LYRE. VACCINATED. NO EVIDENCE OF ADVERSE EFFECTS.* Gervais scrolls through the highlighted information until he comes to the most recent update: *HOME-LAND SECURITY CLEARANCE.*

Devon Lyre.

Daniel rolls the name around for a moment. He repeats it to himself, weighs it, tries to follow it back to its source. Devon Lyre. It's the last name that sparks his memory.

Back when things made sense, Daniel lived with Kit and Ciere. Ciere had a friend. Not just a friend, but an utterly non-crooked, straightest-of-the-straight friend with the last name Lyre. Daniel remembers Kit ranting about it. ("Of all the people," said Kit, "you had to befriend a trust fund brat?") Ciere would hang out with Lyre away from her crew, keeping him on the fringes of things. Daniel never met the guy, and he assumed it was because Ciere wanted something that was wholly her own.

Daniel studies this Devon Lyre, tries to decide if this is Ciere's old friend. Kit's words—*"trust fund brat"*—come back to him, and he sweeps Lyre with a calculating look.

He's checking his watch, tapping his fingers against his thighs, like he has somewhere better to be. The way he glances at the interior of the car—not exactly dirty, but cluttered—with slight disdain. The tag is still attached to his new shirt. And then there's the fact his watch costs more than most people's rent.

Yep, this is Ciere's friend.

For a moment, all Daniel wants to do is come up with an excuse to get this guy alone. To ask him about Ciere—if she's all right, what she's up to, if she ever managed to rob a bank successfully. But—but if he's working for HS now, then that means he's a traitor. Kit is going to be *triumphant*—and Ciere will be *heartbroken*—

And Daniel won't be around to witness any of that.

He's abruptly paralyzed, the sandwich held in one frozen hand. He'll never get to hear Kit's gloating. He'll never see Ciere's reaction to this betrayal. He'll never see any of them again unless they're arrested.

"You're with HS?" Gervais's iron-hard posture relaxes.

Devon Lyre sounds almost embarrassed when he answers. "I'm just an intern." He glances at Daniel and his face creases with concern. "You all right, mate? That sandwich taste off?"

Daniel forces himself to take another bite, chew, and swallow. It slides down his throat like liquid cement. He wrenches his eyes forward so he has something to look at other than Lyre. His gaze drifts to the street ahead and his stomach lurches.

Maya Cooper stands on the sidewalk.

She's pretty, with a rounded figure and brilliant red hair. She's dressed like any of the other people on the street—heavy winter coat, boots, and a scarf. She can't be more than forty feet away.

For a moment, all Daniel can do is stare. Cooper isn't supposed to be *here*, not really. They were only staking out this place as a precaution, but there she is—

"Gervais," says Daniel, his voice cracking with alarm, and Gervais's head whips around.

Cooper strides toward a car parked along the street.

She has a kid with her. A girl, probably around nine or ten. Cooper all but drags her along, and the kid is crying. Tear marks trail down her face and she wipes at her nose with one grubby mitten. Cooper picks the girl up and shoves her into the backseat.

"Does Maya Cooper have children?" asks Daniel.

Gervais twists the key in the ignition. "No."

"Oh," says Daniel. A moment later: "Damn."

"I don't think I should be here for this," says Lyre, his voice rising in pitch. "Um, if I could just get out—"

Gervais ignores him, floors the gas pedal, and the car lurches into the icy street.

14

DANIEL

Gervais swerves in front of a city bus and floors the gas. The bus honks at them, the sound echoing through Daniel's chest like the thrum of a foghorn.

"If we get killed in a low-speed chase, I'll never stop haunting you," says Daniel, gripping his seat hard.

The agent doesn't reply. His fingers dart over the dashboard controls and a voice says, "Yes?" Gervais rattles off codes into his radio—Daniel doesn't know the specifics, but he can guess they amount to: *We've seen the suspect and she's potentially kidnapping a child. Yes, a child—I know it differs from her MO. Would really appreciate some backup right about now.*

All the while, Gervais continues to drive like a madman. Maya Cooper's car is smaller and lighter than the FBI vehicle, and it slips easily between two SUVs. A noise escapes Gervais's clenched teeth and he swerves up onto the sidewalk, nearly sideswiping a biker. The jolt runs through Daniel's bones and he briefly closes his eyes. If they are about to die in a traffic accident, he doesn't want to see it coming.

"I think she's seen us," calls Lyre. Daniel chances a look back; Lyre had the sense to belt himself in. His gaze is focused on a point far ahead and there's no panic in his face. He seems matter-of-fact rather than terrified.

Maya Cooper's car darts through a red light and vanishes behind a stream of traffic. Gervais makes a frustrated noise.

"Turn left," says Lyre. "There's an alley—it'll cut over and we can pick up the street after that."

Gervais hesitates.

"Do it!" cries Lyre, and Gervais grimaces and yanks the steering wheel left.

What follows is a screech of tires as surrounding cars try not to hit them, and the sudden silence as the car speeds down an alley. The car clips a trash bin and Daniel winces away from the screech of metal against metal.

They come out of the alley, Gervais barely pausing to glance both ways before turning onto the street. Sure enough, Daniel sees Maya Cooper's car just ahead of them. Gervais sucks in a breath, hitting the gas.

They're gaining now; so close, Daniel could almost touch the other car if he were standing on the hood.

Cooper must realize, because she speeds up, darting between two cars. In a wild attempt to lose them, she cuts off two other drivers and goes left. Daniel's immunity flares, and he hears the whisper of collision a moment before it happens.

A minivan barrels into her.

The cars collide in a clash of metal and glass. Devon cries out, but Gervais has already hit the brakes. Their own car swoops sideways, skids a few feet, and rocks to a halt. The smell of spilled coffee fills the car and Daniel fumbles for his seat belt.

Maya Cooper is already out of her car. She has the child in her arms and, without so much as a glance back, runs into the crowd.

Gervais lets out a curse. Glock in hand, he pushes his way out of the car—ignoring the fact that it's parked in the middle of the street—and tears after Cooper.

Daniel leans back in his seat. His breathing rattles through his lungs; he's consumed with that unsteady, floaty feeling of having just escaped disaster. He knows he should be following Gervais. He's helping the FBI—he should *help* the FBI.

"What do we do?" says Lyre hoarsely.

Daniel closes his eyes and *listens*. There's no residual pulse of his immunity, no whisper to tell him which way Maya Cooper went. His immunity is silent, while horns blare from all directions.

Daniel looks around, gauges the anger of the other drivers. "I give it five minutes before someone skids on ice and hits us," he says. "I don't know about you, but I don't want to be here when that happens."

He shoves his door open and carefully treads through the slush and gravel. He ignores the angry gestures from the other drivers, looks away from the accident, and hurries onto the frozen sidewalk. Snow catches on his pants and clings to the hem. The cold seeps into his skin, settles in. He isn't dressed for the weather—Daniel thought he'd be spending the day in a warm car.

Lyre trails after him. "Should we go after your partner?" asks Lyre. "I don't know—help?"

Daniel doesn't look back at him. Instead, he makes a sharp right into an alley. He's angry, but he can only feel it in a distant way, like his emotions are coming through a badly tuned radio. Certain words—*betrayal, Homeland Security, Ciere*—manage to come through, and he tries not to listen.

The alley itself is narrow, barely a sliver of space between two old buildings. It's quiet, and more importantly, private. Daniel waits a moment, lets his immunity wash over him, listens for a threat. When he hears none, he whirls around, grabs Lyre by his coat, and shoves him up against the wall.

Lyre's got at least six inches on him, but Daniel catches him off guard.

"What the hell?" gasps Lyre.

Daniel gets his forearm underneath Lyre's chin, pressing him hard up against the bricks. "Do you know Ciere Giba?"

Lyre coughs, tries to shake him off, and fails. "What?"

"Do you know Kit Copperfield?"

This time Lyre manages to shove him off, but Daniel grabs him by the shirt again and throws him back against the wall. Lyre catches himself, hand dragging along the brick in an attempt to stay on his feet. He's unused to fights, part of Daniel thinks. His instincts don't tell him when to duck.

Lyre lashes out with a long leg, but Daniel's immunity warns him and he darts to one side.

"Do. You. Know. Ciere?" snarls Daniel.

Lyre's breath comes in heaves. "Rotting hell. Yes, yes, I know Ciere. Who the hell are you?"

Daniel doesn't answer. He won't give Lyre any more information—not if it means putting Ciere or Kit in danger.

Comprehension sparks in Lyre's eyes. "You—you're him—you're the bloke kidnapped by the feds." His mouth gapes open. "Bloody hell, you're *working* for them now?"

"You're one to talk," snaps Daniel. "What information have you been passing to Homeland Security? You sell out Kit in exchange for some cushy desk job?"

"I haven't told them anything! I would never have worked for them, but—" Lyre's voice strangles out and he looks away. His body slumps and the fight drains out of him. "I'm just an intern," he finally says. "It's just a stupid small division. It's not like I'm working for the UAI or anything. I haven't—I wouldn't betray Ciere." He considers for a moment. "Copperfield, on the other hand..." He smirks just a little.

Daniel flexes his fingers. He's shaking, he realizes, nervous tremors running through his arms. "Where are they? Are they okay?"

Lyre seems to take in Daniel's expression and his face softens. "They're fine," says Lyre. "I haven't seen them since July, but they were both fine then. Last I checked, Ciere's working off a debt to the Gyr Syndicate and Copperfield's off being his usual prattish self."

His words are exactly what Daniel has longed to hear for months. He feels abruptly weaker, tired, but cleaner. They're safe. They're safe. Aristeus kept his word.

"Why are you...?" Lyre seems at a loss for words. He pulls a bewildered face and gestures vaguely back at the direction of Gervais's car.

"I made a deal." Daniel doesn't know why he says the words. Maybe because they're both traitors. "I work for the UAI and in exchange, they don't go after Ciere or the others."

Actually, there was more to his deal than that, but Daniel doesn't want to go into it now.

"That was"—Lyre searches for the right word—"decent of you."

"Yeah, well, I didn't have a lot of choice." Daniel doesn't hide his bitterness.

"If I see her again," says Lyre slowly, "do you want me to tell her anything? From you, I mean?"

"If," not "when." There's no certainty in Lyre's face and it eases some of Daniel's worries. A true fed has more zeal and less hesitation. Lyre may be working for the feds, but he's not one of them. Not yet.

At least they have that in common.

The rest of Daniel's anger leaches away and he shakes his head. He's unsure of what to say. Meeting Lyre has brought back every painful memory of his capture. It's an addictive pain, like scratching at a scab—Daniel wants Lyre gone, but at the same time, dreads seeing him go. Lyre is a link, however small, to Daniel's old life.

He can't deal with this.

So instead of speaking, Daniel walks onto the busy street again. Lyre follows and the two of them find a place to stand, under a plastic awning.

About ten minutes later, Gervais strides around a street corner. He's soaked through with snow and sweat, his jacket pulled at an awkward angle and his shoulder rig clearly visible. Passersby give him a wide berth, but he doesn't seem to notice.

"I lost her," he says grimly. "But we've still got her wrecked car—maybe forensics will get something off that." Upon getting a better look at Daniel and Lyre, his frown deepens. "What the hell happened to you two?"

15

CIERE

The bus from Newark to DC takes about five hours on a good day. On the icy roads, with the sky threatening more snowfall, Ciere spends nearly seven hours crawling toward her destination.

The bus is an older model. The floors are streaked with years of shoe scuffs, the fabric seats are stained, and the windows have a rusted-shut look. Even the emergency door looks as if it would take a bodybuilder to yank it open.

Ciere spends most of the ride trying to doze, tilting her head so that it rests against her seat. When she closes her eyes, she smells old cigarettes. The bus's heaters are on full blast and she finds herself pulling free of her heavy jacket, draping it around her knees instead. The windows are fogged with sweat and breath, and the sound of the windshield wipers fades into the background.

She rouses as they near the DC stop. The brakes let out a soft groan and Ciere wobbles to her feet, gently maneuvering around the other passengers to thud down the bus steps.

The sidewalk is crusted with ice and dirty snow. Ciere steps away from the bus stop, one hand still wrapped around the strap of her backpack. The fresh air is welcome, even if it's so cold, it's almost painful to breathe.

She digs her cell phone out of a pocket and sends a text. *I'm here.* Someone jostles past her and she edges through the crowd, trying to find a still place to wait. But as she turns, she sees a man out of the corner of her eye.

He wears a heavy black coat, and his hair is so blond, it's nearly white. His features are sharp as broken glass—his nose angular, his mouth a thin line.

It's the man who was working for the Alberanis. The gun-runner who shot Ciere, killed Jess, sent even Guntram into hiding—

And he's staring right at her.

Ciere doesn't feel like a person under his gaze. She is nothing but muscle, arteries, and bone—things that can be broken.

How did he find her? Ciere runs a few possibilities through

her mind, but none of them hold up. She's been in hiding for a month. He shouldn't have been able to find her. She glances down at the phone in her hand. A burner, the same one she's had since before Jess died. She meant to replace it, but since Guntram wouldn't let her out of the compound...she never could. Phones are traceable—even burners. That's why she ditches them after a few weeks.

She tosses the phone into the street.

The man weaves through the crowd and Ciere recoils, backing away. She bumps into an older man, stammers an apology, and hurries away from the bus stop.

Fear runs hot through her veins. She wants to disappear, but it's too crowded to illusion herself. Everyone will see her. She needs to slip away, to vanish into the mist, but there's simply no place to go where she won't be observed.

The area is a sprawling mass of buses and travelers, criss-crossing streets and check points. Ciere dodges around a line of people with suitcases and briefly considers trying to slip in with one of the families.

She dismisses the plan almost immediately. It might work on a casual tail, but with the steel-hard intensity of her pursuer, it'll never work. And the pale-haired man might not care about innocent observers.

Instead she heads for a parking garage.

She glances back, hoping against hope to have lost him.

But her gaze immediately finds his white-blond head. He skirts around a group of tourists, eyes on Ciere. His hand is tucked inside his jacket. Exactly where a gun might rest inside a shoulder holster.

Ciere utters a curse and breaks into a run. She barrels through the crowd, pushing past families and tourists, ignoring startled cries. Freezing air scrapes through her lungs, and her feet slip on the sidewalk. She wobbles and steps onto the snowy grass, darting across a would-be lawn. The parking garage looms over her and her heart beats faster. She throws a look over her shoulder, trying to see if the pale-haired man is still following.

With her eyes averted, Ciere never sees the other man who grabs for her.

A hand closes around her arm and yanks her sideways. She opens her mouth to cry out, but a glove muffles her.

"Come on," says a soft, familiar voice. Magnus. She nearly goes limp with relief. Before she can utter a word, she finds herself half dragged, half guided forward. They veer into the parking garage, slipping between two cement pillars. The moment she steps under the wide roof, cold settles in around her. Her breath hangs in the air and the shadows crowd in.

"Vanish us," Magnus says, low in her ear.

Ciere knows better than to argue. There's no time. She draws in a breath, imagines the color of her jacket fading to gray, and pushes out. Her immunity flickers, wavering due to her nerves, but it stabilizes and she knows they're invisible.

It's not a moment too soon. The pale-haired man breaks free of the crowd, stepping off the sidewalk, his gaze tracking left and then right, before settling on the parking garage. It's like he can sense which way she ran, even if she's out of sight. Horrible certainty seizes her. The man's ability to sense her movements is startling, and she's seen instincts like those before.

The pale-haired man has to be an eludere. She suspected it before, but now she knows.

But something makes him pause.

The man hesitates, his hand twitching toward his jacket. Annoyance flits across his face.

"That's right," murmurs Magnus. The whispered words are almost fond, but they're not meant for her. "This is the perfect place for an ambush. Yes, you know better than to come in here. There could be someone waiting for you."

The man's lips twitch, pull back into a snarl. He's not an idiot; he knows better than to run into unknown terrain. A professional, Ciere thinks. He's more than just some gunrunner.

The man throws the parking garage one last furious look before he takes a step back. He vanishes into the crowd, melting away like he was never there.

Ciere shakes herself and lets the illusion go. The moment it dissolves, she sees Magnus again.

He's tall, well muscled, and his dark hair is hidden beneath a woolen hat. His prominent nose is balanced out by wide-spaced eyes and full lips. He's beautiful—even if the shadows beneath his eyes make him look haunted.

"Ciere," says Magnus Fugaré, "you keep the most interesting company."

Getting out of the parking garage is simple—it turns out that's where Magnus left his car. It's an older model, worn with use, and Ciere settles into the passenger seat with a groan. Magnus keeps his eyes on the road as he pulls out, glancing around as if to make sure there are no tails. Ciere waits until the bus station is far behind before speaking.

"How have you been?" she asks. The smile she gives him is genuine.

"Fine." Magnus gently eases the car into heavier traffic, gaze darting to the rearview mirror. "My life has been quieter than yours, I gather. I'm not being followed around by professional hit men."

"You knew what he was," says Ciere. A chill goes through her and settles in her spine. "Old friend of yours?"

Magnus is already shaking his head. "No, but I know what to look for."

"Is this a mercenary thing?" she asks, her voice gone deadpan. "You look into their eyes and see a killer?"

Magnus laughs. "Actually, I saw the gun tucked into his pants."

"I thought he had one under his shoulder," she says, frowning.

"Professionals carry more than one weapon," Magnus says as he brings his coffee cup to his lips. "Who put a hit out on you, anyway?"

Ciere groans and rubs the heel of one hand against her eyes. She's exhausted and smells like a bus. All she really wants to do is curl up and fall asleep. She starts to yawn and turns it into a sigh instead. "It's a long story."

16

DEVON

Devon sits in a hallway of the FBI headquarters. Twin wooden benches stand on both sides of the hall. The floor is scuffed, tiled, and the ceilings high. The building makes the creaky, soft sounds of an old structure. Devon closes his eyes, leans his head against the wall, and listens to the murmurs, the footfalls, and lets the noises lull him into a doze.

That special agent—Gervais or something—insisted on driving back to his work, despite Devon's protests that he had a job, too. "You're technically a witness," Gervais said heavily. "We'll need a statement."

Devon texted Sia the moment he realized he wouldn't be allowed back to work: *Delivered food as ordered and now I'm a witness to child abduction. Delegation sucks.*

That was three hours ago.

Neither Gervais nor Daniel Burkhart has reappeared. Gervais slipped into this building the way Devon's seen ants vanish into anthills; it's obvious the man belongs here. Daniel Burkhart is another story. He edged into the building, his shoulders drawn. "Don't drink the coffee," was all he said before vanishing down a corridor and leaving Devon to his own devices.

Devon plays with his phone until the battery runs out and then he begins tapping his foot against the tiled floor. He's been left alone with his thoughts and he hates that. He's trying not to think, because if he does, he'll have to confront an uncomfortable fact.

Sitting in that FBI car, wondering if he might die in a fiery accident, made something clear.

He doesn't have much left to lose.

His family doesn't like him, his criminal friends told him to piss off, no school will take him, and his life is nonexistent. Devon Lyre's future is one great big blank.

But for a few minutes, in that car chase with his mind racing, calculating those streets and bringing up a mental map, with adrenaline setting fire to his blood—nothing else mattered.

It was exhilarating. It's been a long time since he felt exhilarated. Or felt much of anything, actually.

It was the first time in months he didn't hear *"You don't belong with us"* beating against the inside of his skull.

"How'd you know to take that alley?" asks Daniel. Devon's head jerks up and he sees Daniel walking toward him. He moves quietly, his worn sneakers silent on the tiled floor. He sinks onto the bench opposite Devon.

Devon isn't sure what Ciere told Daniel about him. Better safe than sorry.

Devon puts on a smile. "I've been fetching coffee and running errands in that area for nearly three weeks. I know all the back streets by now."

Daniel eyes him. He's not what Devon expected of him—when he pictured Ciere's description of Daniel, he imagined someone smoother, older, and more obviously a criminal. This Daniel Burkhart looks like any street kid with brown hair and a crooked nose. Quite ordinary.

Except ordinary people usually don't throw other people against brick walls.

Devon can feel the bruises forming on his back and chooses not to mention them. The silence between them is awkward enough.

"Who was that woman?" he says. "The one you guys were chasing."

Daniel pulls a bag of trail mix out of a coat pocket. He rips the bag open and begins rummaging through the contents.

Only after he's found a chocolate piece does he reply. "Maya Cooper. Suspect in a bunch of missing persons cases."

"She's a kidnapper?" Even as Devon says the words, it's hard to believe. The woman he saw didn't look like a kidnapper. Busty and redheaded, she'd looked like a pinup model.

"You saw her do it." Daniel picks a pretzel out of the bag, studies it, then pops it into his mouth.

Devon crosses his arms, tries to find a comfortable spot on the bench. "Didn't that FBI agent want my statement or something?"

"He'll get around to it eventually." Daniel shrugs. "Right now he's trying to figure out who that kid was. It's weird, her taking a kid."

Devon goes still, then forces himself to say casually, "Why?"

"Because," says Daniel, "every person she's kidnapped so far has tested positive for Praevenir. That kid's too young to have been vaccinated, so she breaks the pattern."

Devon's insides seize up. He suddenly feels cold, the scent of the food turning his stomach. "Someone's going after immune people?"

"Looks like," says Daniel. "Maybe they're immune, maybe they aren't. But now that a kid's involved, the FBI's going to come down hard." He looks down at the trail mix and says, "Maybe they'll actually listen to us when we need backup next time." He shrugs and goes back to his trail mix, fumbling for a pretzel. Neither speaks for a good minute.

When Daniel finally says something, his voice is low and his eyes are focused on the bag. "Why'd you choose to work for the feds?"

Devon could ignore the question; he could pretend he didn't hear. With the low buzz of voices, the constant sound of nearby footsteps, the lie might pass.

Instead, he shrugs. "I was kicked out of school again. I couldn't stay with my dad."

Daniel's hard gaze drills into Devon. "No. I mean, why didn't you go to Philadelphia?"

The real question is there, hidden beneath what Daniel isn't saying: *Why didn't you go back to Ciere and Kit?*

Her voice comes back to him. *"You don't belong with us."*

He lets his gaze fall to the floor. Daniel makes a noise, as if about to say something more, but then abruptly rises to his feet. He darts a look down the hall and a moment later, Devon hears footsteps.

A figure strides around the corner and Devon looks up, expecting it to be Gervais.

It's Macourek.

His glasses are tucked against his collar and his dark hair is crumpled on one side, as if he'd been sleeping on his desk.

Devon blinks. Surely the head of Affiliation doesn't usually pick up his interns, does he? Frowning, Devon turns back to say good-bye to Daniel.

The bench is empty, except for the half-eaten bag of trail mix. Devon cocks his head, listens to the sound of faint footfalls. *Criminals*—no matter how much time he spends with them, Devon will never understand them.

Macourek's face tenses when he sees Devon. "I am so sorry," he says, before Devon can say a word. "When I asked Sia to handle the drop—I never thought—" He presses a hand against his forehead and exhales. "Are you all right?"

That itchy, uncomfortable sensation returns. Devon isn't used to having people care about his well-being—well, only Ciere. "Fine, really." He forces a smile. "It was exciting."

Special Agent Gervais emerges from his office. His suit is rumpled and he's running a hand through his peppery hair when he catches sight of Devon. Gervais's eyes travel past him to Macourek, and the agent seems to be making a conscious effort to draw himself together.

"I'll be taking my intern," says Macourek softly.

Gervais's easy expression frosts over and he glances between Macourek and Devon. "I need his statement," he says in what has to be his *open-up, I-am-a-federal-agent* voice. It's firm and unyielding and has absolutely no effect on Macourek.

"Another day," says the younger man curtly. "Devon, come along."

A small part of Devon balks at Macourek's words, but something in the air keeps him quiet. He can feel Gervais staring at him when he turns and trails after Macourek.

Macourek leads him out of the building, down the steps, to a black car. Devon finds himself sitting in a warmed leather seat. Macourek swings into the driver's seat. He takes a breath before shoving the key into the ignition. "This wasn't deliberate," he says. "Just so you know. We don't usually haze the interns with crime scenes."

"I suppose I'm just special then," Devon drawls, unable to help himself.

Macourek shoots him a look; he isn't smiling when he says, "You are."

Devon isn't sure if he's embarrassed or pleased. Both, perhaps. "You didn't have to come and get me. I could've caught a bus."

"It's nothing." Macourek pulls out of the parking spot, easing into traffic. He's a careful driver, always checking over his shoulder before changing lanes, keeping an eye on the other cars.

"It's fine, really," says Devon again. "I didn't mind getting caught up in that. I've always had a...slight interest in criminal justice."

Oh, ha bloody ha, part of him thinks, disgusted at his own little joke.

Macourek's eyes never leave the road. "You like solving crimes?"

"I like puzzles," says Devon, more honestly than he means to. "My mind never shuts up. Not unless it's drunk or doing something interesting. Chasing that woman—that was something interesting."

He expects Macourek to shake his head, the way Mr. Lyre always did. *"You can control your mind,"* Mr. Lyre once said.

"Maybe you're not well suited to an office," Macourek murmurs.

For a stomach-churning moment, Devon thinks Macourek means he's unsuitable for this internship. He can't go home—he just can't. "Looks like maybe I should be sending you out on more errands," Macourek says instead. "Speaking of which, there's an event tomorrow that I can't escape." He shifts, tilting his head so he can look at Devon more closely. "Feel like getting out of the office?"

Devon feels himself frown. "And doing what?"

"It's a political event masquerading as a party," replies Macourek. "Hosted by Aditi Sen—you know, that activist or lobbyist or whatever she's calling herself these days. My bosses have requested I put in an appearance."

Devon stares at him. "You want me to go with you."

"Consider it an apology for nearly getting you killed." Macourek shrugs. "The food will be good."

The drive to Devon's dorm takes less time than he would've guessed. Macourek pulls up at the curb. Devon steps out of the car and begins to walk away. Then another question nags at him and he finds himself turning around. Macourek catches his eye, seems to read his expression, and rolls his window down. "Yes?"

"Is it true?" Devon asks, peering through the open window.

Macourek leans over the seat and quirks an eyebrow.

Devon isn't sure what makes him say it. Maybe he's still trying to hold on to that feeling during the chase—that reckless, wild nothing. "Those FBI agents—they said the kidnapper was going after vaccinated people. I mean, except for that kid—she's too young to be vaccinated."

Macourek's face doesn't flicker. "I've heard about that case, yes."

"What would make someone do that?"

Macourek lowers his gaze to the dashboard.

"Anyone who's been vaccinated could potentially be immune," he says quietly. "It means they're a threat. Taking them, gathering them—it's not the first time something like this has happened."

Devon supposes Macourek would know. Even with Affiliation on the fringes of Homeland Security, he must hear things.

"Do you think someone's killing them?" asks Devon.

Macourek's expression remains unchanged. When he speaks, it's with a clinical detachment. "Perhaps. Or it could be more dangerous than that." His fingers tighten on the steering wheel. "If they're immune, the kidnapper could want them alive."

17

CIERE

Magnus's apartment is a historic remodel in a stately building just off McPherson Square. He murmurs a greeting to the doorman, saying something about his niece visiting for the week. Ciere barely listens; she only really comes awake when Magnus unlocks the door to his place.

It's nice. The furniture looks worn but comfortable, and rugs cover the hardwood floor. It's not a page out of a home and garden magazine, like Kit's house, but it's not a postapocalyptic warehouse, either.

He leads her past a small kitchen and to the end of a hall. She catches a glimpse of a bathroom and makes a mental note before pushing open the bedroom door. It's neat, almost sterile in its cleanliness. There's a desk and a bed and no other personal effects.

After he's bid her good night and she shuts the door behind her, Ciere drops her backpack on the floor. She doesn't bother changing into pajamas; she squirms out of her jeans, tosses her socks down next to them, wriggles out of her bra, and yanks it out from under her T-shirt. All of her clothes are left in a pile on the floor—but she can't bring herself to care. The bed is warm and soft and clean—far nicer than her cot back at the warehouse. She cocoons herself in fuzzy blankets and is asleep within moments.

She drags herself out of bed sometime around seven the next morning. The air is chilled and she wishes she could bury herself beneath the duvet and just stay there, but she's got things to do. People to save. Killers to hunt down. A usual Friday.

When she emerges from the bedroom, it's apparent Magnus isn't awake yet. The lights are all out and a stillness permeates the apartment.

She's used to judging people by their possessions—who owns the gold-plated watch, if the entryway rug is silk. A person's values spill into their everyday lives, even if they don't realize it.

Magnus's apartment is neat and clean and ... stark. Everything has a function—there's little in the way of sheer decoration. The rugs are matte gray, the furniture is heavy and worn, and even the air freshener smells only of clean sheets. Ciere finds the only decoration in the hall outside of Magnus's bedroom. A framed art print—that of a man's portrait. A long, hollow slash goes through the man's face. It's a gruesome little print one that makes her want to look away. But maybe that's the point.

Going on a hunch, Ciere deftly slides her fingernails behind the frame. When she pulls forward, there's a nearly silent click and something unlatches. The print swings forward, revealing a small cupboard. Pinned to the wall are two pistols. Twin cardboard boxes of ammo rest on a small shelf beneath them.

"Francis Bacon," says Magnus. Ciere jerks in surprise.

"What?"

"The art print," says Magnus calmly, as if finding guests rooting through his things is utterly normal. "*Study for Head of George Dyer.*"

She wants to ask about the guns, but what comes out is, "You like art?"

Magnus hides his hand in his pockets, an almost embarrassed expression creeping over him. "No. I've just spent too much time around Kit."

Ciere casts another wary look at the guns. "It's a crappy safe. It's not locked."

He reaches out and gently pushes the print back into

place. "It's not meant to be locked. Few would go looking for it…and if I ever have need of these, I'll want them as quickly as possible." His eyes sweep over the print. "If you're done exploring, I have some information you might find interesting."

"What?"

Magnus strides toward the kitchen. "While you were asleep, I made some calls. I've got information on your new friends."

The dining room is little more than an alcove tucked away near the kitchen. A small, two-seater table takes up most of the space. Magnus already has coffee brewed and Ciere considers his cereal collection. Only after they're settled at the table, food at the ready, does Magnus speak.

He sets a manila envelope onto the table. His pale fingers deftly pull it open and he settles a stack of papers between their cereal bowls.

"Your employer is hard to track down," he says. "Brandt Guntram did his best to bury his records. Luckily for you, I'm popular with politicians."

Ciere does her best not to snort into her cereal.

Magnus is a mentalist. His immunity is more limited than hers—his requires skin-to-skin contact. Through that contact he hears people's thoughts. His talent is a coveted one. If more people knew what he was capable of, Magnus would find himself snapped up by the TSA or a crime family. To support himself, to stay apart from all the danger, he's channeled his telepathy into a different line of illegal work.

He's a prostitute. And an expensive one, if this apartment's location is anything to go by.

Magnus smiles around his coffee cup. "To sum up what I found: Brandt Guntram is the son of a German diplomat. He graduated from Harvard with a degree in political science. He was the adjunct of a New York senator before he was twenty-five—not a small feat. From what I can tell, he was on his way up. He married an elementary school teacher, and since there are no divorce records, I'm assuming they're still together."

Ciere picks up a sheet of paper. It shows a much younger Guntram—his blond hair longer, a tie tucked neatly around his collar. His face is smoother, relaxed. "How does a politician become one of the key figures in a crime syndicate?" She jabs a finger at the paper. "I mean, beyond the obvious jokes."

Magnus straightens. "His career abruptly came to a halt about ten years ago. Apparently, he resigned. Most of the records end there." He picks up another paper and passes it over. "I also managed to find some of the other individuals you named."

Ciere takes the sheet. It features a picture of a younger Conrad. He's still a mountain of muscle, but his hairline hasn't receded quite yet and his expression is that of light amusement. "Conrad Forrester," says Magnus. "He's career military; he spent most of his adult life with the *Kommando Spezialkräfte*." Seeing Ciere's confused expression, he adds, "German Special Forces. He fought in some of the last battles of the Pacific War. As far as I can tell, he dropped off the radar the same time Guntram did."

"And Henry?"

"Henrietta Williams," replies Magnus. "She was in a police academy before she joined up with the Syndicate."

That stuns Ciere. "She was a *cop*?"

"Surprised me, too," says Magnus lightly. "Most cops don't become crooks—even if they are crooked themselves. They'll take bribes, but quit and join up with a crime family? It's unusual."

"So either of them have the experience to shoot someone," says Ciere, stumped. She hesitates, then adds, "Or it could be Guntram."

Magnus nods. "You said you found a money clip?"

"With a hotel keycard," she says. "I'm going to go there. See if there's any record of a Syndicate member staying there."

Magnus stirs his cereal over and over, the moistened flakes slowly melting into a golden sludge. "Do you have a backup plan? What if this Guntram won't accept your evidence...or if he was the one to kill Pruitt? What will you do?"

Ciere sets down the sheet of paper with Henry's picture. She swallows and feels her hands clench in her lap.

"I'll still go back," she says. "I'll get Alan free, even if it means I have to break him out myself."

That earns her a raised eyebrow.

"What?" The word comes out more snappish than Ciere intends.

Magnus rolls one shoulder in a half shrug. "Nothing."

She traces the edge of the bracelet. "If Guntram wants to sic the feds on me, he's welcome to try. I've got enough info on the Gyr Syndicate that I could probably trade it for a cushy deal. What's one minor crook in comparison to a whole crime syndicate?"

Magnus raises his gaze from his coffee and spends a good few seconds simply looking at her. She feels the weight of it, wants to shrug off his attention and have him focus it elsewhere. She knows it takes touch for his telepathy to work, but even so— she's uncomfortable with the way he seems to be reading her.

He hesitates for the briefest moment. He continues stirring his cereal, his eyes carefully fixed on the task. "You've changed. I remember when we first met Alan—you wanted to leave him behind."

Ciere closes her eyes. Gathers herself.

"You're right," she says, surprising herself. "Things have changed."

18

CIERE

Four months after they started working for the Syndicate, Ciere and Alan went to a bar.

And not just any bar, but the creepiest dive Ciere had ever seen. A mouse scurried along the wall; only half the overhead lights worked; the bartender looked as dingy as a dust bunny Ciere had once pulled out from under her bed.

"Stay here," said Guntram.

Ciere didn't sit down. Mostly because she wasn't sure if the barstools could hold her weight. "Why?"

Conrad stood near the door, arms crossed over his chest. His jacket pulled tight around the two guns tucked under each arm. No one gave him a second glance.

"Because," says Guntram, "we need a safe place to stash the two of you while we..."

Alan said, "Do something shady—"

"—that you don't want us to see," said Ciere.

Guntram pressed his lips together, as if holding back a smile. "Yes."

This was the weird thing about working for the Syndicate. They were with the Syndicate, but they weren't *with* the Syndicate—not in any trusted sense. Ciere and Alan hadn't sworn oaths of loyalty or even joined up voluntarily. They were here on a strict need-to-pay-off-a-debt basis. While it didn't matter most of the time, there were occasions when Guntram slipped away, presumably to do mobsterly things.

"Do you need us for anything?" asked Ciere. Her gaze darted over everyone in the room and it was pretty much what she'd expected. Mostly older men, with graying hair and averted eyes. She and Alan were the youngest people here by at least twenty years.

"Like what?" Guntram appeared amused by the suggestion.

She drew up her shoulders. "I dunno. Spy on anyone? Steal from the cash register... if there's anything in there. I mean, is there a reason you're stashing us here?"

Guntram nodded. "The bar's owner is loyal to the Syndicate, as is everyone here. If anything happens, they will protect you."

Prickles of unease ran over her skin. "You think we need protection?"

Guntram finally allowed a smile to steal over his face. It wasn't a reassuring expression. He rested one hand on Ciere's shoulder for a brief moment. "We protect our investments." He gave them one last look, probably meant to be comforting, and then followed Conrad out the door.

"Well, that's vaguely ominous," murmured Alan. "Grab a table?"

They chose one in a corner, deep in the shadows of the windowless room. Alan picked up one of the paper napkins and tried to wipe some of the dust away. Ciere settled uncomfortably in one of the wooden chairs. It wobbled, as if one of the legs was shorter than the others. She rocked back and forth, if only for something to do.

"What now?" asked Alan.

Ciere shrugged. "When in Rome?"

Ciere's original plan was for a tequila sunrise, but the bar didn't carry orange juice. Which was how she and Alan ended up sipping tumblers of straight tequila.

"This is disgusting," said Alan, gagging.

"You get used to it," replied Ciere, taking a sip. Even she had to admit it was pretty bad—good tequila tasted like fire and spice. This stuff just burned. "Haven't you ever drank before?"

Alan swirled his glass. "I spent most of my childhood on the run. I didn't exactly have time for teenage rebellion."

"What was your childhood like?" said Ciere, getting herself another glass.

Alan shrugged. "The usual. We never stayed in one place for longer than a year. We squatted sometimes. There were people who were willing to help us, even if they didn't know who we were. We spent six months living in a homeless shelter once, before my aunt met up with TATE."

"I'm sorry," she said. "About your aunt."

Alan's expression had gone tight, as if he could will away his grief.

"If things had gone differently," said Ciere, trying to change the subject. "If my crew hadn't found you, what do you think you'd be doing right now?"

Alan picked up the bottle, pouring himself another glassful. He picked up his tumbler and grimaced before taking a swig. He coughed and said hoarsely, "Probably be on the run with TATE. Keep out of sight, stay safe."

Keep the formula safe, she thought. She was beginning to feel the warmth of the drinks, the pleasant haze dragging at her thoughts.

"If you weren't here, doing this"—Alan nodded at the bar—"what would you be doing?"

She threw back the rest of her drink, using the moment to collect her thoughts.

"I don't know," she said. "Probably be at the Bolsover house with Kit, waiting for him to come up with his next assignment. If we couldn't find a job, we'd probably be camped out in the living room with all the curtains drawn while he attempted to teach me chess for the thousandth time."

Alan smiled down at the dirty tabletop. "That sounds nice. He's a good teacher, right?"

"Not really," said Ciere. "He's totally cutthroat. You know he once told me that when criminal students graduated, they tried to kill their teachers to take their jobs?"

Alan laughed, looked startled, and then pressed his hand against his mouth as if to stifle the noise. Ciere found herself laughing, too, because something so horribly morbid seemed incredibly funny at that moment. "You probably shouldn't tell Guntram if that's your philosophy," said Alan, grinning around his hand. "Although you'd probably make a great mob princess."

For a second, the fog of the tequila faded, and Ciere looked at Alan—really looked at him. Copper skin and dark hair and a sweater two sizes too large. He was intelligent, quietly focused, friendly but aloof. He was more than a series of numbers and letters, more than the knowledge he carried. He was smart and weirdly beautiful and—

She looked away, a flush creeping along her cheeks.

"I thought you thieves were all about the cutthroat," said Alan. "Take everything you can, sell it for the highest price."

"Thieves are not that evil," said Ciere, trying to sound indignant and failing miserably. "We're multifaceted. Complicated. We do bad things for good reasons…and—"

"Couldn't even finish that sentence with a straight face," said Alan, and he laughed again.

She elbowed him. "Stop ruining the romanticism of my lifestyle."

"Pretty sure the grave-robbing stories you told me a few months ago did that."

Ciere pressed a hand to her mouth, covering her smile. "I have never robbed a grave." A beat. "We robbed a morgue. That's different."

"Entirely different," he agreed. "Much more romantic." He nudged her with a shoulder. "Maybe I'll even get to tag along next time."

Her mouth went dry and she swallowed. "I was just thinking. You know, when this is all over…" Her courage ran out and she pressed her lips together.

"What?" asked Alan.

Her fingers were clammy and she tangled them in the fabric of her shirt, trying to wipe away any traces of sweat.

She didn't think. She just acted. Her fingers touched his and she leaned closer. She wanted this, she realized. She wanted him. And she was a thief—it was her habit to take what she wanted.

Panic flashed through his eyes. He retreated, nearly falling out of his chair. Gaze averted, sounding far too sober, he said, "Ciere."

His voice was sharper than she'd ever heard. "I—I'm sorry," she stammered. "I—I just thought..."

Alan scrubbed a hand over his face. "I know. And I'm sorry. But I can't."

The rejection came like a punch to the gut; she felt achy and breathless. "Why?" She fumbled for an explanation, trying to piece together evidence. He came here, with her. He didn't have to; he could've stayed with Kit or found another place to hide. But Alan had chosen to accompany her, and maybe... maybe she'd hoped it meant something.

Alan kept his gaze averted. "You know where I'd be if I weren't here? If everything had gone the way it was supposed to? I'd probably be in some safe house, under the protection of TATE. When this is all over... maybe that's where I'll end up."

Panic fluttered in her chest. He couldn't mean—she'd always assumed that when this was over, he'd stay with her. She pried her lips open, unsure what she wanted to say. *Stay*, she thought. She could say that aloud, couldn't she? He could stay with her, with her crew.

"Don't you—I mean—" She stumbled over the words. "Don't you want more?"

Alan understood. "No." He shrugged one shoulder. He

lowered his voice, so that only she could hear. "Ciere...I'm the Praevenir formula. I'll never be more than that."

She opened her mouth to argue, but the door banged open. Ciere jumped; the bartender slid an unconcerned glance over his shoulder, then went back to pouring a tall whisky.

Conrad edged through the door—it looked too small for his huge frame. When his gaze alighted on Ciere and Alan, his lips pressed together. "Kitty," he said, waving at Ciere, "go into the back. Brandt would like to speak with you in the bathroom."

Ciere's instincts went on high alert. She rose to her feet and Alan followed. "No, Ashbottom," said Conrad, striding to their table. He put his hand on Alan's shoulder, all but forcing him back into the chair. "You and I will have a drink." He pointed a finger at the bartender.

Alan's gaze flicked to Ciere's, holding it for a brief moment. There was a question in his eyes.

Ciere shook her head, grateful for the chance to retreat. She felt unsteady, both from the alcohol and Alan's words. Gripping the back of her chair for a moment, she tried to compose her face into something resembling normal. Then she turned on her heel and wobbled toward the back of the bar.

The bathrooms were tucked away in a dingy, badly lit corridor. Ciere found the door, hesitated, then knocked.

A raspy voice said, "Giba?"

Ciere hesitated. "Yes." She twisted the handle, peering inside.

"Shut it behind you, please," said Guntram, and for the first time, raw fear spiked through her. Because the moment she stepped into the bathroom, she smelled it. The smoky scent of gunpowder and something…damp. Something she'd smelled only once before.

Guntram leaned against a wall. He wore a red scarf and was smiling at her in an odd way. He reached up and touched a finger to his neck, wincing.

It wasn't a red scarf running down Guntram's chest. It was blood.

"Oh god," Ciere breathed, and pushed the door shut. The lock clicked into place. "What happened?"

Guntram dropped the toilet's lid before sitting down. His left arm flopped limply at his side, while his right hand clenched spasmodically. "Someone aimed a shotgun at Conrad," he said through clenched teeth.

Ciere edged closer. "And you're the one who got hurt?"

"Blast just caught me on the neck and shoulder," said Guntram. "We need to get the shot out."

Ciere heard herself swallow. "We?"

Guntram nodded at the sink. There was a first-aid kit, a pair of tweezers, and scissors.

Ciere's stomach rolled; the thought of touching him, never

mind digging bits of metal out of him, made her feel dizzy. She took a step backward.

"We need to get the largest fragments out now," said Guntram. "You're used to picking locks, right? Small, steady hands?"

Her hands didn't feel steady. She couldn't really feel her hands at all. "Just do it," said Guntram. His voice was strained, soft, but not angry.

She swallowed again—this time she felt something warm and acidic rising in her throat. She tried to force it down. "I've been drinking," Ciere felt obligated to say. "You sure you want me?"

Guntram's eyes lifted at the corners. "Do it."

She picked up the scissors first. She may have never done this before, but even she knew the shirt had to go. It was a mess of warm, sticky cotton. Pushing her nausea away, Ciere tried to focus on each smaller task. Snipping away the shirt, setting it in the sink, surveying the mess before her. She couldn't see the individual wounds through the mass of blood. She wadded up a handful of paper towels and soaked them, dripping the water over Guntram's neck and shoulder until she could see skin. It was dimpled, pocked through with tiny wounds. It could've been worse, but it had to be agonizing. Guntram didn't flinch. His eyes remained on her while she worked, wiping away more of the blood before picking up the tweezers.

Her fingers shook as she pried apart the edges of a small wound, tweezers dipping inside. They touched something hard and she closed the pincers around it, withdrawing a tiny, silver pellet. She dropped it onto the floor and the metal plinked as it hit the ground.

The process repeated itself. Over and over, until it almost seemed like a ritual. Wipe away blood, find shrapnel, pull it free, wipe away more blood. Ciere found herself settling into the rhythm until she almost forgot what she was doing.

Almost. But not quite.

"How are you just sitting here?" she said, once she'd gotten the last shard out. She pressed a fresh bundle of paper towels to his shoulder. "Did Conrad dope you up?"

Guntram's thin mouth twitched. He was far paler than Ciere had ever seen. "No."

"Then you should've been screaming through most of that," said Ciere.

"Pain is an illusion," rasped Guntram. "Pain is in the mind. Pain can be controlled."

She just stared at him, disbelieving.

"It helps to think of it that way," said Guntram, closing his eyes. "Now, get Conrad back in here. He'll give me a new shirt and help clean up the mess. You should wash your hands. And maybe put on his jacket."

Ciere looked down at herself. The front half of her shirt

was stained crimson. Sure enough, a heavy jacket had been tossed in the corner. Ciere hastily ran her hands under warm water, washing away the dried blood. "No one can know about this," said Guntram. "Not even your bodyguard."

If people knew he was injured, it would make him a target. She wiped her hands dry on the last of the towels and reached down, picking up Conrad's discarded jacket.

"You stepped in front of it, didn't you?" She didn't look at him, instead keeping her eyes on the sink. The chipped porcelain was stained a bright pink. "You took the shot for Conrad."

"When things go to hell," said Guntram, voice gone soft and thready, "you'd be surprised what you're capable of."

19

DANIEL

Daniel supposes that the influx of reporters into the city was inevitable.

"Are they all here for the missing girl?" says Daniel. He and Gervais have taken refuge in a cafe near the offices. It's a small, cozy locale with plenty of rickety chairs and a waitress who looks as if she could be Daniel's great-aunt. It's nearly eleven and the breakfast crowd has shrunk to a few people lingering over free coffee refills.

Their table is angled in a corner of the cafe, with a clear view of the exit. In case of reporters, they'll be able to slip out the back. On the table is an open newspaper. The headline catches Daniel's eye: *STRING OF POSSIBLE ABDUCTIONS GOES PUBLIC*.

Daniel says, "Seriously, it's been *twelve hours*. How'd they get the news so fast?" He draws a fingernail along the laminate tabletop. It feels sticky beneath his hands; probably leftovers from some previous customer. The napkins are real cloth, but the white has long since been stained brown.

"Someone at the scene used their phone to capture me running through the streets," says Gervais grimly. He looks like he's been up all night. Probably because he *has* been up all night. "This was supposed to stay under wraps," says Gervais. His hand shakes slightly as he picks up the remnants of his toast. "My boss isn't happy."

"Now that there's a kid missing," says Daniel, "your boss can't blame you for the leak."

Gervais doesn't answer.

"I mean, they *really* can't blame you."

More silence.

"They're blaming you, aren't they?" says Daniel flatly.

Gervais looks at his coffee.

Daniel's frustration simmers to the surface. "Seriously, who did you piss off?"

Gervais glances up, his forehead wrinkling with confusion.

"Because you had to do something," insists Daniel. "The Bureau hates you. They hated you even before your partner was murdered and they thought your 'supposed incompetence' led to his getting stabbed. They hated you back when you arrested me—in June. What'd you do to them?"

"Why do you assume I did anything?" asks Gervais, a slight edge to his words. "What about hating me on principle?"

The waitress approaches and the two of them go silent while she refills Gervais's coffee. Once she's gone, Daniel says, "Maybe. But it seems like there's something personal to this."

"Sometimes," says Gervais, and there's a heaviness in his voice that Daniel has never heard. "Sometimes I don't think I'm very good at my job."

Daniel blinks. Such raw honesty is the last thing he expects from Gervais. The FBI agent has always been solid—always persevering despite the setbacks. This sudden exhaustion makes Daniel frown.

"You caught me, didn't you?" Daniel thinks about it. "Twice, actually."

"The UAI caught you the second time," says Gervais shortly.

Daniel shrugs. "You ever think about doing something else?"

"Like what?" Gervais blows the steam off of his coffee and takes a cautious sip. "All I've ever done—all I've ever wanted to do is protect people. Apparently, I'm just a bad FBI agent."

Daniel considers several responses. "Well, I'm a fantastic con man."

Gervais utters a startled little sound. Then he laughs, and

it's the first truly honest laugh Daniel's heard in weeks. "So how many times have you tried to con me?"

"Zero."

Gervais arches an eyebrow. "Zero?"

"Zero," Daniel repeats. "I wouldn't try it on you."

"Because I'm not rich enough?" Gervais says, still smiling.

Daniel doesn't smile back. "Because I don't do that anymore."

A startled expression chases away Gervais's smile. His lips press together, and the full weight of his scrutiny falls upon Daniel. Daniel doesn't look away. He's got nothing to hide. Not anymore.

It should be a freeing thought. After all, when he was a crook, Daniel was forced to always think. Always be planning, always remember the cover story, always be two steps ahead. Now he can just... be. It should be a relief.

Instead, he just feels hollow.

Gervais looks as if he might say something, but his phone beeps. He checks the screen and some of the tension creeps back into his shoulders. "Text from forensics," he says. "They're done with Maya Cooper's car."

––––––––

The FBI evidence facility is like any other warehouse Daniel has seen—only the security is much heavier, and everyone's required to sign in. Once their signatures and tags have been checked, Gervais and Daniel are ushered down a hallway and led to a room containing the familiar silver car. It still looks dented and pathetic, and it's been stripped. Daniel's reminded of animal carcasses on the side of the road, white bones picked clean by vultures.

A tech stands near the car. She's blonde, probably in her mid-thirties, with premature frown lines forming around her eyes. Waving off their introductions, she says, "You're not going to like it."

Gervais doesn't flinch. "What?"

The tech reaches down and picks up a small ziplock bag. It contains a white sheet of paper. "If you're hoping to track your perp through car ownership, you're screwed. This one's a rental. Pretty sure the ID used to secure it was fake, too."

"And?" Gervais prompts.

"We found hairs," says the tech. "But they could belong to anyone. So many people have probably been in and out of this car that finding a DNA match might not lead you anywhere."

Daniel speaks up for the first time. "What about the internal GPS?"

All new cars are equipped with GPS trackers. For ease, for security... and so the government can track you. The first thing crooks do with a new car is dismantle the GPS. Even if it means fumbling around with maps, it's better than the

184

alternative. An easily tracked criminal is an easily caught criminal.

Daniel glances at the car's dashboard; there's no telltale hole, so this car's GPS must be intact.

"We thought of that," says the tech. "Pulled all the records." This time, she goes for a pocket tablet. She unfolds the screen, flicks it to life, and hands it over. "You see?" Her fingernail traces a line of coordinates. "This car has been all over the city."

"Any point that's been returned to more than once?" murmurs Gervais. "Any pattern?"

The techie shakes her head. "Sorry, Agent. That's your department, not mine."

Gervais frowns down at the tablet. "Can you print two copies?"

That's how Daniel ends up sitting next to a car in an FBI warehouse, papers scattered around him.

"This," he declares, "is too much like my old life."

Gervais kneels some feet away, poring over the papers he has spread meticulously across the cement floor. "What?" he says absentmindedly.

"This," says Daniel. "Grunt work. Finding patterns in people's lives. It's what my old mentor used to make me do—and I hated it then, too."

"The only difference is now you're getting paid." Gervais's eyes continuously scan over the papers and Daniel forces himself to look back at his own work.

"I got paid then, too," he says. "In fact, I got paid better. This nine-to-five stuff may be regular, but it's not…it's not…"

His voice trails off.

Gervais looks up. "What?"

Daniel's gaze narrows down to an address and a name. He shakes his head, rereads the paper, and tries to make sense of it.

"What?" Gervais rises and strides to Daniel.

Excitement unfurls in Daniel's stomach. The sensation is familiar; he experienced it every time he felt the tumblers of a lock slide into place or successfully lifted a wallet.

"You're not going to believe this," says Daniel. "But one of the addresses that Maya Cooper visited once—it's Aditi Sen's house."

20

DEVON

When Devon was seventeen, he met Aditi Sen.

It was at a party. One of *those* parties—the kind with fancy drinks, where a doorman turned you away if your tie wasn't made of silk or your shoes had a scuff. Where everyone was sleek, polished. Where the diamonds were real and the smiles were fake.

Devon preferred the parties where everyone was underage, wearing torn clothing and drinking out of a keg.

His sister insisted on dragging him along.

"You need to get out more," Darla said crisply, her fingers at his throat. She was attempting to fix the crookedly knotted tie, but Devon suspected she was also resisting the urge to strangle him with it.

"I get out plenty," he said.

"Out with people who matter," she said through gritted teeth, fingers working furiously. She wore a sparkling dress of red and silver, and Devon was pretty sure that it was a real emerald around her neck. "Come on, Devon, it's just a fundraiser. Would it kill you to not be pissed and stupid for one hour?"

Devon considered. "It might."

"If you embarrass Dad one more sodding time..." muttered Darla. Her polished accent slipped, roughened into something resembling Devon's.

"What's he going to do?" said Devon. He thought longingly of the champagne he knew must be flowing downstairs. He and Darla stood in a shiny-bright bathroom. She'd commandeered the men's loo, even going so far as to wedge a broomstick through the door's handle. Devon stood next to the row of sinks, eyes wandering as Darla tried to fix his tie.

"It's not what he's going to do to you," said Darla, eyes narrowing. "It's what I'll do." She gave one last yank at his collar and stepped away. She crossed her arms, mouth scrunching up to one side. "Bugger it. Turn around for me."

Feeling a bit like a dog at a show, Devon did a quick turn.

"You don't look half-bad," said Darla. She slid the broom handle free, opening the door.

They walked down a winding circular staircase. The hotel booked for this fund-raiser was top-of-the-line—all gleaming marble and pristine silver. Devon had no idea what the event was for—some environmental charity, he suspected. He only knew it was one of *those* events, the kind where his father was supposed to put in an appearance. To show that rich people still cared about the environment/poverty/little kittens. It was all for show, he thought scornfully. None of these people actually cared. They were just trying to look as if they cared. They were just slipping on masks.

Devon knew all about that.

Darla led him past the buffet tables. She scanned the crowd with a practiced eye, no doubt searching for the best people to talk to. She wouldn't hit up the same ones Dad would; the two would make sure to greet separate crowds, to double-team the charm.

Sometimes Devon envied his sister's rapport with their dad. Mr. Lyre and Darla always seemed to be on the same page.

But when he caught a glimpse of his father across the room, Devon's heart gave an unsteady lurch of panic. If Mr. Lyre saw them, he would give Devon a hard look. The words *Don't screw this up* would be spelled out in his eyes. Devon didn't want to see those words, didn't want to see him, didn't want to be reminded that he couldn't ever belong here.

A waiter with a napkin over one silk sleeve stepped

forward. He balanced a tray of golden wineglasses. "Drink?" he said. He didn't ask for IDs.

"Thank you," Devon started to say, taking one.

Smoothly, Darla plucked the drink from his fingers and replaced it on the tray. "But no thank you," she said to the waiter. The man blinked, then glided away.

"An hour," groaned Darla. She looked as if she knew she was fighting a losing battle. "Just one hour without a drink."

Devon surreptitiously glanced to his left. Sure enough, his dad was still there, still holding a crowd spellbound. "Let's go this way," he said, angling himself in the opposite direction. Darla opened her mouth to ask, but he'd already spotted the bar.

Perfect.

His skin felt dry and the suit too tight. He didn't want to remember whatever happened tonight.

A woman was accepting a glass of red wine from the bartender. She wore a silk sari, a flourished star pendant hung around her throat, and her dark hair was laced with silver. She was comfortably heavy, and her face was lined around the eyes.

"Vodka tonic," said Devon to the bartender.

The woman with the wine smiled at him. "Just arrived?" she said, inclining her head.

He gave her a cautious look. "How'd you know?"

"Because," she said, still smiling, "the first thing everyone does when they get to events like this is make a beeline for the open bar." Her voice was pleasant and something in her demeanor made Devon relax. Maybe it was the fact she didn't know his last name or reputation.

Devon accepted his drink. "Nice to know I'm fitting in. I'm Devon."

"Aditi Sen," said the woman. She held out her wineglass. "To tradition."

Devon gently clinked his own tumbler against her glass and began to bring the drink to his lips, when Darla appeared from nowhere.

She wrenched the glass from Devon's hand and dumped its contents into a nearby plant. The bartender looked scandalized.

"This is Sisyphus," Devon said dryly.

"I don't even want to know what you just called me," muttered Darla, the empty glass still clutched in her hand.

Aditi Sen's dark eyes were fixed on Devon, but not in an accusing way. Her gaze was intense, as if he were worthy of study. "Sisyphus," she said. "A man doomed to roll a boulder up a hill for all eternity." Her attention snapped to Darla. "Your sister?"

"My keeper," said Devon, "but everyone calls her Darla."

Sen smiled slightly. "You're the Lyre children."

Devon opened his mouth to reply, but Darla spoke first.

"You know our father?"

"I know of him, yes," said Sen politely. "We haven't had the pleasure to meet in person. Although he has made some donations to my cause."

A panicky look crawled over Darla's face. Devon recognized it immediately—it was how Darla looked when she forgot someone's name or career. She hated to be caught off guard. He could almost see the sweat rolling down her neck. Of course she wouldn't ask; she'd just pretend to know what cause this Aditi Sen worked for.

"What do you do?" he asked bluntly.

Sen seemed gratified by the question. "I'm an activist. I'm currently working to dismantle the laws that have inhibited the Fourth Amendment."

Devon just stared at her. In his last government class, he had been trying to see what would happen if he mixed vodka and tequila. (Nothing good, for the record.)

Sen must have seen his confusion, because she said, "I'm trying to repeal the Allegiant Act."

Darla choked on her reply.

Devon felt mildly impressed. "Shit."

Sen laughed. She raised her glass as if in another toast. "Shit, indeed. That's what everyone says."

"Bit ballsy of you," said Devon. "I mean, that can't be a safe profession."

Sen's smile widened. "Safe is boring."

Devon decided he liked her.

Darla clearly felt the opposite; he could see it in her stiff posture, the way her expression iced over. "The Allegiant Act is for our own good," she said, her voice gone sugary.

Sen spoke calmly, like this was a practiced dialogue. "The Allegiant Act says that any individual who might pose a threat to American security must have their blood tested and be tagged at all times—and if they *are* suspected to be a threat, they can be detained by the military. Now, tell me what's wrong with that law."

Darla pretended to think it over. "Nothing I can think of."

While she spoke, a waiter drifted by. He carried the usual tray of drinks, but tucked behind his back, nestled in the grip of his left hand, was a full bottle of champagne. Devon snagged one of the glasses as the waiter passed.

Darla hadn't seen a thing. Devon quickly angled himself so that his torso hid the glass from view, his arm awkwardly tucked against himself.

"And you?" said Sen, turning her attention to Devon. He tried to look innocent. His mind replayed her last words.

"The way the law's worded," he finally said. "It's too

open-ended. The way you said it: 'Any individual who might pose a threat to American security'—well, that could be anyone. Anyone could be vaccinated, anyone could be immune. Even if you're not vaccinated, you could be a threat." With a flourish, he revealed the champagne glass and took a swig from it. "We're all walking time bombs."

Darla looked like she wanted to murder him. Taking the glass from him without spilling it was a feat, but she managed.

Sen watched, apparently riveted by the siblings.

"I'm sorry about this," said Darla, once she'd torn the glass from Devon.

"I have five brothers," said Sen. "No apology necessary."

Darla stepped away, went to return the glass to the bartender, leaving Devon alone with Aditi Sen.

"And do you support the Allegiant Act?" said Sen.

Devon grinned. It was his first real smile since setting foot on the premises. With his sister gone, he pulled a full bottle of champagne out of his jacket. It was the one the waiter had been carrying—the one Devon had grabbed, and the waiter hadn't said a word.

"The act doesn't matter," he said, putting the bottle to his lips. Once he'd swallowed, he added, "Those who will abide by the law will abide by it. And those who don't...well, they don't need to fear the feds."

"Not unless they get caught," observed Sen, just as Darla returned. She swelled with indignation.

"If she's Sisyphus," said Sen, "what does that make you?"

"An inanimate object with no free will, meant to be shoved around," said Devon.

Forty-five minutes later, Devon threw up in a houseplant and Darla gave up on him.

He still considered it a win.

21

DEVON

Devon finds the story on his tablet, before he goes to work.

He's sitting on his dormitory bunk bed, quickly scrolling through the news. It's programmed for certain things, certain names—if any of his old friends are arrested, he wants to know.

But this story—he doesn't even have to search for it. It pops up right away.

STRING OF POSSIBLE ABDUCTIONS GOES PUBLIC

"Rotting hell," he murmurs, a chill going through him. There's a picture of Maya Cooper's car, a blurred outline of that FBI agent running after her. Devon's nowhere in the frame and he's grateful for it. The last thing he needs is a picture of him with the FBI splashed across the Internet. He walks out of his dorm, tablet in one hand, still reading as he jogs down the stairs two at a time.

But when he strides into the dormitory's lobby, he comes to a skidding halt.

A large man stands in the foyer. He wears a suit and has a heavy wool coat draped over one arm. "Dad," says Devon.

"Devon," says Mr. Lyre.

Devon's fingers move without conscious thought. When he looks down, he realizes he's texted Sia.

Probably going to be late to work.

"You look good."

They sit in the deserted dormitory common room. There are a couple of sofas, the fabric gone soft and discolored with age. A pool table takes up the rest of the space. Somehow, even in the morning, the scents of perfume, sweat, and microwave popcorn still linger. An empty red plastic cup sits on the pool table, like a small monument to the parties of nights past.

Mr. Lyre sits on the edge of the couch, as if he can barely stand to touch it.

"You mean I don't look hungover and homeless," replies Devon. He makes no effort to sound friendly.

Mr. Lyre folds his hands over one knee. "I was worried about you."

"No, you were worried about your friends finding out you let your son become some vagrant," retorts Devon. "Well, you can tell them that your kid is actually doing all right on his own. Tell them I haven't managed to screw this up yet."

"Devon," says Mr. Lyre, his eyes narrowing. "It's not like—"

"It's exactly like that," says Devon. "I'm fine. I'm wearing normal clothes and working a nine-to-five internship where I'm paid minimum wage and fetch coffees. Most of the time it's boring and I think some of my coworkers are mental, but I'm not in a ditch somewhere."

Mr. Lyre's face tightens. "Don't act so wounded. This isn't the first time you ran off and did something stupid. I mean, last summer you take off, pretending to be at some ski resort in Norway—"

"I *was* in a ski resort in Norway," puts in Devon. It is technically the truth.

Anger flashes across Mr. Lyre's face. "Not for the first half of June," he snaps. "You said you went to a ski resort in Hemsedal—but I did some checking and that ski resort closes down in May."

Devon's mouth drops open.

"And you know what else?" says Mr. Lyre, gaining

momentum. "Your tags show you were in Philadelphia for the majority of June. But then on the fifth of July, you booked a flight to Norway. Which, I might add, is one of the few European countries that actually allows American visas. Since they left the EU, they're fine with us. But you know who doesn't deal with Americans? Most of the countries *near* Norway."

He leans forward, dark eyes ablaze. "I'm not an idiot, Devon. You did something, were involved in something, and you wanted a place to hide from the feds if they came after you."

That was exactly his plan—go to Norway, and if everything went to hell, he could sneak over the border into some country with anti-American sentiments. Even if the feds did find him, extradition would be a nightmare. And he's always wanted to see France.

His father's gaze rests heavy on him.

"I'm not in trouble," Devon says. Again, technically not a lie. He's not in trouble at the moment.

"Then why are you working for the government?" Mr. Lyre says. "Is this part of some plea bargain? Did you commit a crime and offer to work off the sentence?"

Devon snorts. He's trying to picture Macourek strong-arming someone. It's easier to imagine *Sia* doing that. "Is it so unbelievable that I'm here because I want to be?"

"You're wearing a suit, Devon," Mr. Lyre says, waving at him. "You're sober, you're coherent. You can't tell me—"

"That I did it on my own?" he says. And abruptly, none of this is funny. It's not funny at all.

Mr. Lyre falters.

"You can't believe that I'm here because someone wanted to hire me?" says Devon, and he can feel himself cracking apart.

Taking a breath, Mr. Lyre draws himself together. Devon recognizes the look; it's the same one he wears after a social stumble, when he's trying to charm a client. "You're smart," he says. "Devon, you're a bright boy. But working for the government like this—it isn't safe—"

"What is *safe*, Father?" Devon says, unable to keep the hostility from his voice. "Keeping me hidden? Telling me to be a failure so no one will notice me? Only thing is, you don't really like failures, do you?"

Mr. Lyre rises to his feet. "If you were going to become a government puppet, we could've stayed in London. We came here for you, so you could be free."

"Free to do what?" Devon says, with a strangled little laugh. "To pretend to be normal?"

"It's better than the alternative!" Mr. Lyre's voice rises and he makes a conscious effort to lower it. "Devon, most people like you are rounded up by the government, used as spies or special ops or security. And those are the lucky ones. You know how many people find crime families at their doors? How many times I've heard about people gone missing because they seemed too talented, too knowing—"

"So you think it's better for me to spend my life pretending to be normal?" Devon shakes his head. "Well, I'm not *normal*, Dad. I've tried my whole damn life to be normal and I *can't*. You want to know how I know that? Because when I was five years old, you sat me down on your knee and tested me. Gave me phrases to memorize, to see if I could recite them back to you. Because I was too intelligent to be *normal*—"

"Devon," says Mr. Lyre, but Devon barrels over him.

"And do you remember the first thing you asked me to memorize?" Devon's lips peel back, and he knows he's grinning. Because that's how he deflects things—with humor and jokes. Even now, when every word cuts into him, he can't stop smiling. "*'We are unfashioned creatures, but half made up, if one wiser, better, dearer than ourselves—such a friend ought to be—do not lend his aid to perfectionate our weak and faulty natures.'*"

Mr. Lyre's calm mask drops away, and there's anger and hurt there, too. "I'd forgotten," he says.

"Good for you," sneers Devon.

Mr. Lyre spreads his hands, palms out. "It was the first book that came to mind."

"Frankenstein," says Devon. "That's the first thing that came to mind when you thought your son might be immune." The words form a knot in his throat and he shakes his head.

"I've got to go," Devon says, cutting his dad off before he can respond. "I'll be late for work."

He's on his feet before Mr. Lyre can protest, moving toward the front doors. The sky is steel gray and the old snow has been churned into a freezing, dirty sludge. He inhales, tasting exhaust and moisture, and he doesn't stop walking even when his father calls after him.

22

CIERE

There are two key elements to a good crime: timing and location.

The timing part is obvious. You don't pick someone's pocket if there's already a hand in there. (Ciere learned that the hard way when she was eleven.) There's a rhythm that good crooks learn to pick up. Human nature is predictable, and playing off someone's inattention, their impatience, their exhaustion—it makes duping them easier.

Location is a bit harder.

When the target is a person, the location of a crime is simpler. The whole "getting mugged in a dark alley" is a cliché for a reason. It works. The target is isolated, out of the line of sight, and usually the sound of distant traffic covers up any suspicious noises.

Fixed locations are harder. Crooks have to carefully gauge the places they want to hit—see if security is worth getting around. The best location is one that is crowded, unfamiliar to its occupants, and appears safe.

Nine times out of ten, hotels are great fixed locations. The bustling activity, filled to the brim with strangers, and the constant comings and goings means that no one is truly safe. Doors are left cracked open, maids can be bribed, and there are plenty of exits to slip through.

The Arata Suites is tucked into one of the expensive tourist districts, surrounded by upscale shopping centers, cutesy little boutique shops. The hotel is beautiful, massive, and Ciere suspects the parking lot is hidden somewhere in the back. There's a valet in front, and marble steps lead up to two broad doors.

Ciere does her reconnaissance from a nearby park. It's a quaint little square of lawn, complete with a designer playground. She climbs a tree and illusions herself into nothing. She shivers, her gloved hands fumbling with a pair of binoculars. What she sees isn't encouraging.

There are cameras; the doorman is obviously ex-military; even the boys running the valet look vigilant. When a couple walks up to the front door, the doorman takes their tags, scanning them both before allowing them inside.

This is a hotel where security isn't an afterthought—it's a feature.

She weighs several options. She could steal a keycard and attempt to slip in under the guise of an employee. One of those red jackets the valets wear couldn't be that hard to find. But she's never been a good driver and accidentally crashing a guest's car might prove problematic.

Ciere leans back against the tree trunk, crossing her arms over her chest. Whoever killed Pruitt did a good job of picking the worst hotel for Ciere to investigate. Either it's coincidence or the killer is used to operating in high-security places.

Someone like Guntram, part of her pipes up.

"Or Henry," she mutters to herself. "Or even Conrad."

She spends an hour in the tree, watching the hotel. Her legs go numb with cold and her mind wanders, but she tries to simply observe. This is what good criminals do. They watch. They take in a location and look for patterns. They calculate the right moment to strike.

As she puts the binoculars back to her eyes, a large utility truck pulls up to the valet. It's white, with some kind of food logo painted across the side.

One of the red-jacketed valet boys runs up, gesturing wildly at the truck. He points around the corner, as if trying to direct them somewhere else. After a moment, the truck moves on.

Interesting. Ciere would expect a hotel of this stature to cater its own parties and meetings. Outside catering means someone wants something distinctive, presumably for a special event. And if these caterers don't know the service entrance…maybe, just maybe, there is a chance here.

She wishes she still had her phone; she could just look up the hotel website and scroll through their event calendar. She scurries down the tree and out of the park, all the while keeping a careful eye on her surroundings. If that Alberani hit man is still after her, she doesn't want to be caught off guard.

Even in this weather, there are a few kids bustling around the swing set. Parents cluster together in groups, talking among themselves and sipping specialty coffee drinks. They're distracted, eyes always on their children. Perfect.

One of the parents leaves his bag on a bench as he runs after a particularly rambunctious toddler. Ciere, still invisible, digs into the bag and finds a tablet. She quickly boots it up, praying it won't be password protected. It isn't.

She scrolls through to a search engine and quickly types in the hotel's name. A pristine website pops up, complete with a picture of the hotel's front entrance. *ARATA SUITES,* it reads. *COMFORT AND SECURITY.*

For those willing to pay for it, Ciere adds mentally. But her fingers are already moving, tracing a line to the button labeled EVENTS. A quick scan of the dates and she finds it.

ADITI SEN ADDRESS. 7 PM–12 AM.

Aditi Sen. Ciere recognizes the name—she's some kind

206

of politician. Ciere returns the tablet to the bag and hurries away, just as the dad returns with the toddler in his arms. Ciere watches them for a moment, then shakes her head and moves on, the snow crunching beneath her feet.

Magnus is doing the dishes when Ciere stomps into his apartment. "You find anything?" he says, tossing a dish towel over his arm. Ciere yanks off her jacket and hangs it on a hook.

"Magnus," she asks, "just *how* popular are you with politicians?"

23

DEVON

It's a Friday, and Devon can feel it in the air. There's a hum of anticipation and everyone seems a little looser, a little more relaxed. Devon is on data entry duty. It's not riveting work, but it does keep him occupied. He tries to focus on the task at hand and shuts out all other distractions.

Lunchtime comes and goes and he ignores it. He was about an hour late to work, so it's the least he can do—but that's not why he does it. The tedious work, the constant rhythm of his fingers over the keyboard, is all that's holding him together. His body feels fragile, ready to break apart if anything more happens. So he won't let it. He will narrow the world until it consists of nothing more than simple statistics.

Sia stops by his desk once. "See you," she says. She has a purse over one shoulder and her white cane in hand.

"You headed out?" he replies.

She nods. "It's a slow day. Macourek said we could duck out early—well, except for you, I guess."

He narrows his eyes. "And what's that supposed to mean?"

"I mean," says Sia, "I heard Macourek's taking you to the event tonight. You should try to have some fun."

Devon can't hold back a snort. "Then why aren't you going?"

"Date night," says Sia, grinning. "And I've had my fair share of these events. Just don't dump a drink on anyone's head and you'll be fine."

The event is being held in exactly the kind of place Devon has come to expect: some ritzy hotel with far too much security. After giving his keys to a valet, Macourek climbs the stairs, Devon at his heels. Getting into the hotel takes a few minutes. The doorman—heavily muscled, with a telltale bulge under his arm—scans their tags. Then he examines Macourek's invitation, as if trying to determine if it's real, before waving them through to the metal detector.

"Mind holding this for a second?" says Macourek, handing Devon the invitation before taking off his watch. Devon mentally checks himself over for metal and then decides he's fine. While Macourek takes a money clip from his pocket, Devon examines the invitation.

One of the names catches his eye. "Aditi Sen," he says. "This party's for Aditi Sen?"

"You've heard of her?" Macourek pats down the rest of his pockets, as if checking for any stray items.

"I've met her, actually," says Devon. "At a party last year."

The look Macourek aims at him is uncertain.

"Don't worry," he says. "That night I managed to throw up in a planter rather than on someone."

Oddly enough, this doesn't seem to reassure his boss.

"Just don't be startled if she starts calling me Boulder," Devon adds.

Macourek squints at him, then he shakes his head. "I'm not going to ask."

"Better that way," says Devon cheerfully.

"Imagining your childhood frightens me." Macourek gives his invitation to another one of the doormen.

"It's not that exciting. Sometimes I got drunk at school. And then other times my dad was yelling at me for not living up to the family name."

Macourek slides his tags back around his neck, tucking them out of sight. "My childhood was firmly middle class, so I can't say I know much about fancy parties. The father thing, though, I know all too well."

Devon smiles tightly. His voice thins out when he says, "Is that why you decided to hire me?"

Macourek glances at him before looking back to the hallway. "One of many reasons." But he's moving before Devon can say another word.

The hotel's foyer expands into a sweeping hallway. It's a gorgeous building. Some architect must've had a field day with it. As they stride deeper into the hotel, a flash of black and gray catches Devon's eye. There are a man and woman standing by a wall. Their backs are rigid, and there's something in their expressions that makes Devon pause.

Macourek slows a step. "Looks like the FBI has been taking an interest in Sen's movements of late," murmurs Macourek, nodding at the agents by the wall. His fingers clench and he shoves them into his pockets. "Bold of them to stand in plain view."

"They're not invited?" asks Devon, chancing a look at the agents.

"No," says Macourek. "But that won't keep them away from an event like this. They must have an arrangement with the hotel."

Devon glances back at the agents and tries not to feel shaken by their presence. It's not like he's a criminal—well, not anymore.

The party is exactly what Devon expected: extravagant and boring, crowded with men in custom-made suits and women in cocktail dresses. The place is tastefully decorated and someone erected a stage with a podium and microphone. His eyes wander to the bar, like a compass drawn to north.

The urge to drink is overshadowed by the memory of his father. He won't drink. He won't get fired.

If only so he never has to go home again.

He's still glaring at the bar when a crackle of static draws his attention. Several people stand on the stage.

One woman is standing at the podium.

Aditi Sen hasn't changed. She still wears a sari, and looks ready to take on the world. She knits her fingers together and smiles at the crowd. The murmurs die away.

"I see quite a few old faces"—she inclines her head and a few people wave—"and many new ones. I'd like to thank you all for coming tonight.

"I'm not going to bore you with speeches. I just wanted to tell you that I had some trouble getting into this party." She smiles, as if sharing a joke. "Despite the fact that it's being hosted for my benefit, I had to have two separate people vouch for my identity before the doorman would let me in." She touches a finger to a lock of hair that's strayed across her ear. "Maybe I'm graying more than I thought."

Laughter rings out.

"But no," Sen says, still smiling. "I know that's not it. Here—I'll show you why." And she pulls down at her sari's neckline. For a second, Devon isn't sure what she's trying to show them. Her collarbones? He sees a flash of silver, and realizes it's her pendant necklace. But that can't be it, because now she's holding up each wrist. Empty. Nothing on them.

That's when it clicks and Devon understands. He draws in a sharp breath.

"It's not what's here," Sen says. "It's what isn't. See what's missing?"

Devon mouths the word at Macourek, unable to help himself: *Tags.*

Macourek's mouth draws tight.

Other people catch on. There are a few uncertain noises, a quiet hum of conversation as the point sinks in.

Aditi Sen isn't wearing her ID tags.

"I took them off this morning," says Sen. "Left them on my kitchen counter." She surveys the crowd, waiting for them to fall silent. "Do you know the original use for dog tags?

"They were worn by soldiers for identification." Sen reaches out to one of her aides, who hastily pulls off his own tags and hands them to Sen. Sen holds them up, the twin slips of metal catching the light. "If a soldier was killed in battle, one tag went to the family and the other was kept on the body to identify it. Which, I suppose, is now the point as well."

The smiles drops from her face. "We are all soldiers. The government has declared war upon its own citizens when it decided we were more useful as weapons than as people. You may think I'm just speaking for those with adverse effects, but I'm not. This constant surveillance, this tracking, the fact that it is illegal not to wear dog tags at all times, affects every one of us." She sweeps her free hand across the room, taking in the crowd. "Every time we enter an elsec, every time we get pulled over for speeding, every place we go—these get scanned and logged. Our locations, our very lives are subject to scrutiny. And if we're deemed a threat, the military has the means and laws to come after us."

Sen grips the tags tightly, jabbing at the sky with them. Her voice rises in pitch. "As long as we wear these, we're not free. We are not equal. We are things to be requisitioned and used. I think it's high time we reminded the world that we are people—not soldiers."

She throws the tags onto the floor.

Silence weighs heavy on the crowd. Devon holds his breath, unsure what to do. Then Macourek begins clapping. It's a slow, deliberate sound—not the frayed excitement of applause, but more of a steady beat. Slowly, others join in until nearly the whole room thunders with it.

It's a dangerous speech. Sen's putting herself on the line by not wearing her tags and encouraging others to do the same. She could easily be imprisoned.

She's rich, Devon reminds himself. She's connected. She's

probably safe. The most that'll happen is she spends a few nights in jail for not wearing her tags.

The clapping slowly dissolves and Sen nods at her audience, stepping away from the podium.

The aide doesn't retrieve his tags. They remain on the floor, and everyone seems to give them a wide berth. Tension leaks from the air until people are chatting, the throngs milling about. Devon tries to shake off his own unease.

"This isn't a party," he says. "It's a political rally." He finds himself squinting at Macourek. "Are you here because HS is keeping an eye on Sen?"

"Homeland Security isn't fond of her, that's for sure," says Macourek, eyes still fixed on Sen. "She's been arrested several times—she'd probably be charged with treason if she weren't so powerful."

"But you like her," says Devon. It comes out more accusing than he intends.

Macourek takes a crab puff from one of the waiters. "I respect her work."

"So why am I here?" asks Devon. He wants it clarified, because he's acutely aware of his own tags hanging around his throat. They mark him as vaccinated, as potentially dangerous.

Macourek takes a sip of his champagne. "You are here so that when someone greets us, you can step in and give your name first. That way if I forget someone, it won't be obvious."

This startles a laugh out of Devon. "You want me here in case you forget someone's name?"

"It's more a question of 'when' than 'if,'" says Macourek delicately. "I've probably met at least a quarter of the people here…and I'll remember about two of them. You, being new, can introduce yourself and get their names in return. And you're a bright young man—you'll probably remember them."

Macourek has no idea. Devon chokes down another laugh. "That I can do," he says.

Macourek drops his empty champagne glass onto a waiter's tray. "Tell you what—I'm going to visit the restroom and then we'll make the rounds. I'll talk to those I have to, we'll grab some more food, and then duck out early. Good?"

Devon agrees and Macourek slips away, easing through the crowd. Devon smiles to himself. He grabs a crab puff and a glass of water from two more passing trays and tries to make his way to the fringes of the party to find a quiet place to wait and—

That's when he sees her.

A gray dress clings to her shoulders, floats away from her waist. Thin stockings of silver thread cover her legs and glint like chain mail. Her eyes are heavily lined and her thin mouth is bare.

Ciere.

Her blonde hair is longer, shoulder length, and she looks

different. He gives himself a shake. It's been less than a year since he saw her—she can't have aged that much.

It's the way she moves that throws him. Ciere was always skittish and quick. But now she eases through the crowd with a firmer step. A predator on the prowl, rather than someone looking for the exits.

His body locks up, all the joints cemented in place. He can't move—it's all he can do to follow her with his eyes. Ciere. Ciere. He hasn't seen her since that horrible day, since they tried to dump a federal agent's body and he screwed everything up. Since she abandoned him. Since she chose Fiacre.

That last thought is what frees him. He finds himself moving. He knows he should turn around and get out of here, but it's almost as if someone's tied an invisible string around them both—he has to follow her.

She strides up to the bar, begins pointing at bottles. The bartender seems thrown, probably unused to girls in frilly dresses asking for a shot of whisky.

Devon's mouth feels clumsy, and it takes him a moment to think of something to say.

"C-Ciere," he croaks, and she whirls to face him.

24

CIERE

"So let me get this straight," says Ciere. "To get into his party, you're going as this senator's date and I'm your assistant?"

It takes all her self-control not to put her hands up and form quotation marks around the word *date*.

Her dress is an empire waist, made of gray silk and tulle. It reminds her of the dirty snow outside. Magnus wears a tuxedo. She has to admit, he looks fantastic in it, his body all hard angles and hair smoothed back.

"Technically." Magnus pulls into the valet parking and his car glides to a halt. "You're my date. Or that's what my invitation says, anyway."

"The one the senator managed to get for you," says Ciere.

"Yes."

"But you're really his date."

"Yes."

She squints at him. "Won't his wife mind?"

"I've been her date as well," says Magnus lightly, stepping out of the car and handing his keys over to a red-jacketed young man. Ciere scrambles after him. The air outside is bitingly cold, but they should only be outside for mere seconds. "I was a birthday present at some point," he says mildly. "They both ended up becoming regulars."

She tries to come up with a response and fails. "So after we get into the party," she begins to say, and lets the sentence trail off.

"You're on your own." Magnus nods to the doorman, who takes their tags and the invitation Magnus managed to wrangle. He begins scanning both. Only after they've passed inspection are Magnus and Ciere directed to the second security checkpoint. Magnus murmurs, "I'll be spending the night elsewhere. You still have the key I gave you?"

One of Magnus's apartment keys is safely tucked into the lining of Ciere's bra. "Go back if you need to," says Magnus as they approach the checkpoint. "If you need a place to stay." He holds out his tags for the second time.

"Hopefully, I won't need to," says Ciere. "I'll get the evidence and catch the next train up to Newark." She smiles brightly at the bouncer. He holds out a hand for her clutch and she obligingly gives it up. He conducts a brief search before returning it. Their heavy winter coats are taken, and they're given tickets to retrieve the garments later.

Magnus offers his arm. "Ready?"

Ciere accepts the gesture, her fingers sliding around his silken sleeve.

Together, they stride into the hotel proper. In other such places Ciere has visited, there's usually just a check-in desk, a concierge station, maybe some free coffee, and a sign for the hotel's bar.

This hotel more closely resembles a museum. The arched ceiling stretches high above her, and there are actual columns descending from it.

"Jeez," she says, without meaning to.

Magnus laughs softly. "Kit will be furious when he finds out you pulled a job in here without him. He's always loved places like this."

Someone calls out and Magnus looks up. She sees the change in him. It's fascinating—Magnus's mild expression smooths out, lights up from the inside. He moves sinuously, reaching out to clasp the hand of the approaching man. The reserved mentalist is suddenly *warm*, charming.

He's working, Ciere realizes.

"You're late," the senator says fondly.

Magnus smiles back. "Have we missed anything important?"

The senator laughs. "Just Sen's speech—so no." He gives Ciere a polite nod and rests a hand on Magnus's elbow. "Shall we?"

Magnus nods at Ciere before following the senator through one of the arched doorways. Ciere hesitates, suddenly unsure. It's not like she's never been alone on a job before, but this is the first time the stakes are so high.

Alan.

She inhales, braces herself, and some of her nerves fade away. *On the job*, she thinks, and tosses her hair back. *Just another job.*

She steps into the ballroom.

Ciere has spent several years living in an elsec. The elite sectors always remind her of those old pastoral paintings—carefully crafted scenes of brightest beauty. Fields and trees, women in flowing dresses on swing sets and men in suits having picnics. Elsecs are worlds unto themselves, where the wealthy try to pretend they are just like everyone else.

No one pretends here.

The chandeliers cast glittering lights over the floor and walls, their spinning shadows making Ciere dizzy. The floors are a deep marble, so reflective she can see the crisp outline of her ballet flats and the hem of her dress. If elsecs are those pastoral paintings, then this scene resembles the ancient paintings Kit likes to collect—the ones of empires. Rome,

Paris, Russia. Those paintings are all red and gold, like the last rays of a sunset. An ember burning itself out.

There's another thing those scenes of decadence have in common.

All those empires fell.

She ventures into the crowd, mindful of her surroundings. She feels out of place here; she's spent so long in warehouses, not showering, and eating raccoon burgers. When a waiter passes by, she snags a crab puff.

The plan is simple; having used Magnus's connections to get into this party, she'll linger until everything is in full swing. Then she can slip out and begin her search in earnest. No one will question a well-dressed teen girl wandering through the halls. Especially not with a party going on.

The mysterious hotel key is safely tucked into her clutch. Her fingers dig into the beaded fabric. She'll need it later.

She drifts through the throngs of well-dressed elite. She glides to the bar and orders a shot of whisky. If she's caught in the hotel, a little alcohol on her breath will help her cover.

The bartender blinks. His hands stray toward a half-empty bottle of champagne. "Are you sure you wouldn't like...?"

Ciere gives him a look and he hastily grabs a shot glass. Ciere toys with her clutch, waiting for the shot. She's entirely unprepared for someone to say her name.

"C-Ciere?"

The voice is familiar, low with that faint accent.

She whirls. Standing behind her is a tall young man. He looks different; his hair is clipped neatly and he's wearing a gray suit jacket. Even so, she recognizes him immediately. "Devon."

25

DEVON

The shock welds Ciere in place. She stands, frozen, even when the bartender slides her drink across the bar. Her lips twitch, as if trying to say something, but nothing emerges.

Devon has rehearsed this conversation in his head countless times. He's considered what he would say to Ciere, how he would've said things differently. He's spent entire nights rehashing their last encounter, trying to pick it apart in case there was something he could've done differently. He's come up with lectures, with insults, with pleas, with arguments.

What he ends up saying is, "Bloody hell, Ciere. You look like the ghost of prom past."

That seems to bring her around. She blinks several times. "I—I thought you were in Norway."

Devon replies, "Well, I came back."

And that brings their conversation to a standstill.

Awkward silence.

Devon opens his mouth, then closes it. All of his imaginary conversations seem to melt away.

The party carries on around them, ignorant of the little drama playing out before the bar. An older woman sidles up to order a martini and Devon jumps out of the way. He snatches up Ciere's drink and hands it to her. They fall into step, drifting away from the bar and toward a wall. A quiet place, Devon thinks. They both have the same idea—find a quiet place and regroup.

They still think alike, and that gives him courage.

"Your hair is longer," he remarks.

Ciere's hand drifts to her shoulder-length curls. "It keeps my neck warm," she says dazedly. "And Kit's not around to insist on cutting it."

Which means she's still with the Syndicate. She's still working off their debt, one incurred when they robbed a bank in Syndicate territory. Devon feels a twinge of guilt and tries to ignore it. She's paying for *their* mistake—not hers, but *theirs*. He was able to leg it to Norway, while she had to stay behind and play nice with a bunch of mobsters.

But then again, considering her current location, she can't have had too hard a time of it.

"The Syndicate has business here?" He gestures vaguely at the room.

Ciere bites her lip, then shakes her head. "No. It's—uh, personal."

"Are you nicking something?" He takes a drink of water, just for something to do.

Another head shake. "Finding a murderer," she says, and he nearly chokes on his drink. "It's a long story," she adds, twitching one shoulder in a half shrug. "What are you doing here?"

"You probably won't believe it...but I'm working," says Devon dryly.

Ciere gapes. "I *don't* believe it." Her gaze sweeps over him. "Are you a valet or something?"

"I don't work for the hotel," says Devon, a little offended. But then he realizes his mistake. He doesn't want her to ask where he works. Because then he'll have to tell her and she won't like it. Interning for Homeland Security is a betrayal—or at least that's how she'll see it.

He speaks before she can, the words slipping out in a tangled rush. "You here alone? Or is that creepy shark-toothed guy with you?"

Her brow wrinkles. "You mean Conrad? No, he's in Newark. I'm here with Magnus. He's technically here on different business, but whatever." She lifts her drink and points over his shoulder. Devon turns and sees a familiar figure. Magnus is standing in a group of well-dressed men and women, chatting amiably. Ciere's wave must catch his eye, because he glances up and sees Devon. His lips part, his mild expression tinged with surprise.

Devon's arm flails in what he hopes is a casual greeting. It's possibly the most awkward wave in the history of waving. If there is a history of waving.

Devon shakes his head and tries to draw his scrambled thoughts together. "H-how's the others?"

"Others?"

Devon clears his throat. "The wanker and Anastasia."

Kit Copperfield and Alan Fiacre.

Ciere gives him a dirty look. It's possibly the most beautiful thing he's ever seen, because it means she's dropped her guard. The walls between them are crumbling. "Kit is fine," she says tartly. "Still in Philadelphia. And Alan"—she drops her voice—"is with Guntram and the others."

That's interesting. "He's not into finding murderers?" he says, smirking a bit. "He always did seem a bit squeamish. Not up to this sort of thing."

Ciere's grip tightens on her drink. There's no humor in her face when she says, "Actually, I'm here to prove he didn't kill someone."

Devon takes another drink and wishes it were stronger than water. He feels like he might need a drink after this conversation, good intentions be damned. "Anastasia killed someone?"

He can't help but use the nickname, even if Ciere hates it. He began calling Alan Fiacre Anastasia months ago because it seemed to fit—last surviving member of an infamous family.

"No," says Ciere instantly. A pause. "Well, I'm pretty sure he didn't."

Devon lets out a low whistle. "You've had an interesting few months, haven't you?"

Ciere's shoulders slump. It's a small gesture and he wouldn't have noticed if he didn't know her so well. "You could say that." She scratches absentmindedly at her left biceps and he sees a thin, angry red line denting her skin. It looks like a healing scar.

His stomach twists and he feels a little sick. He's being an idiot, he knows it. Making light of things that are deadly serious. He reaches out, hand hovering over the scar. Ciere flinches, then drops her hand. She doesn't pull away when he lightly traces the line with a fingertip.

"Are you all right?" he says softly.

When she looks up at him, he knows all the walls are down. They're back to normal, back to the way things should be. "Not really. Everything's gone to hell lately." She sounds tired and she drains the whisky shot in one go, clutching the empty glass between her fingers. "The Syndicate doesn't trust us, I've got an Alberani hit man on my back, Guntram might be trying to blackmail me, and I'm probably on a wild-goose chase."

Her use of the plural doesn't escape him. He tries to ignore it. "I'm sure everything will..." His voice trails off when a familiar figure approaches. Macourek's thin form materializes in the crowd, walking toward them. He comes up on Ciere's back, smiling.

"Already making friends, I see," he says lightly, striding around Ciere and coming to a halt at Devon's shoulder.

Ciere's glass hits the marble floor and shatters. It's a small sound in a large, crowded room, and hardly anyone notices. Devon glances down and sees her hands are shaking, fingers clawed in fists. She's staring at Devon, openmouthed and deathly pale. Like a black hole has opened up behind him and he doesn't know it.

Devon glances over his shoulder to see if there's a gunman or mobster or something to fear, but there's nothing—just Macourek. A Macourek whose face has gone bloodless.

And then Magnus is there, probably drawn by the sound of breaking glass.

Magnus edges forward, putting himself in the midst of the three of them. His eyes are cold, focused on the man just behind Devon.

"Hello, Aristeus," says Magnus.

PART THREE

We will then be forced on our part to take those measures we deem necessary and sufficient to defend our rights. To this end we have all that is necessary.

—First Secretary Nikita Khrushchev,
Letter to President Kennedy,
October 24, 1962

26

CIERE

Aristeus.

Aristeus stands before her, one hand on Devon's shoulder like it belongs there. All of his attention is on Magnus. He opens bloodless lips, but Magnus speaks first.

"You say that name here and I will silence you," Magnus says, his tone quiet and deceptively calm. But his shoulders are rigid with tension. "It's Magnus now. Call me Magnus."

Aristeus's mouth moves silently, shaping a word that is definitely not *Magnus*. He swallows the unsaid name. When he speaks, his voice is coming apart at the seams. "What are you doing here?"

"Freelancing," says Magnus. He sounds strangely toneless.

Aristeus gapes at him.

Magnus's voice remains level, almost soothing. "It's nothing that would harm your precious cause."

"The illusionist," Aristeus says jerkily.

"Stays with me," replies Magnus. His tone becomes a shade colder. "Anyway, I see you've been busy recruiting."

Devon stands poised as if to move but unsure where to go.

Magnus has no such uncertainty. He takes a few slow, deliberate steps forward until he and Aristeus are almost nose to nose. Aristeus doesn't recoil; he edges forward so that he stands between Devon and Magnus, his stance almost protective. Countless emotions play out over his face and he can't seem to settle on one.

"Tell me that you won't say a word," says Magnus, his voice just above a whisper.

Aristeus swallows, his eyes flickering down Magnus's body before returning to his eyes. Ciere wants to reach out and grab Magnus, to tell him not to look into Aristeus's eyes.

Aristeus is a dominus, the rarest of all the immunities. With a single moment of eye-to-eye contact and a verbal command, he can take control of a person's mind. It's a deadly skill, one she's seen him employ without mercy. But Magnus shows no fear.

"Aristeus," murmurs Magnus. His hand reaches out and he grasps Aristeus's forearm. His fingers worm under the man's sleeve, and Ciere knows he must be touching bare skin. "Are you going to tell anyone I'm alive?"

Aristeus's mouth works silently. But Magnus must hear his answer.

A silent conversation passes between them. Ciere watches it play out in the creases of Aristeus's forehead, the way Magnus's body relaxes. They're safe for the moment, she realizes. The specifics are lost on her; all she knows is that somehow Magnus has ensured they won't be arrested...or killed.

Magnus releases him and takes a step back. "Wait." Aristeus grabs for Magnus's jacket, but Magnus twists out of reach. "What about the others?" says Aristeus raggedly. "Are you...are you the only one left?"

Magnus doesn't meet his gaze this time. Every muscle in his face draws tight and he says curtly, "Don't try to find anyone else. Don't try to find me. Don't come near the girl." Without looking back, Magnus takes Ciere by the arm and begins to walk away.

"Hey," says Aristeus. His expression is cracked open, and Ciere sees something exposed in his eyes. A tentative flash of hope. "I'm glad you're alive."

This time Magnus does stop. He closes his eyes for the briefest second and his grip on Ciere tightens. "I wish I could say the same."

Ciere chances a look back. Aristeus makes as if to take a step forward, but thinks better of it. His mouth snaps shut and he pivots, as if determined to be anywhere but there. He walks away, his gait unsteady.

Magnus's stride lengthens and Ciere finds herself nearly jogging to keep up. They brush past the other party guests. Once they're free of the reception hall, Ciere hears footsteps ring out. Magnus whirls, mouth drawn up in a snarl.

But it isn't Aristeus following them. It's Devon. He's out of breath and there's something wild in his expression.

"What is it?" says Magnus. Not unkindly.

"I—I can't." Devon looks stricken. "You're wrong. They're not..." His accent thickens and he stumbles over the words. "It's not—*they're* not the UAI. Macourek and the lot—they're with something called Affiliation."

Magnus looks at him with pity. "The Unification and Affiliation of Intelligence. What did you *think* UAI stands for?"

"United American Immunities," says Devon desperately.

"Devon," says Magnus, "the U.S. government doesn't acknowledge the term 'immune.'"

Devon backs up, his fingers tightening around his forgotten tumbler. "They're normal," he says.

Magnus remains silent.

Ciere knows Devon, knows him well enough to see the thoughts play out behind his eyes. He bites his lip, twists it

between his teeth. "He can't be a dominus," he says. "He's...
he's just some bloke. His name is Macourek."

"That's his birth name," replies Magnus softly. "Aristeus is
what he chose for himself."

Devon glances from Magnus to Ciere, growing more
desperate. "No."

Revulsion takes root somewhere inside Ciere. She can feel
it, growing into full-fledged horror. Devon's with the UAI.
Devon, who's her best friend, whom she took home, took on
jobs, confided in.

"That man tried to kill—" she says. "He thinks he *did*
kill—you haven't...you haven't told him—" She bites off the
words, making them nearly unintelligible.

"A single damn thing," snaps Devon. His own voice is
shaking. "I wouldn't betray you, even if you did abandon me."

She barely manages to find her voice. "What?"

"Beside that river," says Devon, and there's a new emotion
in his voice. "You took off with Fiacre."

She stares at him, dumbfounded by his harsh tone. She
can't believe this; she did that to save his life, to keep him out
of jail. The feds were going to take them all down, and the
only chance was a gamble that even Ciere hadn't counted on
working.

"I screwed up your crooked plans and you left me," says
Devon, face twisted with anger.

"This is not the time," Magnus tries to break in, but Ciere cuts him off.

"I didn't want you to get hurt!" she cries.

"YOU CHOSE HIM!"

The words echo through the marble hallway. She opens her mouth to deny it and finds that she can't.

"I haven't betrayed you," says Devon. He speaks the words quickly, spitting them out like they're burning him. "I would never betray you. I didn't know who that man was, and I would never tell him—"

"He could order you to," says Ciere, and abruptly all the anger leaves her. It's replaced with cold, sickening fear. She knows what it's like to be held under a dominus's sway. He could be working for Aristeus right now, even if he doesn't want to. Aristeus could be controlling him.

"He's never used his immunity on me," Devon says.

"He could've ordered you to say that." Ciere takes a step back.

Devon winces. His tirade crumbles. "You're wrong," he repeats hollowly. "He hasn't—but you're not going to believe me, are you? Macourek... Aristeus—*FUCK!*" The curse bursts from him and he throws his tumbler against a wall. It shatters. The broken glass skitters across the floor, but Devon doesn't seem to notice. He's gasping for air, and a soft noise escapes his lips.

Ciere steps forward and her hand comes up. She's not sure what she wants to do—she only knows he's in pain and... and...

He's been working with the UAI.

Her hand falls back to her side.

"Come on," says Magnus quietly. His steely grip fastens around her wrist and she is drawn away.

She forces herself to come back to the moment. It's true. They need to leave now, to get away from Aristeus. Even so, she can't help herself. As she walks away, she glances back over her shoulder.

Devon doesn't follow. He's staring at the shattered glass, and his whole body quivers uncontrollably.

Part of Ciere wants to go back, but Magnus's grip is unrelenting. He doesn't stop until they find a door marked EMPLOYEES ONLY. Magnus tests the door, finds it unlocked, and steps through.

The room is obviously storage: stacked metal chairs, folded tables leaned up against a wall, and heaps of linens. Ciere lets herself sink into one of the chairs. The world tilts oddly to one side and she blinks to clear her vision. Her mind feels heavy, overburdened by too much knowledge. She's never wanted to unlearn anything before; knowledge is power—that's what she's always been taught. But tonight she's drowning in it.

"Kit's not answering his phone," says Magnus. She looks up to find him standing with his cell phone pressed against one ear. She hadn't even realized he'd gotten it out. "It's probably nothing, but I need to get to him. He needs to know."

Despite not having much alcohol, she feels drunk. Her insides are churning and cold sweat breaks out along her neck and back. Her fingers flex and she almost wishes there were a glass still in them. Another shot might take the edge off the yawning emptiness in her chest.

"We've got to go," says Magnus, and she realizes it's not the first time he's said it. "It's not safe here."

Ciere shakes her head. "I can't go." Her fingers tighten around her clutch. "I need to find proof. I can't go yet."

Magnus kneels before her. "Ciere—"

She cuts off any argument he might make. "Is Aristeus planning on calling the cops?"

Magnus waits a moment. "No."

"Then I'm not leaving yet." Ciere leans forward, takes Magnus's hand, and goes still.

She's doesn't try to control her thoughts. She just lets him in, lets him see the depth of her desperation. She has to do this.

A shiver runs through Magnus. His eyes slide out of focus. Then he's blinking rapidly, and a bitter smile touches his lips. "Ah. I see." His grip tightens, winds around her wrist. He reaches into one pocket and withdraws a pen.

"If you find what you're looking for, go here," he says, scribbling out an address on her wrist. The pen's tip digs in and she winces. When she glances down, the street name catches her eye.

"Kingston," says Ciere, and it triggers a memory. "You said something to Kit about it in June. Where is it?"

Magnus huffs out a breath.

"It's a graveyard," he finally says. "It's where Kit is supposed to be buried. The first time, anyway. Back in the day, if we couldn't get ahold of each other, we'd leave messages on each other's headstones. Just little notes no one else could decipher."

She gapes at him and she's not sure if she's amused or disturbed. "That's a little...creepy."

Magnus doesn't look fazed. "It's better than smoke signals. I need to make some arrangements before I head up to Philadelphia. I'll stop by the graveyard before I go. If you want to come with me, meet me there before an hour is up."

"Not back to your apartment?"

Magnus shakes his head. "No. I'm probably just being paranoid, but don't go back there. Aristeus might come looking...or send someone." His hand tightens around her wrist, holding her in place.

"You think he's coming after us?" asks Ciere, trying to keep the fear out of her voice.

Magnus tries to give her a comforting smile, but it fractures down the middle. "Don't go back to Philadelphia right away. Actually, the Syndicate might be the safest place for you right now—a few dozen mobsters might make even Aristeus pause.

"Be careful," he says. "Promise me you'll be careful."

The touch isn't just meant to convey his words; he's actively listening to her thoughts. Ciere realizes this, realizes she can't lie to him.

"I'll do whatever I have to," she says, and means it.

27

DEVON

Devon finds a bench in the hallway. His legs give way and he collapses onto it, fists pressed into his eyes. His skull feels hollow, a sensation he associates with regret and hangovers. Pain flickers at his temples and part of his brain begins to dredge up a medical textbook on stress headaches.

Everything's gone wrong.

He breathes a curse and opens his eyes. He can't stay here. He needs to find a way back to his dorm—he needs to get his stuff and run. But—where? He can't go to Philadelphia, not to Kit or the others. He can't go back to Boston, either. Devon can only imagine the look of scorn on his father's face, the derisive *I told you the government was trouble.*

Devon scrabbles around in his brain, trying to think of

somewhere—anywhere. He doesn't have friends from school. His closest relatives are in London.

A sense of loneliness sweeps through him; he feels utterly adrift.

Stand up, he tells himself. *Find a taxi. Get back to your dorm.*

Small steps. He can manage those.

He does manage to stand. He's about as coordinated as a zombie, but he's moving. It's a start.

He makes his way toward the front hall, but a noise draws his attention. There's a soft grunt and the snip of metal cinching into place. Devon drags his gaze up from the floor and sees three people.

Before him is Aditi Sen's aide flanked by the two FBI agents. The aide stands with his shoulders thrown back, chin jutted defiantly. But there's something off about the way he stands and it takes Devon a moment to see the real picture.

The FBI agents are cuffing him. "...be charged with insufficient identification and failure to produce your tags," the first one, the woman, is saying. "And you don't have your boss's protection."

The aide's eyes blaze at her.

"Fine, then," says the second agent. "Let's see how well that loyalty serves you. Come on."

"Not going to read me my rights?" says the aide. He allows the agents to grasp him by the arms, herding him in the direction of the main entrance.

"You aren't wearing tags," says the first agent, her voice surprisingly bright. "You don't have any rights."

"The Allegiant Act at work," Devon says dully. He realizes he spoke the words aloud only when both FBI agents glance at him.

"You need something, kid?" says the second agent. His grip on the aide never relents.

Devon shakes his head and averts his eyes. He feels something like shame when he walks away. That man probably isn't immune, probably hasn't done a criminal thing in his life. But he'll be held in prison, possibly charged with something—if only to tarnish Sen's political agenda.

If I were really a UAI agent, could I have helped him?

Devon's steps slow and he finds himself frozen, paralyzed by this thought. How the hell did that even occur to him? Devon isn't a revolutionary—he's not even a fed. Not really.

And abruptly, he's furious. It isn't fair. That aide shouldn't be sent to prison for a political statement; Devon shouldn't have to feel guilty because he's free and that man isn't; Macourek shouldn't have lied; the UAI should just be the bad guys.

Everything should be simpler.

28

DANIEL

"Seriously?" says Daniel. It's the fifth time he's said it. "Seriously?"

"We can't let you in, sir," says the doorman. He looks a little unsettled; he's not used to dealing with FBI agents and their teenage sidekicks.

The Arata Suites is abuzz with excitement. Daniel can feel it, hear it, the sound of anticipation a constant whisper in his ears. There's some kind of event going on. If this were any other hotel, that would've made sneaking in a much easier task. But this hotel scans tags at every entrance, and only guests or invitees are allowed in.

"We have reason to believe one of your guests may be in danger," says Gervais. His voice has sharpened into the tone he uses to tell criminals to drop their weapons and put their hands on their head.

Daniel knows this from experience.

"I can't let you in, sir." It's probably the fourth time the doorman has repeated himself. They're all running out of words, repeating the same phrases again and again. Stuck on repeat, Daniel thinks.

"If a crime goes down in that hotel tonight and we aren't there to stop it," begins Gervais, but the doorman doesn't budge.

Back in the old days, Daniel would've stolen a valet jacket and made off with a Porsche. Now he stands next to the hotel's front doors, arguing with a man who looks like he has a boulder for a head. Being a criminal was easier.

"Come on," mutters Gervais, and they walk away from the hotel's entrance. Standing on the slushy sidewalk, Daniel tries to come up with an alternative plan.

Daniel shivers and it has nothing to do with the cold. "We can't break in."

"Obviously," replies Gervais. He already has his phone out. He hesitates, as if unsure whom to call.

"We don't have time for that," says Daniel, nodding at the phone. "This Maya Cooper's a ghost. If she is after Aditi Sen, we need to be in there. Now."

Gervais utters a soft curse and goes for his phone again.

Daniel lets him; might as well try everything. He takes a step back, eyes going to the first-story windows. Every building has a weak point; it's just a matter of finding it. But this hotel is as heavily fortified as most banks. Breaking in will take time.

Also, it would be technically illegal, a little voice says, *and wouldn't hold up in court.*

A second little voice says, *Since when do we care about that?*

"Well, tell them it's an emergency," Gervais growls. A pause, then: "Fine." He jabs his thumb into the phone, ending the call.

"Bad news?" says Daniel, still eyeing the windows.

Gervais's mouth twists into a snarl. "You're not going to believe this, but there's already a team inside."

Daniel brightens. "But—but that's good! They can let us in, vouch for us!"

Gervais glowers at the hotel.

"They're not going to vouch for us, are they?" says Daniel, flattened.

"No," says Gervais through a clenched jaw. "And they won't protect Aditi Sen, because they're too busy arresting one of her assistants. Like *that's* the priority."

Daniel lets out a low whistle—he's seen the way Gervais's

colleagues eye him. They regard him with distrust, with thinly veiled fear. Daniel has seen such looks before; it was how his former friends looked at him once they realized he was working with the feds. But this—this is stooping to a whole new level.

"Seriously, what did you do?" he says.

This time Gervais doesn't pretend to misunderstand. His fingers tighten around the phone. He looks tired and old.

"A family escaped me," he says quietly. "They were criminals—all of them. Petty crimes, but they were obviously immune. A dauthus and an eludere, I think. My partner and I were one of the teams chasing them. During the chase, we lost track of them and had to choose a direction to go: right or left. I said I thought I'd seen them going left, so we went that way. They'd gone right."

Daniel knows he's gaping, his mouth hanging wide open. Gervais glances at him and looks away. "That's it," says Daniel incredulously. "That's—that's your big, dark secret. That's the reason your colleagues don't trust you? *You made a wrong turn?*"

"My colleague said she'd seen them go right," Gervais replies, eyes downcast. "She said that I deliberately let them go. That I was obstructing justice. That's when I was...well, that's when they partnered me up with Carson. He had his own issues with the Bureau. And..." He doesn't finish his thought.

Daniel does it for him. "Carson got killed during a shady investigation last summer." He snorts, another piece of the puzzle falling into place. "And now you're partnered up with a well-known ex-criminal eludere who works for the UAI—the agency that likes making your Bureau its bitch." He lets out a bitter little laugh. "They think you're an immune sympathizer. That's why they hate you?"

Gervais looks around him—at the darkened, snowy street and the glittering hotel. At the doors barred to them. "If you were partnered up with anyone else, you wouldn't be stuck out here."

If Daniel were partnered with anyone else, they wouldn't be having this conversation. A lesser man might've taken out his anger on Daniel, but instead Gervais directs it inward.

He's a good person.

And luckily for him, Daniel isn't.

"Come on," says Daniel. He straightens, pushes his shoulders back, and forces a grim smile onto his lips. He strides back toward the hotel entrance.

The doorman eyes them beadily. "I can't let you in."

"Oh, shut up," says Daniel brightly. "We both know that's not true. You could let us in."

"If I wanted to get fired," retorts the doorman.

"Which I'm sure would be tragic." Daniel beams. "Because

I'm sure this job pays so well and comes with amazing benefits. Out of curiosity, do you get dental?"

The man just glares.

"See," says Daniel, still grinning, "I think you want a crime to go down. That's the real reason you won't let us in.

"I mean..." Daniel continues. He's relaxed now. This is territory he knows well. It's just another con. "This job is nice and all, but you could do better. Look at those muscles." He takes another step forward, hands exposed and posture friendly. It won't do him any good to be put in a choke hold. "You're ex-military. Probably left a few years ago to freelance as a bodyguard. Somehow you ended up here. Want to know why?"

The man's jaw works.

"You're squinting at me," says Daniel cheerfully. "Which means your glasses prescription is probably a little out of date. What's eye insurance these days, anyway?"

The man glares down at him. "Glasses aren't expensive," he says.

"No, but the surgery to correct your vision will be," says Daniel. "And that's what you really want. No mercenary with an eye problem is hirable. That's why you're working for rich assholes in this dump."

"Dump" is a bit of a stretch, but Daniel's point is made.

"If you ever want a better job than this, you need to fix your eyes," says Daniel, still smiling. "And to do that, you need money. Money you won't get from this job. Now that's a conundrum. But if someone were to slip you a little bribe... you know, don't let the feds in while a political activist is kidnapped..."

Comprehension dawns on the man. He looks so startled by the idea that Daniel knows he's honest.

"That's not true," says the man.

Now Gervais is smiling. Not a happy smile, but a smile nonetheless. "But that's what it'll look like to a judge."

Daniel can see the thoughts working themselves out behind the man's eyes, carefully weighing the risks. *He's definitely military*, Daniel's instincts whisper. The man's hand twitches to his belt and Daniel tenses. But the man reaches for a radio. "I'll call the night manager," he growls.

With the doorman's back turned, Gervais's smile widens into something more honest. He squeezes Daniel's shoulder.

"Don't take this the wrong way, but you make a surprisingly good federal agent."

Gervais's words burrow beneath Daniel's skin. His grin brittles and he shrugs off Gervais's hand. It was meant as a compliment, he tells himself. Not a barb.

"My old mentor used to say the only difference between

being a criminal and a cop was who paid you," says Daniel, making no effort to keep the bite out of his voice. "And before you start fitting me for a suit and a badge, you should know that if that guy didn't take the bluff, I was going to steal a caterer's jacket."

Gervais's smile drops away.

The night manager turns out to be a woman. She's dressed in strict business clothes, with a metal name tag clipped to one lapel. The moment he sees her, Daniel knows they're not getting inside.

"I'm sorry," is her clipped response. "But no one enters the hotel without a valid room booking or a warrant." Her professional smile is as thin as a blade.

Daniel clears his throat. "Can we book a room?" he says, with his most insincere smile.

She turns on one polished heel, barely deigning to reply. "Booked through May."

Which is how they end up on the sidewalk again, staring at the hotel.

A long minute passes.

"What are you planning?" says Daniel.

Gervais stares upward. "You think those third-story windows are locked?"

Daniel shakes his head. "Trust me—the only windows

without sensors will be near the top floor, and we'd need a fantastic levitas to get that high." He trusts only one levitas, and that man is in Philadelphia.

Daniel grimaces and begins edging to the left. "Come on."

Gervais hesitates. "What are *you* planning?"

Daniel tries to smile and isn't sure he succeeds. "Attempting to steal a caterer's jacket."

29

CIERE

C iere leaves the storage closet behind, taking a moment to straighten her dress and run her fingers through her hair. She needs to look normal, even if normal is a stretch.

As she walks, she leaves some of her fear behind. Action takes precedence over thought. She can worry about the UAI and Devon later—for now, she's going to find Pruitt's killer.

The heart of the hotel is located just behind the lobby. The security is lax, but Ciere understands why. They're not expecting danger from the inside, since getting in is such an ordeal. They think of this place as impenetrable. Safe.

They're wrong.

She stops near one of the large columns, ducking into the shadows. She pulls an illusion over herself, coloring her skin and dress to resemble the wallpaper. She crosses her arms and simply watches for a good five minutes. The key to any crime is to observe, to calculate habits and exploit them.

From what she can see, there are two employees working the check-in desk. A young man and woman, both dressed in crisp business wear. They're startlingly beautiful, posed like models. Ciere studies them, watches as the man sips at a cup with the hotel logo emblazoned on the side, watches the way the woman yawns when she thinks no one is looking, watches where they clip their ID cards to their belts.

Ciere waits, heart beating hard, until the man sips at his mug and appears to empty it. He says something to his coworker and she nods, eyes on a magazine. The man eases out from behind the desk, and strides in the direction of the reception hall, no doubt to refill his mug with whatever he was drinking. Probably not coffee.

Lifting his ID card is a simple matter. She's glad for the thousands of times Kit made her practice it. Only the tips of her fingers touch the card and it comes free in her invisible hand. She tucks it into her palm and steps away. The man pauses, as if feeling a draft, then shakes his head and moves on.

Ciere steps into the space between the wall and a large potted plant. She closes her eyes and lets her first illusion fall away, replacing it with the young man's polished features. Still holding the ID card, she walks behind the check-in desk. Behind the marble counter, the young woman is reading some sports magazine. "Snag me any food?" the woman asks, never looking up.

Ciere hesitates, then grunts a negative. Her voice isn't deep enough to pass for a man's, but the grunt seems to satisfy the woman. Ciere quickly takes the place of the young man. His computer is in sleep mode and there's a place for a keycard to slide. Ciere does so, easing his ID card through. The computer wakes up instantly.

Ciere hesitates. She's never pulled a heist like this; she's unsure what buttons to press and she can't ask for help without giving herself away. With a tense little exhale, she retrieves the hotel key and runs it through the computer. The menu wobbles, its screen quickly replaced with new options.

IDENTIFY CARD / DEACTIVATE KEY / HELP

Ciere presses the first button, hoping it won't ask for a password. It doesn't.

Room Number: 302
Check-In Date: November 21, 2034
Scheduled Check-Out: Indefinite

Ciere tries to work out how much an indefinite stay at a place like this would cost, but she has no idea. She grits her teeth; it does seem like the ideal location for Guntram. Maybe the owners are also under Syndicate protection. Maybe they're letting him keep this room in case he needs a secure place in DC.

The young man appears, striding down the hallway, his mug in hand. Ciere's breath catches and she turns away. There's a service door behind her, probably leading to some staff offices. She pushes it open and walks through. As the door slides shut, she hears the woman's voice. "What? Weren't you just...?"

"What?"

A moment of hesitation. "Um, never mind." The woman sounds bewildered, not suspicious, and Ciere's grateful for it.

Ciere finds another door and hurries out of the office. The illusion sloughs off. She strides to the stairs—elevators are too dangerous. The long hallway stretches out before her and she finds her step quickening. She's so keyed up that she takes the stairs two at a time, hurrying up them in less than a minute.

Room 302 is a corner suite, at the end of the hall. The door frame is made of polished metal, roses worked into the design. Ciere shakes her head in disbelief. If she weren't already here on a mission, this hotel would be the ideal place to rob—all these rich tourists clustered into one location.

She knocks once, twice. If anyone answers, she'll pretend she got the wrong room. But there's no sound, not even the soft footfall of someone coming to check the peephole.

Ciere waits another few seconds, counts them to herself, then brushes the key against the lock. It blinks red.

She sucks in a breath and holds it. She waves the key before the lock. This time the sensor catches it. The light glows green and the lock makes a whirring sound. Ciere grabs for the doorknob and twists it open. Elated by her success, she steps inside.

The bed is rumpled, the duvet tossed every which way. There's a duffel bag resting near the small table. Judging from the smell coming from a garbage can, room service hasn't been here in days. Ciere covers her nose with a hand, trying to block out the scent of rotting food. The room itself is everything the hotel website promised—extravagant and tastefully decorated. Ciere pauses to admire the decor for the briefest moment before moving on to the duffel bag.

The first compartment she unzips is full of clothes. Jeans, flannel shirts, completely normal clothing that has no place in this luxurious hotel. She delves deeper into the pile, but there's nothing. Just clothes.

She rocks back on her heels, balancing there for a moment. She racks her brain, tries to come up with something—anything. She needs more.

Searching the room takes little time. There are only a few places to hide things in a hotel; that's why they're so easily burgled. Between the mattresses, under the sink, in the closet, under the dresser, even inside the overhead light—she checks everywhere. The only thing she finds are a few dead flies in the light.

Jumping off the chair, she stands in the middle of the room. Her jaw aches and she tries to unclench her teeth. She leans against a wall, eyes going out of focus for a moment. One of the paintings hanging on the wall across from her becomes little more than a green-and-blue blur.

"Come on," she mutters. "Think. If I was Guntram, where would I..." Her voice trails off and her vision snaps back into focus.

The paintings.

Magnus's apartment comes flooding back to her. There are two paintings here—both landscapes. Ciere walks up to one, digs her nails beneath its frame, and pulls.

The first painting doesn't budge. The second comes off its hinges easily. She sets it on the floor, hoping to see something behind it.

Nothing.

Disappointment washes through Ciere, wiping away what's left of her determination. She stays in place, just staring at that stupid wall. Her limbs go heavy with exhaustion, and a headache begins chewing away at her concentration. She's used too many illusions in a short time.

She looks down, ready to put the painting back on the

wall, and freezes. Because this room's secrets aren't behind the painting; they're carefully taped to the canvas itself.

A small pistol and an envelope.

The first thing she thinks is, *How the hell did Guntram get a gun past hotel security?* The second is, *Yes, that could definitely have killed Pruitt.*

Ciere moves on to the envelope. Inside are small slips of paper—just construction paper. She picks one out. On one side, there's a hand-drawn star, the edges flourished. She wouldn't have given it a second glance, but the sight of it makes her pause. She knows that symbol. She's seen it before.

A flourished star spray-painted onto the side of a train. Where Pruitt was killed.

A shock goes through her. It means something. She doesn't know what, but it means something. She takes out another one of the slips of paper and stares at it. The hand-drawn star looks just the way she remembers it. Maybe it's a calling card—serial killers are supposed to have patterns; maybe this marks the locations where people have been killed. Ciere wonders if there are other places in the city with that mark, the star fading into the background of other graffiti.

She takes a few of the papers and quickly replaces the gun and envelope, setting the painting back on its hinges. As she works, she runs through her recent memories, trying to remember where else she's seen that emblem before.

A soft click makes her whirl around. Her eyes snap to the door. She hears the telltale sound of a card being slipped from the lock before she throws herself to the floor.

There's no time for a better hiding place. If this person is one of Guntram's colleagues, they'll know how to get around illusions. They might be scanning every room with a camera or phone lens. She scrambles beneath the bed, curling up and rolling to one side. Maybe it's a maid or maybe it's Guntram himself—but either way, Ciere cannot afford to get caught here.

The mattress frame scrapes her shoulders as she presses herself to the floor. The scent of carpet cleaner and dust fills her nose and she draws in a sharp breath and holds it. Anticipation tightens her chest; despite herself, she's itching to peer out from under this bed, to see the face of the person striding into the room.

The footsteps are nearly silent and Ciere is surprised to see a pair of pink sneakers. Not exactly the footwear she would expect of a serial killer—and definitely not something Guntram owns. A second pair of feet follows. They wear black formal women's shoes.

Two women. Not Guntram.

A shiver of pure relief goes through Ciere. She can deal with this: with crooks and crimes and mysteries. So long as she's not dealing with Guntram—deadly, in control, and a far more capable illusionist than Ciere has ever been—she'll manage.

"I'm pulling out of DC tonight," the first woman says. Her voice is clear and young; Ciere doesn't recognize it. "It's not safe here anymore. I'll get this shipment out and then move down the coast."

The second woman speaks. This voice is older, slightly hoarse. "Are you sure you can get out tonight? The feds are everywhere."

The first woman laughs. "Like that'll stop me."

"Taking the child was dangerous," the second woman says, after a moment's pause. Ciere watches the black shoes as they stride toward the door. "They're looking even harder for you now."

"They can look all they want," the first woman replies.

That's when Ciere feels it. A pressure, like someone's pressed a tuning fork to her skull.

The pink sneakers shimmer and then vanish.

Ciere's breath lodges in her throat. She clamps her lips together, holds in a gasp.

An illusionist. That woman is an illusionist.

Ciere's mind fixates on the word. Illusionists are rare— not to mention expensive. If there's one working in DC, killing people, leaving behind calling cards, Ciere might have stepped into something larger than she could've imagined. This could be a hit, a gang war, or...

...Or maybe the Alberanis have stepped up their game.

The second woman lets out a small laugh. "Maya," she says, "be careful."

A noise comes from the direction of the first woman. There's still no visible sign of her, but the voice is close and amused. "Always am."

The second woman's feet move again, this time vanishing around a corner. There's the click of a doorknob.

The pressure in Ciere's head intensifies, heightens to an almost painful pitch, and then releases. The pink shoes wink back into view. The woman slips them off, revealing pale bare feet.

Ciere tenses. Heart in her throat, she tries to angle herself so that she can catch a glimpse of the illusionist. She can just make out the woman's reflection in the full-length mirror.

This woman is plump, probably in her late thirties, with auburn hair and large eyes. She's dressed casually, in a nondescript coat and pants. She walks to the bathroom door, pulling it shut behind her. A moment later, there is the distinct sound of a fan, followed by the splatter of water.

Ciere remains crouched beneath the bed.

30

DANIEL

Daniel sits on a bench by himself. The hotel stands proudly on the other side of the street, bright and unreachable. Gervais is in the car, parked somewhere behind the building. This two-man surveillance crew isn't exactly professional, but it's the best they can manage.

Daniel's valiant attempt to get into the hotel began with them trying to bribe a bellboy into stealing a caterer's jacket and ended with him and Gervais being chased out the back by a sous chef brandishing a cleaver.

They agreed to never speak of it again.

"We'll guard the two main entrances instead," Gervais said. He looked as dignified as a man could, when he'd just been bested by someone who spent his days chopping lettuce. "Call me if you see either that Maya Cooper or Aditi Sen."

The bench is freezing. Daniel can feel the cold creep through the heavy fabric of his coat and settle into his bones. He inhales and tastes stale snow and gasoline fumes. The overhead lamp isn't working, but it doesn't bother him. The darkness feels like an old friend. He's safe here, out of sight.

It feels like days since he's had any time to himself; he's always running around on someone's orders lately. He should be welcoming the solitude. Instead, he just feels lonely. It's a sensation he's beginning to grow accustomed to. He and Gervais may not be on horrible terms, but it's not like they're friends. Daniel's contacts in the UAI are dubious at best. Most of that office is in Aristeus's thrall—taken in by his immunity, no doubt. Ciere's friend, that Devon Lyre, is probably under Aristeus's power, even if he doesn't know it yet. *Poor bastard.*

As if summoned by his thoughts, Daniel's phone rings. A glance at the caller ID and he winces. Aristeus. Probably checking in on the Maya Cooper situation. Well, at least Daniel has something to report this time.

He snaps the phone open. "You working late again?" he says glibly. It's best to go on the offensive during these calls. "It's nearly seven—you should go home once in a while. Take a load off, get drunk, do something that's not—"

Aristeus's voice is so ragged, he barely recognizes it. "Where are you?"

Daniel's fingers tighten on the phone. He won't break it. He *can't*, not anymore. (Daniel went through three phones before Aristeus gave him that particular order.)

"Outside some fancy hotel. Think it's called Arata or something," says Daniel.

A pause. "Where?" Aristeus sounds disbelieving.

Daniel repeats himself. Then adds, "Arata Suites. We're following a lead. The GPS in Maya Cooper's car—"

A beep cuts him off. He glances down at the phone and sees the call has ended.

"That's polite for you," mutters Daniel. At least he's not the only one having a bad night, if Aristeus's harassed tone was anything to judge by. That thought almost makes him smile.

It's not even a minute later when Daniel sees him—the man rushing from one of the hotel doors. He sprints down to the slushy sidewalk before pausing to look around.

Daniel feels his jaw slacken. Even at this distance, there's no mistaking that dark hair or skinny frame. He's wearing thick-framed glasses—*that's new*—but it's still Aristeus.

It takes Aristeus a moment to find Daniel. He barrels across the street at a reckless speed, ignoring the cars. His skin is the same color as the snow.

"You're *here*?" says Daniel incredulously. "You were actually inside that hotel? How the hell did you get in?" A new thought occurs to him. "Can you get me and Gervais in? Because Aditi Sen might be in—"

Aristeus ignores him. He seizes Daniel's coat, forcing Daniel to slam his back into the wooden frame of the bench.

"Your crew," he says, and his frantic, furious expression is something Daniel's never seen before. It's close to panic. "Tell me about them."

Daniel should feel fear, he *knows* he should feel fear, but all he can muster is shock. "What?"

"That illusionist," snarls Aristeus. "The one we met at the docks last summer—she was part of your crew, right? You knew her."

Daniel's incredulity blooms into defiance. "You said I wouldn't have to talk about them," says Daniel.

He stares at Aristeus, takes in the man's fresh suit, the new glasses, the hair sticking to his sweaty neck. Anger travels down Daniel's arms, into his wrists and hands. He wants to move, to lunge, to do anything but answer. "You said you wouldn't ask about my old crew—you said they'd be safe."

Aristeus has always been in control. Even when angry with the FBI, it was a quiet, contained emotion. This man is unraveling, eyes bright and lips pressed tight. It's enough to make Daniel feel a real twinge of fear.

"What happened?" Daniel asks, unable hold back the question. "What's going on?"

Aristeus shakes his head once. "They are safe," he says hoarsely. "They're safe and they never told me."

Despite his confusion, Daniel almost wants to take a step forward. Not to comfort Aristeus, but the exact opposite. All his old instincts clamor to the surface; desperate men are easy marks, and part of Daniel can't help but wonder if he can use this somehow.

Aristeus's expression hardens. His anger seems to focus, to pinpoint on Daniel. "Your old crew," he says, and while his voice is smooth again, his fists are shaking. "You're going to tell me about them."

"No," says Daniel, twisting away.

Aristeus's hand comes down on his shoulder, and their eyes meet. *"Tell me,"* Aristeus says, and this time it's not a question.

31

CIERE

Ciere can't move. Her muscles lock in place, and she finds the mere thought of shifting positions impossible. An illusionist. Pruitt's killer is an illusionist. That's why Ciere thought she felt an illusion at the scene—she *had* felt one. It just hadn't belonged to Guntram.

She tries to think back to the woman's words, to sort through what few facts she has. The murderer—*Maya or whoever she is*—is leaving DC. Getting some kind of shipment out of the city, and then abandoning it tonight.

If Maya runs, Ciere will never catch her. Not unless—

"Oh, shit," she whispers as a thought occurs to her. A truly damning, completely insane, probably-doomed-to-fail—and also *horrible*—thought. Because she hated Guntram once. Hated him for doing it to her. Hated his cold calculation, his sincere words when he said, *"We protect our investments."* She's done this before, done it when Guntram told her to. But she's never taken this step on her own, and she could always hide behind that.

"Shit, shit, shit." It's almost a chant as she hurries to the closet door. A quick glance up to check that Maya is still showering, and then Ciere opens the closet door.

She places her wrist between the door and frame, tries to judge the angle. If she does this right, maybe she won't shatter her bones.

She begins to move, but her muscles freeze. Her body rejects this plan, refuses to go along with it on the basis that it doesn't want to get hurt.

Alan, she thinks, and holds the name close.

She slams the door shut. On her wrist.

She hopes the sounds of the shower and Maya's humming will cover the noise. It isn't loud, just a sickening crunch.

Pain flares up Ciere's arm in a blindingly, utterly agonizing torrent. It takes her a moment to catch her breath. She drags her eyes open; she'd shut them at some point. When she looks down, she sees the bracelet is smashed beyond repair.

The interior of the tracker bracelet is all wires and gleaming metal filaments. Something deep inside the wiring begins to glow red.

Her wrist aches and she's not sure if she's broken a bone or just sprained it. Either way, she'll have to deal with it later.

Gritting her teeth against the pain, she kneels beside Maya's duffel bag. She slips the bracelet into one of the deepest corners, jerking the zipper shut when she's done.

She slips out of the room, quietly pulling the door shut behind her. The hallway is nearly deserted—only a well-dressed couple strolling to their own room. Ciere keeps her gaze lowered and hurries to the stairs. Maybe it's the adrenaline trying to stave off the pain, but she feels dazed, separated from her physical body. The skin around her wrist is paler than the rest of her arm. It feels raw and new, like a wound after the bandage has been removed. It's been months since Guntram put that bracelet on her. She almost forgot what it feels like to be free.

She goes out the hotel's back door, into the parking lot. The doorman bids her a polite good night and she mumbles something in response. The cold air is a shock to her system and it brings her back to the moment. She walks down a line of cars, past Lamborghinis and Mercedes, and takes a sharp right turn. There's an alley she can cut through, then she'll be back on the street.

She'll find a quiet place, she thinks. She'll find a coffee shop or a cafe and then she'll call Guntram. She'll tell him what she found. He'll send a team after that illusionist.

Alan will be safe. Everything will be all right.

Of course, that's when the Alberani hit man appears from the shadows, his hand going for her throat.

32

CIERE

Ciere has never been a fighter.

She's small, for one thing. Just two inches over five feet, she has the perfect build to slip through windows and under security wires. Her hands are nimble and petite, good at picking locks and slipping into pockets. The idea of punching someone has never been appealing; she prefers to become a shadow on the wall and evade any chance of being hurt.

But Ciere hasn't spent the last five months living with bloodthirsty mobsters for nothing.

So when the Alberani hit man comes after her, time snaps to a standstill.

She ducks to one side and her small stature works in her favor. His hand whispers past her throat, missing by inches.

She takes in the alley, observing the heaps of dirty snow,

and the broom that someone propped up against one of the trash bins. She lunges for it and holds it in both hands. A crappy weapon is better than no weapon. She brandishes it at him, holding it like a makeshift spear.

The pale-haired man sees and a smile cracks his mouth. He rushes at her and she jabs at him, trying to hit him in the chest.

The man moves too quickly for her to keep up—he dodges around the space, one hand grabbing her dress. Then she's pressed up against the wall, bricks digging into her back. A cry bursts from her mouth and fresh adrenaline spikes through her blood. She whips the broom at his face.

He moves like a shadow, slipping out of reach before she can hit him. The broom feels clumsy in her hands and she knocks over a trash can. The clang and clatter of the metal drown out all other noises and she finds herself desperately wishing that someone would hear.

She swings at him again, and he ducks. One leg comes out, catches her ankle, and she wobbles, caught off balance. He lunges and she retreats, barely out of reach. She lashes out one more time.

When she hits him, it's more luck than skill. One end connects with his temple and he grunts, retreating a step. The blow rattles up her arm, jolting her injured wrist. Blood wells up from a shallow cut and it trickles down his face.

Ciere uses the distraction the only way she can.

She brings to mind a fun house, one filled with mirrors. Illusions appear all around the hit man. Too many Cieres to count, all identical and moving in dizzying circles. She hopes they'll confuse him. If nothing else, they can provide a distraction while she runs.

The man's eyes flit back and forth between the illusions. He feints right, then left. The illusions whirl around him—bobbing blonde girls all wearing the same dress. He speaks for the first time.

His voice is rusty, with an edge of gravel to it. "Nice try, but there's a reason I was hired to go after you."

His eyes drift out of focus. His lips part, and he inhales. It reminds Ciere of the way a snake tastes the air, its tongue a blur. His limbs tense and his gaze snaps to attention.

He makes a grab for Ciere—the real Ciere. She cries out, and the end of the broom hits him in the chest. The plastic bristles soften the blow, but it's still enough to knock his lunge off balance. He stumbles and falls against one of the trash cans, knocking it over. Papers and rotten food slide along the ground, mixing with the dirt and snow.

Ciere barely manages to stay on her own feet. The illusions flicker and vanish, leaving behind the single girl.

Which means—

To test her theory, she turns to run. The hit man moves

before she does. Because he can sense what she's going to do before she does it.

She was right. He's an eludere.

Which means Jess dying wasn't her fault. The thought is a comfort, even in this situation. The Alberanis must have wised up and begun sending immune soldiers with their gunrunners. That's how they managed to react so quickly to the trap. The pale-haired man sensed the danger moments before the Gyr Syndicate struck. Jess's death truly wasn't Ciere's fault.

The man takes a step forward. Ciere hits him again, but this time his fist fastens around the broom handle. There's a moment where they're both connected, yanking hard on the broom in a macabre game of tug-of-war. The man's mouth twitches and a chill goes through Ciere. She doesn't like that look, doesn't like it at all.

She pulls hard on the broom, trying to wrench it from his grasp. He lets go.

The world tilts at an odd angle and Ciere falls hard. The pavement slams into her back, knocking the breath from her. Agony lances up her arm and she gasps for breath, trying to sit up.

And Ciere finds herself staring at a gun.

It has a military-grade suppressor and the hit man aims with both eyes open, finger steady along the barrel.

Ciere freezes. "Finally," the hit man says. "I was supposed to be done with this job a day ago."

"How did you follow me?" Ciere says frantically, because this has been eating at her. She can't figure it out. She has no traceable technology, has vanished herself, traveled by bus, by car, on foot, gone places she's never been before. There's no pattern to follow. Even a professional shouldn't be able to find her so easily.

The hit man barks out a laugh.

"Should've known better," he says. "Tagging members of your own crew with trackers. It was only a matter of time until someone hacked the system."

Oh god. The bracelets.

They've hacked the bracelets. That's how the Alberanis have been following her.

If the Alberanis have hacked the bracelets, then they're all royally screwed. The Alberanis know the location of the Gyr Syndicate's teams—where the members are, where their targets are. Guntram needs to know now. She needs to warn him.

It almost makes her laugh. The tracker bracelets have been the Syndicate's ace in the hole for months. Having another crime family turn the bracelets against Guntram is almost poetic. She could've appreciated the artistry, if not for the fact that it was going to get her killed.

Alan has a bracelet, too.

"Don't feel too bad about being caught," says the man. "Your friends are probably dead by now." He smiles, the expression edged with triumph. He's won and he knows it. There's no hesitation when he raises the pistol.

Panic creeps up the back of Ciere's throat and she swallows it down, refuses to let it paralyze her.

She thinks of Guntram, Conrad, Henry, even Cole—*Alan*, she won't let herself think about Alan—being killed. Her fear drains away, leaving behind something harder. Her fingers grasp at the pavement, dig into the snow, and she readies herself to move. She reaches for her immunity and *pulls.*

The barrel levels with Ciere's collarbone.

If this were a movie, Ciere thinks wildly, the hit man would say something witty. He would try a quip before killing his enemy. But the hit man doesn't say a word. He just pulls the trigger.

The suppressed gunshot echoes down the alley, where it might be mistaken for a backfiring car. The bullet passes through Ciere and doesn't leave a trace. It smashes into the brick. Dust scatters into the air.

She isn't injured; she doesn't move or speak. The afterimage hangs there, like the flicker of a television screen in the instant before it powers down, and then the illusion vanishes. The hit man utters a curse, spins around, trying to find his target.

He doesn't move fast enough.

Ciere swings the broom like a baseball bat. She brings it down on the back of his skull, and the sound it makes—she knows it'll haunt her dreams for weeks to come.

He goes limp instantly. His body folds into the pavement. Blood drips down his neck and she tries not to look at it.

Part of her wants to lean down, to touch his neck and feel for a pulse. She knows a blow like that can kill—she's heard Conrad lecture Alan on pressure points. But a bigger part of her doesn't want to know. Because if she has killed him, even in self-defense, it means she's crossed the line she told Guntram she never would.

So long as it isn't a certainty, she's not a killer.

33

DANIEL

For nearly half an hour, Daniel talks.

The words flow from his mouth like blood from a wound. He would do anything to stem them, to place a hand over his mouth and stop talking. But he can't. His body is rigid, straining against the invisible bonds. He can't move. He can't stand up or run or fight. All he can do is sit on a bench in downtown DC and spill everything.

He tells Aristeus about finding Kit. Tells him about Ciere. Tells him about the safe houses he knows about. Tells him about past jobs and scores. Tells him about stealing beer from Kit's liquor cabinet and drinking it when Kit wasn't around. Tells him about the time Ciere scared the life out of Daniel by illusioning herself to look like a cop.

Tells him the big things and the small.

Aristeus listens with greedy attention. He never directs the conversation, simply lets the words wash over him. Only when Daniel begins rambling about the time he locked Kit in a closet does Aristeus finally raise a hand to stop him. Aristeus's furious energy has faded and he looks more resigned than angry. He turns to look at the passing traffic, slumping against the bench, his stiff posture relaxing. He closes his eyes.

Daniel's dry throat aches. He licks his lips, feels them crack under the attention. "That good enough for you?" he rasps. He's been speaking too long. It hurts.

"Yes," says Aristeus, still not looking at him. "Unless you have something to add." He gives himself a little shake, as if trying to snap out of something.

"Fuck you," says Daniel, but without any real heat. His own anger is gone; he just feels wrung out. Aristeus won. He's taken everything from Daniel: his freedom, his friends, his life, even his memories.

Something must have happened. He doesn't know what, but something happened. Aristeus may be a conniving, murdering sociopath, but he has always stuck by his word. For him to break their deal...he shakes his head in confusion.

"Shit," he mutters. "First Gervais loses his nerve and now you flip out on me—apparently the crazy is catching."

At this, Aristeus glances at him. "What?"

Daniel scrubs a hand over his face, trying to work his

expression back to normal. He doesn't want to answer; this is another secret yanked from between his lips. "I think he's depressed. This job's getting to him."

Aristeus's gaze is flat and hard. "You think he might betray us?"

Daniel just shrugs. The question is too open-ended for Aristeus's orders to kick in. He doesn't think Gervais would ever betray Daniel. But if he had to, Gervais would definitely go up against the UAI. He's not exactly fond of them.

Aristeus takes Daniel's silence as confirmation. "If he makes any move against us, stop him," he says. "Consider that an order."

"Us?" says Daniel. The word tastes bitter in his mouth.

Aristeus rises to his feet. He's straightening his tie, trying to draw himself together. "Yes, us. If he betrays us, don't hesitate." He smooths a hand through his hair. "I have to go. Loose ends to tie up."

Daniel doesn't say a word and Aristeus doesn't expect a good-bye. He strides down the sidewalk, vanishing back into the Arata Suites. Belatedly, Daniel realizes he never got an answer as to whether or not Aristeus could get them inside.

Even more belatedly, Daniel realizes he can't bring himself to care. Not about this case, not about Maya Cooper, not even about the missing people. None of it matters. They're all just pawns, little pieces to be moved around a chessboard played by people much higher up. Nothing Daniel has ever done matters—he's a petty criminal at best and an FBI assistant at worst.

He yearns to call Ciere or Kit. To warn them, to talk to them, to just remember what it feels like to not be miserable. They won't know what's coming. They have no idea Aristeus is after them. And it's his fault. If Daniel never let himself be caught by the FBI, he would still be in Philadelphia and no one he cares about would be in danger.

Daniel shivers, tries to push his thoughts away. He needs to focus, needs to return to the problem at hand, needs to... needs to...Something flickers on the edge of his awareness. A nagging little whisper. He glances up, eyes scanning the street. A passing minivan crunches through the snow, but that can't be it.

Daniel closes his eyes and listens, senses movement on the opposite sidewalk. He opens his eyes and squints through the dim lamplight. But no one is there.

Daniel feels himself frown. "I'm losing my mind," he mutters. But he can't shake it—can't shake the feeling that he's not insane. His fingers go for his phone without him consciously deciding to do so. He unfolds it, flicks the camera to life, and stares at the screen. He drags the phone's sight along the opposing sidewalk. When the camera focuses on a long figure, he nearly drops his phone.

Because Maya freaking Cooper is striding up the street. He glances at the phone screen, then at the sidewalk in real life. Because she's not there. And then she is. His gaze darts between each image and it takes a good second before he understands what his immunity was telling him.

It's an illusion.

"Oh," he hears himself say.

His hands move without him thinking about it. He presses the first speed dial, and a second later, Gervais picks up. "What is it?" he says, sounding tired. "If you'll hold on a sec, there's some kind of medical alert that's gone off—"

"Maya Cooper is across the street from me and she's on the move." Daniel says the words in a rush.

Gervais doesn't waste any time. "I'm on my way. Do not let her out of your sight."

"Do we call for backup?" asks Daniel.

Gervais understands immediately. "You mean do we call for one of the agents who have ostracized us?" he says delicately. "So that they can arrest Maya Cooper and be a hero?"

Daniel feels himself grin. "Gervais, that's selfish and conniving. I've never liked you more."

34

DEVON

This late, the Affiliation office is locked tight, but Devon manages to break in. It's a simple matter of hacking two keycards and stepping over a laser tripwire. When he strides down the hallway, he expects to see it dark and deserted. Instead, Sia sits behind her desk. *She isn't supposed to be here,* a distant part of him thinks. *Date night.* But like everything else, it must have been a lie.

She cocks her head at the sound of his footsteps. "Lyre," she says, and just like that—he *knows.*

"Sia," he says, understanding. "It's short for Tiresia. The blind seer. I should've guessed." Everything comes together, the way it does when he's looking at a puzzle and sees exactly how the lines will fit. "You're a mentalist."

A smile blossoms on her face. "Devon Lyre," she replies.

"An eidos who dropped out of high school. I have to admit that I like the irony."

Her beam infuriates him. His mind races, trying to catalog all the times she touched him. What was he thinking at the time? How much does she know? About Darla? About his family, surely. About Ciere and her crew, all the people he swore he would never betray. Has he passed along the knowledge of their existence to the UAI?

But—no. He's been trying not to think about them, if only because it hurts.

"You know what I am." His voice is flat. "Have you all been laughing at me? The blundering intern who didn't know he was working with the UAI?"

"Most people don't, not at first," she says. "Say the letters *UAI*, and people panic. We like to bring in new recruits slowly. That's why the more…infamous agents will use their birth names at first. We like to let new interns see we're not a group of superpowered psychopaths."

He snarls, "Then what are you?"

She rises to her feet, steady and certain, and walks around the desk. "We're people, Devon," she says. "Just people doing a job."

"And Macourek?" Devon barely manages to say the name. "What about him?"

"He is," Sia says gently, "just as human as the rest of us."

286

Devon can't think of anything else to say. The swelling sense of betrayal blocks everything out. He should be running, he should never have come back to this building, with its dangerous occupants inside. He shouldn't be here.

"You don't belong with us."

The words come at him again and he closes his eyes. "Is this how you were hired? Brought in as an intern and lied to?"

"We've never lied to you," says Sia. "We just didn't…share everything."

"Yeah." Bitterness leaks into Devon's voice and he lets it. He glances toward his desk, the files he left resting next to his computer. "Data collection and analysis—that's what Macourek said you did."

"It's technically true," says Sia. "We've put together databases of census information, created algorithms to determine who might be immune."

All those files, all those nameless genders and ages and occupations and *people*—Devon forces himself to think the word. He's been inputting that data for weeks, and it's being used to find people just like him. Cold sears through him in a nauseating wave. For one horribly long moment, he thinks he might actually vomit.

"Unification and Affiliation of Information," says Sia. She speaks conversationally, as if they're back in that coffee shop. "Most people don't realize what *UAI* actually stands for. But then again, most people also don't know what *NSA*, *USDA*, or the rest stand for, either, so why should we be any different?"

"Why would you do this?" he says, a little desperately. "Why did you stay, after you found out?"

Sia runs her hand over the desk, her fingers finding the metal nameplate. Her fingertips trace the embossed lettering, and her stance shifts into something defiant. "I wanted to be a doctor, you know."

He goes still, stymied by the subject change. "What?"

"When I was younger," says Sia, and there's anger in her voice he's never heard before. "I wanted to be a doctor. I thought my ability to read minds would be an asset. I could touch a patient and feel exactly what their pain was—I could diagnose more easily, cut through the guesswork. Even see if patients were lying to me. I'd keep my immunity a secret and use it to help people.

"But when I was fifteen, I was outed by one of my friends," she continues, "someone I thought I could trust. But then she told everyone, and the others…they were afraid of me. I spent months as a complete pariah. When the kids weren't ignoring me, they'd steal my lunch or misplace my gym clothes, or write up petitions to get me expelled because I was a freak. They'd go to teachers and claim I cheated on tests by reading minds." The corner of her mouth twitches, as if she's barely holding back a grimace.

"I snapped after six months," she says coolly. "I was furious, so I went to my friend and threatened to reveal all of her secrets if she didn't stop harassing me. She told her boyfriend. He— he…" She touches a finger to her temple. "He and his friends cornered me outside of the school. Said people like me shouldn't exist and then hit me over the head with a brick."

Devon sucks in a sharp breath.

Sia's hand drops to her side. "I woke up four days later. They'd had to drill a hole in my head to relieve the pressure from an internal bleed. And when I opened my eyes, all I could see were distant shapes and colors. My sight has never fully returned."

"You're blind."

"Visually impaired," Sia replies. "And you want to know the best part?" Her mouth twists. "I never knew any of my friend's secrets. I didn't have to—just the threat was enough to make her so afraid of me that her boyfriend tried to kill me."

"So you joined up with the UAI." Devon shoves his hands into his pockets. He can still feel his anger, but it's more distant.

"Aristeus offered me a home," says Sia. "A place where I'm valued for what I can do, where people aren't afraid of me. In return, I work as his PA and use my immunity to screen anyone that walks into the office." She touches the nameplate again. "You want to know why I stayed? Because no teenage girl should have to be afraid that someone's going to kill her with a brick. That's what I'm working to change."

Devon can't think of a reply; he can barely form a coherent thought, never mind an eloquent argument. "Is he here?" he finally says.

"Just got back," she says.

Maybe it's Devon's imagination, but Macourek's office looks foreboding cast in the light of his newfound knowledge. Its stark interior, the line of wire bonsai trees, the glass walls surrounded by ice and darkness. The office itself is unlit.

Macourek stands, staring out one of the windows, his back to Devon.

Devon considers the ominous scene before him for a moment. Then he flicks on the light. Macourek winces slightly, his shoulders hunching. "Took you a while to get here," he says.

"I walked," says Devon. He doesn't add that he wasn't in a hurry to arrive. "You took the car." He makes no effort to hide the anger in his voice. "My friends say you're Aristeus."

Macourek doesn't turn around. "And you're acquainted with some very dangerous criminals," he replies. "I'd known you had a shady past, but…" He shakes his head. "How did you even meet that illusionist?"

"She robbed my house when I was a kid," says Devon. "I let her. It was a bonding moment."

Macourek turns. He appears older somehow, his youthful features crumbling with exhaustion. A scar creases his lower lip, dimpling his chin. It's faint and Devon has never noticed it before. "Let me guess." Macourek settles into his chair, resting his fingers comfortably beneath his chin. "She was the first immune person you'd ever met—besides yourself, of course."

A moment of uncomfortable silence settles between them. "Yes," says Devon, because he's tired of lying.

Macourek nods. "That's the way it usually goes. The first immune person you'll ever meet will either pick your pocket or arrest you. It's always the same. Immune people are either crooked or straight. Either criminals or cops. And those are the ones lucky enough to survive." He gestures at the chair before his desk. Devon doesn't move.

"Why'd you drop out of school?" asks Macourek.

Devon crosses his arms. "You've seen my records. I didn't drop out, I was expelled."

"You got yourself kicked out of six boarding schools," says Macourek dismissively. "And that's since you were twelve. Before that... well, I was unable to acquire your records before you moved to the U.S. Unfortunately, the UK isn't exactly happy to give us intelligence these days." His lips twitch. "But I'm going to hazard a guess. Don't feel obligated to answer—just listen."

Devon still doesn't move.

"You were a perfect student in your childhood," says Macourek quietly. "You did exceptionally well in school, you learned to speak and read at a young age, and rather than be overjoyed, your parents were terrified of your successes. Your school probably tried to put you in gifted programs but your parents stopped them, insisting you be placed with the normal students. You were barred from any intellectual competitions—no math teams, spelling bees, even pop quizzes were things to be warned about. Your parents told you to do well, but not be perfect. When you were twelve, someone tried to recruit you—maybe it was a crime family, maybe it was MI6. Your parents moved your entire family to the United States to escape that.

"After the move, you decided to take your parents' advice and stop excelling. You began drinking when you figured out that inebriation muddled your eidetic memory. You didn't drink to get drunk, you drank to be normal."

Devon's throat constricts. He tries to lock down his emotions, but this is the problem with being an eidos—he remembers it all. Every painful detail comes rushing back, just as clear as the moment it happened.

"Not quite," he says. He manages to keep his voice steady. "My mother wanted me to work for the government. She thought it was the patriotic thing to do. My father divorced her and brought me and my sister with him when he moved to Boston. He lost a good bit of business since then—people think he evaded taxes or some rubbish like that."

"Ah." But Macourek doesn't sound surprised. "You think it's your fault."

Devon's legs finally refuse to hold him. He sinks into a chair. It's one of those moments, the kind where it feels as if time has stopped and cannot move on. The world has gone askew and nothing will ever set it right again. It's a stupid thought. Things will go on—they always go on. But Devon can't picture anything beyond this conversation.

It's how he felt when they moved away from London.

It's how he felt when he answered Eduardo Carson's phone.

"Maybe if I tried harder," he says, "none of this would've happened. I know I could—I could make more of an effort. I could just try to fit in—" His words are disjointed, but Macourek seems to understand.

"Devon Lyre," says Macourek sharply.

Devon's head snaps up. Macourek, no, *Aristeus* gazes at him. Not with pity. It's more like...understanding.

"There is nothing wrong with you," Aristeus says.

It's like there's something breaking in Devon's chest. It hurts and it shouldn't, because he knows that Aristeus's words are just that—words. They're just jumbled-up syllables that shouldn't mean anything, but Devon's spent his whole life with his own family trying to hide him away, like they were ashamed of him, ashamed of what he could *do*, what he could *be*—

A knock comes from the door and Sia is standing there. "Sorry to interrupt, but Morgan's back," Sia says. "She wants to talk to you—she says it's urgent. Something about TATE hacking the customs website again."

Aristeus rises from his chair. "Thank you, Sia. I'll be out in a moment."

Sia nods and pulls the door shut behind her. Aristeus straightens his tie—he's still wearing his clothes from the party, Devon realizes. It humanizes him somehow, the fact that Aristeus hasn't had time to change clothes. "You can stay here," says Aristeus, "for as long as you need to. If you need a ride back to your dorm, you can take my car. I won't be needing it tonight." He gestures to a bowl on his desk, where a number of keys are tangled together.

It's a generous offer. Devon should feel grateful, he knows that. But all he can muster up is a numb sort of curiosity.

"What's the name Morgan goes by?" Devon asks tonelessly.

Aristeus freezes in the doorway. "Morana."

A Celtic goddess of death. No need to ask about Morgan's immunity.

"Dauthus," says Devon, and Aristeus nods before walking away. He softly shuts the door behind him, as if wanting to give Devon privacy.

Sitting alone in the office is surreal. Part of Devon is screaming at himself that he's behind enemy lines and he should do something—see if there's a file on Ciere. Steal important data. Something.

Another part of him just wants to curl up on the floor and never leave. So long as he's sitting here, he doesn't have to think about his next move. He doesn't have to think about the decision he's going to have to make.

A loud ringing makes him flinch. Aristeus's mobile flashes angrily up at him. He must have forgotten it.

On a whim, Devon picks it up and glances at the caller ID.

DANIEL BURKHART.

Devon's stomach leaps. He stares, remembering the last time he answered a phone that wasn't his.

Oh, screw it.

He flips the phone open and attempts an American accent. "Hello?"

"Aristeus," says a familiar voice. It takes Devon a moment to place it. It's not Daniel. It's that FBI agent—Gervais. "We've found her, we've found Maya Cooper. She's on the run, but we think she's going to try to kidnap Aditi Sen or something— we don't know. But"—a horn blares on the opposite end of the line and Devon winces—"we're on her trail and we'll try to stay on it—I wanted to tell you that we haven't called this in yet. If you want to question Cooper, you should get down here now—hell, Daniel, I told you to drive the car, not crash it—"

The line goes silent.

Devon watches the phone's screen dim and then fade to black. "Well, that's interesting," he says. And it is, because anything that means he's not thinking about his own life is definitely interesting.

Devon pockets the phone and the car keys, and strides out of the office.

35

DANIEL

T his is becoming scarily routine," says Daniel, taking a turn too tightly. The FBI car clips the edge of the sidewalk and he and Gervais bounce in their seats.

Gervais clutches at his door handle, all the while still holding his phone aloft. He has it raised to eye level, despite the fact that they're still trailing the same taxi. It would be hard to illusion something that big—Daniel remembers how much trouble Ciere had with simply illusioning herself.

"I thought you said you could drive," says Gervais, wincing as Daniel hits the brakes.

Driving the FBI car is both a challenge and a pleasure. It's got more power than any car Kit ever owned, but driving it feels like sitting on a particularly skittish horse. One tap to the gas and it jolts forward, the steering wheel jittery under his fingers. The dashboard is unfamiliar. There are more buttons on the GPS screen than Daniel is used to—and one of them keeps blinking red. Daniel tries to ignore it and hopes it's not the "check engine" light.

They're a few car lengths back from the taxi, trying to stay hidden in the traffic. Which might be easier if the Friday night traffic weren't hell-bent on getting out of the city. Trailing a lone taxi is difficult enough without following traffic laws. Even so, it's better if Daniel drives. With his immunity, he can try to sense which way the taxi will go. Then there's the fact that should Maya Cooper be armed, Gervais will need both hands. His jacket is crumpled in the backseat, the black Glock tucked under his arm.

"She was at the hotel," says Daniel. "So Maya Cooper is definitely tailing Aditi Sen. Do we know why?"

Gervais shakes his head, eyes locked on the taxi's taillights. "There are plenty of people who want Sen gone."

"I thought she was just a lobbyist." Daniel hits a patch of ice and feels the steering wheel jerk under his fingers. He grips it harder. Driving quickly amid this slush and darkness feels like teetering on the edge of disaster. All it would take is a single slip and the car could be out of control. For just a moment, Daniel wonders what that might feel like—the weightless roll, the shattering glass. When he takes another turn too quickly, his stomach flips. It's not altogether unpleasant.

"Aditi Sen is an extremist," says Gervais grimly. "She's spoken out against everything from the titer test to the tagging system. The only reason she's not in jail is because she has connections."

"Is that disapproval I hear?" A green light winks yellow. Daniel frowns at it, judging the distance. Then he hits the gas.

Gervais makes a soft sound of distress as they pass through the intersection, under a firmly red light. "The tagging system is put in place for everyone's safety," he grits out. "It makes it easier for me to do my job." The dashboard's red light winks on again, blinks a few times, then vanishes.

Daniel laughs. "Yeah. Because I'd hate for your job to be difficult." The taxi takes a right turn and Daniel swerves right, cutting off another car.

Gervais's depression seems to have gone, left behind at the hotel. He's focused again. Daniel feels it, too—the addictive high of the chase. It's different being on this side of one. He's used to being the hunted, not the hunter.

"Maya Cooper is kidnapping people who could be immune," Gervais muses. "She's also chasing a lobbyist. This could be a political thing. Maybe a rival politician is paying her off."

The taxi takes a left turn and Daniel follows. From what Daniel can tell, Maya Cooper is taking a circuitous route to somewhere. She's probably directing the taxi driver in circles, hoping to evade any potential tails. The FBI car is unmarked and a sedate black; it looks like half the other cars on the street. She probably hasn't realized that Daniel and Gervais are following her, and Daniel wants to keep it that way.

The light on the dashboard winks on again. Daniel glances at it and nearly clips a Ford. The other driver makes a rude gesture, which Daniel returns with vigor.

"Both hands on the wheel," snaps Gervais.

"Driving might be a little safer if the dashboard weren't angry at me," Daniel bites back. "Please tell me we aren't out of gas or anything."

"It's the medical alert I mentioned before," Gervais says dismissively. "A patient escaped or something—all cop or FBI cars are programmed to pick up the signal. Not for us to deal with."

"Could you please shut it off, then? It's kind of distracting."

Gervais sighs and touches the GPS. A map appears, all dark lines and faded blues. Except for a brilliant speck of red—

Which, if Daniel isn't mistaken, is dead ahead of them.

Daniel looks at the taxi. Then back at the GPS. Then back again.

"Oh," says Daniel, "you've got to be kidding me."

"What?" Gervais looks at him, as if expecting disaster. Daniel shakes his head.

300

"Bear with me for a moment," he says, and then yanks the car down an alley.

The taxi vanishes from sight and Daniel feels a rush of apprehension. He's taking a gamble. Out of the corner of his eye, he can see Gervais's jaw working, as if he has lost all ability to speak.

The silence spans only a few seconds. "What the hell?" Gervais all but yells.

"Trust me," says Daniel. "I'm testing a theory here." The car jostles and twitches beneath Daniel and he slows down a fraction. The snow is thicker in the alley, more solid and less worn down. There hasn't been enough traffic to smooth it out completely.

"That was our only lead!" says Gervais. He sounds appalled rather than angry. And just a little betrayed.

"Didn't I just tell you to trust me?" Daniel slows the car to a crawl as they exit the alley. He glances down at the dashboard, sees the red light winking two streets down. He turns in that direction, ignoring the oncoming traffic. He's alight with energy, invincible.

Gervais swears softly. He apparently doesn't share Daniel's optimism.

Daniel maneuvers the car down another street, keeping an eye on the GPS. The red dot blinks closer and closer until Daniel sees it make another turn—right in front of them.

Daniel turns to Gervais and doesn't bother to hide his grin.

Gervais doesn't get it, not at first. Daniel's gaze darts between the road and Gervais, so he sees when Gervais catches on.

"You've got to be kidding me," he says, echoing Daniel's earlier words. "The medical alert...it's from her?"

A laugh bursts from Daniel. "She's been kidnapping people, Gervais. She's probably pissed off hundreds—one of them might belong to a crime family or something."

"Someone's tagged her," says Gervais, aghast. "They put a medical tracker on her and set it off. Probably hoping that someone will pick her up. That's—that's—"

"Really underhanded," says Daniel.

"I was going to say 'ingenious.'" Gervais looks as if he just found out he's won the lottery. "This means—she can't get away from us. We could literally lose her right now, but we won't lose her. Which means you can stop driving like a maniac," he adds hastily.

Daniel reluctantly slows down.

"She doesn't know she's being tracked," says Gervais. "I'll call in the med alert and let the local cops know it's being handled. We'll stay out of sight, wait for her to go wherever it is she's going."

"Then what?" Daniel slides a glance toward Gervais.

Gervais's smile is thin and drawn tight. "Then we take her down."

302

36

CIERE

She leaves the hit man's body in the alley.

Ciere uses what's left of her concentration to vanish herself. She's a shadow, moving down the dark street, and she prefers it that way. A frigid wind claws at her dress and she wraps her arms around herself. Her jacket is back at the hotel. The only thing she has left is her clutch and its contents.

She illusions herself into a man's guise, wearing a waiter's uniform. There are plenty of restaurants to choose from and she settles on an upscale Italian joint. She strides through the door, past the greeter, and no one questions her. She hurries into the coatroom. It's small, little more than a closet, filled with wool and polyester. She grabs the heaviest coat she can find and delves into the pockets of the others. She comes up with about fifty dollars in cash and someone's cell phone. Then she vanishes herself and darts out a side door.

Once back on the street, she pulls on the coat and pockets the cash. She might need it later. The cell phone is put to immediate use. She's been without a phone for nearly twenty-four hours—and it turns out there wasn't any need to smash her last one. The Alberanis were never tracking her phone. She punches in Guntram's number.

The phone rings once, twice, three times, and then goes to voice mail. Her heartbeat picks up, thumping painfully. She tries again. Still no answer.

Uttering a soft curse, she dials Alan's number.

Your friends are probably dead by now.

Four rings. She's expecting it to go to voice mail, when a voice says, "Hello?"

Relief sweeps through her. "Alan, it's me," she says, but that's all she gets out.

The noise Alan makes—it freezes the words in her mouth. If she didn't know better, she would think he held back a sob. "Ciere," he says breathlessly. "Oh, thank god. You're okay—tell me you're okay."

"Alan," she begins to say, but he cuts her off.

"Get your bracelet off now," he says. The words come out so fast, they're almost unintelligible. "I don't care what Guntram told you—get it off now. Smash it, do whatever you have to. Leave it in a garbage can and get the hell out of there."

Her steps stutter to a halt. She moves quickly to one side, until she's pressed up against a store wall, out of the foot traffic. Leaning on the bricks, she says, "I know—the Alberanis, they've been tracking them. They hacked them somehow, I don't know how—"

"Jess's phone," says Alan. "They took Jess's phone. When she died, her bag was left behind—her phone must have been in there. The Alberanis must have found a good hacker and figured out the system."

"I don't have my bracelet," she replies in a rush. "I broke it—it's a long story, but I'm safe."

Alan doesn't speak and his silence sends a jolt of pure panic through her. Her fingers tremble and she presses the phone harder to her ear.

"They found you, didn't they?" she manages to say.

It takes him another moment to answer. His voice is barely a whisper. "At the warehouse. Boxed us in. Guntram tried to vanish everyone, but they had cameras and heat sensors. It was like…they knew. They must've known what he can do. Or maybe they thought you'd be there, so they came prepared."

Her heart lurches in her chest and she finds herself sinking toward the ground, her back sliding against the brick wall.

She's conspicuous like this—a lone girl crouching next to an empty storefront—but she can't bring herself to care.

"What happened?" She feels the words slip out without meaning to say them.

"Cole's dead," says Alan softly. Ciere wraps both hands around the phone to keep it steady. "Along with four of Henry's team. I—I'm not sure about Henry herself. I think Conrad and Guntram got out. I was with Cole, but after he was shot, I broke my bracelet and got out through a vent." He makes a soft, pained sound. "I heard some of them talking through the walls. That's how I knew about the bracelets. I tried to call you, but your phone... you haven't been answering your phone—"

"I thought maybe it was being tracked," says Ciere. "I—I broke it—"

"I thought you were dead." Alan says the words so softly that Ciere strains to hear them. "After the raid, I couldn't find any of the others. We all ran in different directions and I thought—I thought if you were hurt—"

"Where are you?" she says, unable to hold back her fear.

It's a moment before he answers. "On a bus. About an hour away from DC."

With nowhere else to go, Ciere looks up the address scribbled on her wrist. She gives it to Alan, tells him to meet her there. The Kingston Cemetery is only a few miles away. Magnus will be long gone by now, but the cemetery is the only place she can think of to hole up.

She throws her stolen phone into the street and a passing car runs over it. The last thing she wants is for some business-man to track her down because she pocketed his work phone. Glancing up at the street signs, she orients herself and begins walking.

Holiday decorations are out in force here—shiny bright lights are coiled around the streetlamps, and most of the storefronts have holly or tinsel. Late-night shoppers carrying paper bags hurry past her.

Ciere feels removed from it all, like she's gazing into a wholly different world. Christmas shopping and holiday dec-orations seem out of place in the same city where a mobster hit man just tried to kill her. And where she's pretty sure she killed him, instead.

She tries to lose herself in the walk. She tries not to think but finds she can do nothing else. All she can do is remember Magnus's toneless voice or Aristeus standing over Devon, his hand on Devon's shoulder. Proprietary—almost protective. So that is where Devon went. That's where he vanished to. He's with them now.

It hurts. It shouldn't, but it does.

She told him to leave. She did it for his own good. She couldn't be responsible for him, not when the stakes were as high as they were. Devon wasn't raised to be a crook. And as much as he wishes he could be, he doesn't have the instincts for it. She wishes he did; it would make life easier.

She tries to think of other things. In her mind, she goes back to the hotel room. She tries to focus on the memories of Pruitt's killer, of the gun she found behind the painting, the two pairs of shoes, of the papers with the stars on them.

Her legs feel wooden, her body exhausted but her mind ever working. Her shoes are soaked through with slush and dirt; she isn't dressed for a long trek across the city.

The cemetery looks relatively new. The ground is still smooth, and most of the markers are the kind that lie flat against the earth. Only a few raised statues even give away the fact that it's not a park. Snow covers the grass, but someone has swept the headstones clean. Ciere hefts herself over a short stone wall, dropping to the other side with ease. The gates are locked tight.

She's not sure what grave belongs to Kit, so she finds one of the larger statues. The ground beneath it is free of snow. Shivering, Ciere sits on the ground, drawing her legs up under the woolen coat.

She tries to relax, but her limbs won't stop twitching. Her fingers keep grasping at the coat, trying to draw it closer. Her body is still hyper-alert, even if her mind isn't. Vaguely she wonders if the hit man had friends, and if they might come after her.

Sucking in a freezing breath, she decides to bow to her own paranoia. Conjuring an illusion isn't easy. Her mind feels fractured and useless, but months of Guntram's training have hardened her. She casts a thin illusion over her body, so at first glance she'll just be another shadow. Knowing she's out of sight makes her feel a little safer.

Sleeping is out of the question. Even if she wants to, she can't keep her illusion up while unconscious. She lets her mind wander instead, eyes drifting out of focus. The city lights become a blur and she watches them through barely open eyes.

Alan arrives sometime after midnight.

He wears a coat that's too big for him. His short hair is sticking up in every direction, and there's a wariness to his face as he pulls himself up and over the cemetery wall.

Ciere drops her illusion. Her legs are numb and stiff, and it takes two tries to get to her feet.

She waves at him and the fear falls away from his face. His lips move, forming a few silent words, and then he's hurrying over. He's hurt, she thinks. He's limping. She wants to ask if he's okay, but never gets the chance. Alan's arms are around her before she can say a word. She closes her eyes, lets herself relax into his embrace, and holds on to him as if he's the only thing anchoring her to the world.

37

CIERE

They find a twenty-four-hour diner.

It's part of a chain, cheap but clean. At this hour, the hostess looks a little bleary-eyed and the only other occupants are a drunk man and a cluster of college students. The table is plastic, the menus laminated, and Ciere requests a table near one of the side doors. The fare is basic, and Ciere orders a sandwich, a cup of soup, and a whole pot of coffee.

Only after the food is on the table and the waiter has gone to help someone else does Ciere finally talk to Alan. They haven't really spoken until now; the silence was too comfortable, and delving into the events of the last forty-eight hours seemed like a daunting task. She fortifies herself with a cup of coffee before even attempting it. Hands cradling the warm mug, she says, "I found out who killed Pruitt."

Alan has been eating a turkey sandwich like it's the last food he will ever see. He pauses, mid-bite, and then swallows. Setting the sandwich down looks like it takes supreme self-control. "Who?"

"A woman called Maya," says Ciere. She keeps her voice quiet, even if there's no one near enough to hear. "She's an illusionist."

Alan's copper skin goes a little pale. He reaches for a glass of water, like he needs something to do while he comes up with a response. "Did you...confront her?"

"No," says Ciere. "I broke my tracker and put it in her things."

Alan begins coughing and puts the water down. His full lips are twitching, as if he's trying to smile through the coughing fit. "That's—that's—"

"Pretty desperate, I know," says Ciere. Her wrist is swollen, despite the cold. It must be sprained. She tells him the rest of the story, skimming over the details. Alan goes still when he hears Aristeus's name, but he doesn't interrupt. Only when she's finished does he speak up.

"I don't think the Syndicate is in any condition to come after us." He picks up a spoon and goes to work on his chicken soup. "They'll regroup, but by then we could be long gone."

"Or we could wait for them to regroup, and I'll tell

Guntram everything I found," says Ciere. "Go back to Philadelphia and hang out there until the Syndicate gets back on its feet."

Alan sets the spoon down. He leans forward, head tilting downward.

"What?" Ciere says, confused.

"You want to stay with them?" Alan says, his tone careful.

Ciere feels herself frown. "No. But Guntram needs to know an illusionist has it out for his team. I owe him that much."

"You don't owe him anything." Alan's lips press together and there's something in the set of his shoulders that makes Ciere think he's readying himself. "I know you like him—"

"I don't like him," says Ciere. And it's true; she doesn't like Guntram. It's more a grudging respect. And now that she knows that he didn't kill Pruitt, that he hasn't been trying to entrap her, she feels a little guilty for suspecting him.

"*The devil you know,*" Kit once said, and now she completely understands. She says, "You don't need to go back. You can stay with Kit—"

"What?" Alan says incredulously.

"You were the one they were threatening," says Ciere. "You can stay behind while I tell Guntram what I found. If he's still alive."

Alan sounds almost insulted by her words. "I'm not going to—"

"Put the formula in danger again?" Ciere whispers.

That shuts him up. Because he must know it's true.

Resentment flickers across his face so quickly she almost doesn't catch it. "I thought you," he says, "of all people, didn't care about the formula."

That's true. Beyond her initial astonishment that he has it memorized, the only thing she's ever felt about the formula is fear—for Alan. He has the instruction manual for the world's most deadly weapon inside his skull and there are people who will kill for it. One of them already tried to kill him to keep it out of the government's hands.

Ciere has little use for the formula. If she were truly a master thief, she might consider selling Alan. She might use a mentalist to draw the secrets from his mind, sell them to a foreign government, then buy a private island.

But Ciere's never been that ambitious, and the thought of selling Alan makes her feel sick. The formula is just another part of him—like his dark hair or dislike of eye contact.

"I don't care," she says simply. "You do."

That clearly throws him. His brow knits together in confusion.

It sends a sharp spike of anger through her, the thought that he's only ever had people care about the formula. Like the rest of him is irrelevant, so long as he carries the weapon in his mind. He's more than that.

"I know you don't want the formula to fall into the wrong hands," says Ciere, "so you can go back to Kit. I'll find Guntram and let him know about Maya." Seeing his distress, she quickly adds, "I'll be okay. I've handled jobs alone before. This is just another messaging job. I promise I'll be careful."

"Where will you find him?" asks Alan, and Ciere's grateful that he seems to have accepted her plan.

"Where else?" she replies. "Gettysburg."

They leave the diner, paying for their meal with the crumpled bills Ciere stole. It's nearly four in the morning; she feels the late hour as a heaviness in her limbs. She wants to lie down and sleep, but it's not safe. Their plans are made—they just need to carry them out.

Alan will take an early morning commuter's train to Philadelphia. He'll be safe there. Ciere will take a bus to Gettysburg.

They walk down the street, toward a bus stop. The traffic is sparse, only a few passing taxis and the early commuters. The snowfall has started up again—just a few thin flakes drifting through the air. Ciere feels better on the move. Once she has a purpose, she can forget everything else.

Well, almost everything.

"Do you still have your phone?" she asks, turning to look at Alan. He ghosts along, half a step behind her. The way a real bodyguard might, she realizes. Conrad's training must be sticking with him.

Alan nods. "Do you want to try calling Guntram? He might have his phone...I admit, I didn't try hard to get in touch with him." He reddens. "I mean—I wasn't planning on letting him handcuff me again."

"Later," says Ciere. "I already tried, but he didn't answer. He's probably ditched his phone." She hesitates. "Devon. I—I want to see if I can talk to him."

The memory of him, standing in that hotel hallway, won't leave her alone. He's her friend, and if he's under Aristeus's control, then she needs to know that. If only so she can kidnap and find a way to deprogram him.

She waits for an argument. Calling Devon is risky; he's had contact with Aristeus, and his mind might not be his own. But Alan simply nods. "He's your friend."

They stand next to a lamppost, glad for the illumination. The trickle of snowfall is becoming steadier, the air churning with fresh winds. Ciere senses the change in weather; they might be in for a storm. Alan hands her the phone and she dials Devon's number from memory. The phone's metal is cold against her bare ear.

It rings once. Ciere edges her weight from foot to foot. She's nervous, even if she can't settle on why.

"Hello," says Devon's familiar voice. "Before you say

a word, are you calling to talk to Macourek/Aristeus, or a charming fellow named Lyre?"

"Devon," says Ciere. She opens her mouth to ask if he's all right, but finds herself saying, "What?"

"Ciere!" He sounds delighted. "Ah, good. You're still talking to me. That's a start, I suppose." He clears his throat. "As for the greeting, well, most of my biggest blunders occurred because of a case of mistaken identity. That and the fact that I keep finding myself with federal agents' mobiles."

His meaning sinks in. "Wait—you have *Aristeus's phone*?"

Alan draws in a sharp breath and Ciere turns away, trying to focus on Devon's voice. He sounds…not drunk, exactly.

"Nicked it," says Devon brightly. "He'll notice eventually, but whatever. We need to talk, right?"

Ciere closes her eyes; feels that old ache inside her chest. She misses him, misses her best friend. "Yes—"

"Good, good," he says vaguely. He draws the words out, as if distracted. "But not now. I'm kinda busy." A horn rings out and Ciere winces.

"Where are you?" she says. Because it's finally registered—the sounds on the other end of the line. There's the sound of cars, and his voice echoes strangely.

"Chasing people instead of thoughts," says Devon.

"What?"

Devon laughs, but it sounds forced. "It's all part of my

brilliant plan. I'm going to help catch a kidnapper. Mostly because it's either this or I drink so much, I risk alcohol poisoning." There's a sound on the end of the line, like that of a door opening. "Now if you'll excuse me, I have a date with a couple of FBI agents and one Maya Cooper."

The name punches through Ciere like a bullet. She feels it go through her, leaving a gaping hole. Her breath leaves her in a rush.

"Devon," she croaks, "no, you have to listen to me—"

There are footsteps; she can hear them clearly. He's on foot.

"We'll talk later," says Devon, and hangs up.

Ciere holds the phone tight against her ear, even after it's gone silent. Everything is moving too quickly. She's caught in a world of light and noise, and it blurs together until she can't hear anything else. Alan's saying something, but the words are hazy and she can't hold on to them. Her heart feels like it's turning over and over, pounding so hard, she thinks it might give out.

She redials Devon's number, fingers stiff and clumsy. It goes straight to voice mail. She closes her teeth around a frustrated cry and tries again. Nothing.

No matter what's going on between Ciere and Devon, she's known him for years. Since she was a kid, on one of her first thefts, he's always been there.

Maya. He's going after Maya—the illusionist. The one who killed Pruitt.

She realizes she's repeating these words aloud, over and over, until Alan says, "Come on."

She can still feel Pruitt's blood flowing over her hands, soaking the scarf, feel his heart stutter and go silent. She felt it when he stopped breathing. Her terror shifts, focusing on a new nightmare: Devon, bleeding out into the snow, silent and still.

"We have to find him," she says. Her voice comes out jerky, in little stops and starts. "She'll—she'll kill him."

"No, she won't." Alan's face is hard and he takes his phone back. His fingers blur over the menu, switching through options. "Before Pruitt died," he says quietly, "I made sure to see how the tracking system worked. I might have...downloaded the system without Guntram knowing."

She gapes at him. "It was insurance," says Alan defensively. If he thinks she's about to rebuke him, he's wrong.

"That's genius," says Ciere. "You can find the illusionist—and Devon." Another ripple of fear goes through her. "But the tracker's active; it'll be drawing in the cops—"

"So you'll hide us," says Alan, as if that's a sure thing. He hands her the phone and she stares at it. The screen shows a blue grid, the city in miniature. There's a glowing red dot blinking in one corner. She squeezes the phone, some part of her afraid to let go.

38

DANIEL

A parking garage," says Gervais. They're parked a block away from said garage, sitting in the car while the snow gently begins to blot out their windows. Gervais hits the windshield wipers and they creak in protest.

The cold seeps into the car. Without the heaters to keep it at bay, Daniel shivers and draws his coat closer around himself. Going out into that frigid air isn't a pleasant prospect.

"Do you think she knows she was followed?" asks Daniel. They're in a grungier district of DC, filled with factories and the telltale signs of the homeless. Graffiti marks up nearly every visible surface. In summer, this neighborhood will smell like hot cement, burning plastic, and unwashed bodies. The snow smooths out some of the rough edges, but it also makes Daniel wonder if there are any frozen bodies around.

It wouldn't surprise him. Before he joined up with a thieving crew, he spent several months on his own. He learned quickly how deadly a cold winter can be—and how exposure can kill just as easily as a gun or knife.

"She's been taking different taxis around town for hours," says Daniel, when Gervais doesn't respond. The FBI agent runs a hand through his silvered hair, his face creased with thought.

"She might have been biding her time," he says finally. "If she needs to be at this place now, maybe her safest bet was to keep moving and out of sight. Or maybe she just wanted to stay warm."

The "out of sight" thing isn't an exaggeration. In between cab rides, Maya Cooper walked several blocks, invisible all the while. Only the medical alert kept Daniel and Gervais on her trail—and even then, it took some creative maneuvers to keep up.

Daniel is pretty sure he'll never be allowed to drive Gervais's car again.

Gervais checks the GPS; the red dot hasn't moved for five minutes. "We should call for backup," he says quietly. "Going in there without help is suicidal."

"Aristeus might be sending someone," says Daniel. Gervais received two texts from Aristeus, both asking for updates on their location. They gave Aristeus the parking garage's address moments after they pulled up. It makes Daniel uneasy to have Aristeus following them, but there's little he can do about it.

"We can't rely on the UAI," says Gervais. "We should call in my colleagues." But he doesn't make a move toward his phone, and Daniel knows why. If they call it in, if they get everyone here and Maya Cooper manages to slip away again...it might be the last straw. Gervais is balanced on the edge, and all it will take is one last slip for him to be fired.

And Daniel will be assigned to someone new.

"We should get eyes on her first," says Daniel. "Hell, send me in alone. If she sees me, I'll blend in."

Gervais turns narrowed eyes on him. "No."

Daniel stares right back. "I had a life before I was arrested, you know. Some of it involved pretty sketchy places."

"Weren't you high up?" asks Gervais, his frown deepening. He knows a little of Daniel's criminal background. "You were involved in art heists, jewelry cases, and some confidence work. Your file was mostly white-collar."

"Yeah, but I started out in places like this," says Daniel. "I spent nearly a year pickpocketing and breaking into cars in crime family territory. If I can survive that, I can survive a bit of recon in a parking garage."

"With a kidnapper," says Gervais flatly.

Daniel offers him a smile. It's not a genuine expression, but it's all the reassurance he can muster. "We need to get eyes on her, then we can call in backup. I'll speed-dial you the moment I see her, I promise."

Gervais's gaze sweeps over Daniel, as if trying to see him the way a stranger would. Daniel is well aware of how he looks: old pea coat worn over a faded hoodie, dingy sneakers, crooked nose, green eyes, and a wary expression.

He looks like he belongs here.

"If anything happens—" says Gervais.

"I'll call the cavalry." Daniel raises two fingers in a mock salute.

Gervais frowns. "I was going to say that if anything happens, I won't forgive myself."

Daniel's stomach tightens. He can't think of anything to say, so he doesn't.

The inside of the parking garage is exactly what he expects.

It's a shantytown. This garage is large and sturdy enough to hold up through winter, and those who have nowhere else to go have taken up residence. Daniel walks through one of the doors. He half expects to be challenged. Small gangs have been known to claim buildings like this. But the only person who gives him a second glance is a small child. She sits with another girl, both of them huddled near a fire.

There was security, once upon a time. Daniel can see that most of the doors have broken locks, and there are no windows on the first floor. But the remnants of wealth are long gone, just like this neighborhood's previous occupants. The cars are old and cheap, some with broken windows, some with tents extending from doors.

A bitter smile pulls at Daniel's mouth. Just like the wealthy have their elsecs, the poor have their neighborhoods, too.

He pulls his hood up over his head. He's careful to stare straight ahead, shoulders thrown back and his walk brisk. He glances around for any sign of Maya Cooper and finds none. Taking a breath, he heads for the stairs.

The stairs are a risk; if any gangs have claimed this territory, he might find himself cornered. The concrete steps are icy and the handrail red with rust. Daniel hurries up to the second floor. The door to this story is marked up, its window shattered. He pushes it open and steps inside.

Immediately a man appears. "This is our floor," he says flatly. He's dressed like Daniel—all layers and fingerless gloves. "Find your own place to sleep."

Daniel holds up both hands. "Sorry, man. Just looking for a friend."

The man glares at him until Daniel backs into the stairwell. Little chance Maya Cooper is on this floor, anyway. He hurries up another flight of stairs. The third-floor door's window is unbroken. This floor is entirely dark. Daniel puts a hand to the door and then freezes.

His immunity whispers to him. Daniel closes his eyes, reaching out with his senses. He hears a shuddering exhale that could be a laugh or a sob.

Daniel's hand jerks back. Instinctive dread coils in his stomach. He will not open this door, not for anything.

The fourth story's door is barred.

The fifth's isn't. Its door is marked up, someone having taken a can of blue paint to it. The word *five* is scribbled across it in stylized letters. Beneath it, someone has painted a star. Probably not a gang sign—or at least it's not one Daniel recognizes.

He steps through, even more cautious than when he first entered the garage. There are lights set up—someone wound Christmas twinkle lights around the concrete pillars. It gives the cavernous room a strangely surrealistic feel. There are a few cars, mostly deserted. Broken glass crunches beneath his feet.

He senses her presence first. It's the same sense of purpose, like a silent drum beating in his ears. Daniel darts behind one of the columns. A woman is leaning against one of the walls, her arms crossed over her chest. Her lips are pursed and she checks her watch.

Daniel scrabbles for his phone. *she's on the 5th floor. i think she's meeting someone. maybe accomplices. call for backup or come here yourself?*

There's no answer. Daniel silences his phone; if Gervais does reply, he doesn't want a telltale beep to give him away.

Daniel edges back toward the door, making sure to keep to the shadows. He pulls it open, glad for the silent hinges, and steals back into the hallway. He needs to talk to Gervais.

The moment he steps into the stairwell, he nearly runs into someone else. Daniel jumps back, fists coming up defensively. He'll run upstairs if he has to—he can go up to the sixth floor and take one of the other exits down.

But before he can either fight or fly, he recognizes the newcomer. He's tall and black, and wearing an expensive wool coat.

"What the hell are you doing here?" snaps Daniel.

Devon Lyre blinks at him. "Same thing you are, I expect." He digs around in his pocket and comes up with a phone. "You texted me the address."

Daniel feels his jaw drop. "That's Aristeus's phone." A beat. "Wait, I was texting *you*?"

Devon beams at him. "Yes." He looks ludicrously proud of himself, as if lifting a federal agent's phone is a neat trick. Daniel narrows his eyes and reaches out with his immunity. Devon's heartbeat is quick; his hands are balled and he's breathing in quick, sharp bursts. There's a twisted, desperate yearning coming off him in waves. Daniel shakes his head.

"You stole Aristeus's phone," he says flatly. "Does he know anything about where we are?"

"No," replies Devon. Some of the wild energy fades from his eyes when he takes in Daniel's wariness. "Aristeus isn't coming. Does that scare you?"

Actually, the thought makes him feel lighter. Daniel pauses to collect himself. "Not as much as it should," he says. He shakes his head. "Seriously, you stole Aristeus's phone? Why?"

"Because I just found out who I was working for," says Devon. "Thanks for telling me, by the way."

"I thought you knew." Daniel tries not to smirk and fails. "So you got revenge by stealing the bastard's phone."

"And his car," adds Devon brightly.

Now Daniel understands why Devon looks so gleeful.

Daniel tries not to laugh. The sound that escapes his lips sounds like a strangled snort. "Are you insane?"

Devon grins broadly. "Probably."

This time Daniel makes no attempt to stifle his laugh. Devon joins in, and for a moment, the world seems to right itself. Daniel looks at Devon Lyre and understands why Ciere chose him as a friend. Hell, if things were different, Daniel might have picked Lyre to be on his crew.

"Come on," he says, heading down the stairs. "You're here,

you might as well be useful. You can wait next to the car and direct the reinforcements in after us. How'd you find me, anyway?"

"Only so many entrances," replies Devon. He walks with one hand skimming a cement wall, as if for balance. He doesn't have gloves, Daniel realizes. And his coat, despite the wool, doesn't look too heavy. Devon isn't dressed for the weather, which means this was probably a spur-of-the-moment decision.

They slink out of the building, doing their best to go unnoticed. Once back on the street, Daniel makes a beeline for Gervais's car.

It's empty.

Daniel's heart turns over. He snatches his phone from his pocket. There's a message—and he missed it because he silenced the damn phone.

> *i'm coming in to confirm the ID. i've called in backup. do not move.*

"Oh, crap," says Daniel. "He's gone in there. We need to—" He's about to say something more, but a whisper from his immunity cuts him off.

His whole body goes cold. He *senses* her presence even

before he turns around, knows who it will be long before he sees her.

A petite blonde girl wearing an overlong coat stands in the middle of the icy street.

"Ciere."

39

CIERE

Ciere has never liked the early morning hours. They are the in-between time, the moment the night holds its breath until dawn arrives. It's technically dark enough to pull a job, but the threat of morning and early risers means she can never relax. She prefers midnight, when the darkness is impenetrable. She can slip away into that darkness, sure that no one can see her.

She learned at a young age not to fear the dark. It makes for better cover.

Alan emerges from the taxi first, paying their cabbie with what's left of their cash. Ciere follows, stepping out into a neighborhood that the cabbie is clearly glad to escape. It's not even really a neighborhood—more like a cluster of long-abandoned buildings. It's a factory district, much like the one the Syndicate took refuge in.

Ciere eyes the landscape with a practiced eye. The roads are unplowed, the few cars all but buried in snow. The city avoids this place, which means that other people have claimed this territory.

She swallows. This is the perfect place for Pruitt's murderer to hide.

"You ready?" says Alan softly.

Ciere sucks in a breath, tastes fresh snow and the smell of something burning. "After you."

Venturing into this neighborhood is a risk. Knowing the kind of desperation that lurks within these buildings sends little jitters of fear through Ciere. She'll vanish herself and Alan, if necessary. But in this snow, two sets of footprints will be obvious.

Alan points at a parking garage a block away. "There."

Ciere ends up leading the way. She keeps to the shadows, moving in quick bursts between buildings. As they approach the garage, she sees something out of place: a car that isn't covered in snow. There's the thinnest layer of white, as if the car has only been here a short while.

And standing beside it are two teenage boys.

Ciere's heart lurches into her throat.

Devon Lyre stands with his hands in his pockets. He's alive, unhurt. All the breath rushes out of her. Beside him is Daniel Burkhart.

She hasn't seen Daniel since the horrible night she met Aristeus. All the fear of that night comes back to her and she feels dizzy, nearly sick with it. If he's here, maybe Aristeus is, too. And Alan—

She throws out an arm, catching Alan in the chest. She walks back until the two of them are nearly pressed up against a wire fence.

"Daniel can't see you," she hisses. "He knows about the formula—he thinks you're dead. If he finds out you aren't, he'll tell Aristeus."

"Are you saying I should stay here?" he whispers back. He's mere inches from her, his breath spilling from his lips in a cloud.

Ciere hesitates. She can't leave him behind. Not only is that dangerous, but she doesn't want to. "I'll vanish you. Stay behind me, so no one accidentally runs into you. And walk where I do, so you don't leave behind another set of footprints."

Alan nods. "Do it."

She reaches out, places a hand over his chest. She doesn't need to touch him, but his presence anchors her. She centers herself, draws upon her immunity, and pushes outward.

Alan's hand comes up, covering hers. He gives it a squeeze.

His image flickers and fades from sight. She can still feel his solid form beneath her fingers. She doesn't move for a moment; she's not sure if she can move. Turning around means facing Devon and Daniel—her former best friend and a boy she once thought of as family.

Something touches her chin and she flinches in surprise. Alan's gloveless hand is nearly as cold as the snow. She shivers again. His thumb strokes a line down her jaw, leaving heat in its wake. "It'll be all right," comes his voice, close to her ear. "I'll be behind you."

She nods and the movement dislodges his hand. She retreats a step, heart thumping hard, and turns to face her two oldest friends. They're still next to the car, and she hears Daniel's voice. "Oh, crap," he's saying, and the familiarity makes her throat hurt. "He's gone in there. We need to—"

Ciere jogs toward them. "Hey!" she shouts.

Devon whirls and Daniel turns so quickly that he nearly slips.

"Ciere," he breathes, and he doesn't look happy at all. Fear flits across his face.

Devon breaks into a smile. "Look, the gang's all together again!"

His flippant tone is like a spark. It sets Ciere's temper ablaze, reminding her why she's here and what she's set out to do. Devon doesn't belong here, in this neighborhood, with

Daniel and the FBI or the UAI or even the crooks that are no doubt holed up in the nearby buildings. She wants him safe; she left him behind so he'd be *safe*. But here he is, chasing danger like it's some kind of game. Fury takes hold in her chest, driving away the cold, the fear—everything. She takes one step, then another, and then she's running.

She rushes at Devon, grabs him by the collar, and shoves him against the side of the car. "What the hell, Devon?"

Devon gapes at her.

Daniel glances from Devon to Ciere and back again. Clearly, this wasn't what he expected.

"Chasing a murderer?" Her voice climbs another octave and she doesn't bother to keep it down. "Even for you this is stupid!"

Devon's shock falls away, hardening into anger. "What's that supposed to mean—even for me?"

She tries to shake him. It doesn't work too well, which shouldn't surprise her, given their height difference. Her frustration swells; she wishes she were big enough to physically drag him from the scene.

"Ciere," Daniel begins to say, but she heads him off.

"And what are you doing here?" she snaps, glaring at him. He takes a step back, which is somewhat gratifying.

Daniel holds his hands up, palms out. "My fed handler and I were assigned to this case. We're to locate Maya Cooper and then call in reinforcements."

"Is Aristeus here?" she snarls. She needs to know, if only for Alan's sake.

Devon lets out a snort. "Considering I stole his phone and his car, I'm going to say no."

Ciere releases Devon, shoving him a little as she steps back. "Are you both suicidal?"

"No," snaps Devon. "And what—why are *you* here?"

"That woman, that stupid woman you're chasing, she killed a member of the Gyr Syndicate," cries Ciere. "Shot him in the chest. He bled out through my hands—" She nearly chokes on the words, then forces herself to go more slowly. She needs them to understand. "She's a murderer and an illusionist and she'll kill you."

Something occurs to her. "Wait, why are you chasing her?" She directs the question to Daniel, who fidgets under her gaze.

"She's been kidnapping immune people," says Daniel. "The fed and I have been trying to tail her."

"And I just happened to tag along," adds Devon. "Seemed like fun, so here I am."

"Fun?" Ciere snaps, her anger returning. "You think this is fun?" She delves into her coat pocket and comes up with the papers she took from Maya's hotel room. "You know what I found in her hotel room? These stupid papers and a gun. You know—something to *kill* people with."

Devon's attention snaps to the papers.

"I've seen this star before," he murmurs, as if to himself. He reaches out to take a paper.

"So not the point," says Ciere.

"Wait," says Daniel. "I've seen that, too. It's tagged on the door where she's hiding out up there." He points up, at the parking garage.

"It was also on the train where my colleague was killed," says Ciere, frustrated. "So what? It's probably just her signature. Like, I don't know. A serial killer's secret way of bragging about her victims."

She turns to Devon, expecting him to confirm her theory. But his expression is strangely blank. She recognizes it; she's seen it when he sifts through his memories. He once described his immunity like a scrapbook—everything is in there somewhere; it's just a matter of finding it. His eyes move quickly, unseeing, before understanding dawns on his face.

"She wore a necklace with a star," says Devon, dazed.

"Maya Cooper?" says Daniel.

Devon shakes his head. "Aditi Sen." His eyes go wide. "They're not kidnappings."

Daniel and Ciere exchange a look. She can feel them settling into old rhythms and it's almost like there's been no separation. He's the closest thing Ciere's ever had to a brother.

When he cocks an eyebrow, she can clearly read his unsaid words: *Does he do this often?*

"We've got to stop your handler," says Devon, and takes off at a sprint toward the parking garage.

"Should we go after him?" says Daniel, gesturing like Devon's a runaway pet.

Ciere is already running, her soggy ballet flats slapping against the sidewalk. She makes a mental note to never wear anything but tennis shoes ever again.

"I ever tell you about the time I helped people sneak out of school?" Devon says over his shoulder. "I could get people in and out of the dorms, past security, and off campus any time of night. I set up several routes and calculated when each one could be taken based on when the security sweeps would happen."

"I'm sorry," says Daniel, "but what the hell does this have to do with anything?" They rush through the garage door, past tents and rusting cars. Ciere catches only a glimpse of a few people before she finds herself in a stairwell.

"I'm getting there," says Devon, not turning around. "Point is, the system had to constantly change. We couldn't always use the same routes because patterns are how people get caught. I set up some marks. They were symbols I drew— little things that could be mistaken for flyers or tagging. That way the routes were clearly marked, so people could follow them without needing a guide. In exchange, they smuggled me things like vodka and candy. Which I then sold to my classmates."

"Fascinating," says Ciere. "Still not really sure how relevant it is, though."

"You said you saw the mark where your mate was killed," replies Devon grimly. "And that Maya Cooper had those cards with the same symbol. And—and that star. Aditi Sen was wearing a star necklace. They're marking things, like I used—"

A shot rings out. It echoes down the stairwell and Ciere stumbles to a halt. "Shit," says Devon, and scrambles on.

Daniel rubs his ears and says loudly, "Maya Cooper is a smuggler?"

Devon doesn't reply; he pushes open the door and, sure enough, Ciere sees the faintest outline of a star, its edges flourished.

When she rushes through the door, she nearly runs smack into Devon. He's come to a standstill, frozen mid-step.

A man with silver hair stands in the middle of the floor, gun held in both hands. A plump, red-headed woman that Ciere recognizes as the illusionist stands near a black van.

A strange hissing noise emanates from the van and Ciere's eyes flit over it, drawn to the tires. One of the tires is blown apart, and another is leaking air fast. The FBI agent must have shot it.

"GUN ON THE GROUND NOW," shouts the man.

The illusionist, Maya, is completely still. She also holds a gun, but it's lowered and aimed at the floor.

"PUT IT DOWN!" The man's voice echoes off the walls, loud enough to make Ciere wince.

Slowly, the illusionist does as he says. Once the gun is on the floor, the FBI agent kicks it away.

Standing next to the black van is another woman. She's probably in her mid-fifties, her black hair edged with gray. She has skin nearly the same color as Alan's—a slightly darker copper. Her eyes are trained on the gun-toting man, but there is no fear in her face.

It's not her face that Ciere recognizes. Her gaze scans up and down the woman, finally settling on her feet. Black shoes, shiny and feminine.

The other pair of shoes Ciere saw while hiding under a bed.

"Ms. Sen," says the man, in a different voice. Still the voice of a federal agent, but more gentle. "Step away from the van and get behind me."

Aditi Sen. That's who the woman is.

"I'm sorry, sir," Aditi Sen says. She has a nice voice, one suited to speeches and banquet halls. "But I think I belong over here."

That's when Ciere sees them.

A group of five people huddle by the van. They're clutching bags—one even has a suitcase.

"Smugglers?" says Daniel.

"Actually," says Devon, panting for breath, "I think *they're* what's being smuggled."

PART FOUR

Seventeen years ago, the government decided that its own citizens were its greatest threat.

I hope we can live up to those expectations.

—Aditi Sen, July 20, 2034

40

DEVON

Aditi Sen and Maya Cooper stand frozen in place. Cooper's face is that of angry defiance, a cornered animal ready to bite back. Aditi Sen's hand rests on Cooper's arm, holding her still. Sen's expression is that of dignified tranquillity.

There are people behind them, huddled near the van. Sen probably brought them, Devon thinks. It makes sense. She picks up the passengers, brings them to drop points, and then a guide takes them to the next drop point. They're probably utilizing everything from cars to boats—any way to get people to the border.

It's exactly how he would do it.

"All of you," says Special Agent Gervais, "step away from the woman. I'll protect you."

He still thinks they're victims. He hasn't figured it out yet.

"They're not being kidnapped," pants Devon, taking a step forward. Ciere reaches out to grab him, but he shakes her off. "They're leaving the country." He glances to the two women. "They're smuggling them out, making it look like kidnappings so no one'll suspect." He hurries forward, conscious of the gun in Gervais's hands. "Please, don't hurt them."

The FBI agent barely gives Devon a glance. "You're that kid from the UAI," he says shortly.

"Who apparently didn't know he was working for the UAI," supplies Daniel.

Devon's composure cracks. "Did *everyone* know but me?"

"Pretty much," says Daniel.

Gervais swallows audibly, clearly ignoring the little diversion behind him. He takes a step forward, gesturing with his gun at the men and women behind Maya Cooper. "They're victims of a crime."

"No, they're not." Aditi Sen holds up a hand, rings glittering in the dim light.

"Are any of you here against your will?" says Gervais, directing his words at the passengers.

The five people—two women and three men, Devon counts—all shake their heads.

"Come on," says one man, giving the two women a fond, somehow rueful look. "You really think the two of them could overpower all of us?" His voice shakes, but he seems to be making an effort to stand tall. He's obviously terrified, but not of Aditi Sen or Maya Cooper.

It's a good point. Most of the people near the van are young, fit. Not the easiest of targets.

"You can't be serious," snarls Gervais. "That kid—you've been taking people—"

"Willing people," says Maya Cooper. She has a clear voice. "People who asked Sen for help. They knew she would do what she could—and she knew me."

"An illusionist," says Daniel.

Maya jerks her head around and stares at Daniel. Her eyes narrow and Daniel smiles slightly. "Eludere," he says, by way of explanation.

"This cannot be happening," snaps Gervais. "That woman is a criminal."

"No, she's not." Sen takes a step forward, palms out.

Gervais grips the gun more tightly.

"You want to know how it began?" Sen says, her eyes never leaving Gervais. "An eighteen-year-old girl came to me. She had applied for federal aid in order to pay for college. Along with her family's financial records, she had to include a copy of her blood work. Six months later, a federal agent approached her. Her titer tested positive for the vaccine and she had a 4.0 GPA. They thought she was an eidos."

A chill works its way through Devon's skin. "Was she?"

Sen makes a furious sound. "Does it matter if she was? All that matters is they thought it and they wanted her. She came to me—she'd read an interview I did in some teen magazine. She came to me and begged me to save her from the very government that was supposed to protect her."

"You've been smuggling people out of the country." Ciere says the words with a faint smile. She tips her head as if to acknowledge some great feat. "Mexico?"

"Canada," Sen says curtly. "From there, they can fly anywhere they want without having some mentalist rummaging through their heads. We've been using cargo trains up and down the eastern seaboard."

Ciere steps forward, hand extended toward Maya Cooper. "Wait." She swallows, her hands twisting together. "Did you kill a man in Newark?" she says. "Near a train station."

Maya Cooper hesitates. "Yes."

A harsh breath rattles from between Sen's teeth. "Maya."

"He saw me at a train station I was scouting for a drop," says Maya. "I was careless letting him see me, I thought the place was deserted because of the weather. The man was armed and I thought he was a fed. He pointed his gun at me..." Her chin snaps up. "I'm not sorry."

"He wasn't a fed," says Ciere quietly. "I knew him."

Gervais looks as if the walls around him are ready to topple. "Y-you haven't been kidnapping people?"

Maya Cooper meets his eyes squarely. She doesn't look away. "No."

"That—that child—"

"Was given to me by her parents," says Maya. "I was to take her to a checkpoint and they would follow. Smaller groups are easier to transport."

His wavering gun goes still again, aimed directly at Maya's center of mass. The agent's training must be kicking in, Devon thinks. He can't process this, so he's falling back on old habits. "But you *did* kill a man. You just admitted it."

"How are you going to arrest us all?" calls one of the passengers—a woman this time. She sounds more defiant than the others. "There's one of you, even if you do have a gun. We could just walk out of here."

It's a good question. Devon sweeps the area again, calculating the odds. If Gervais goes up against them all, even with Daniel on his side, his chances aren't good. Not against an illusionist—and whatever those passengers might be, if they are immune at all. There are too many variables; Gervais can't be sure of victory.

Aditi Sen opens her mouth to say something, but she never gets the words out.

Because that's when they hear the sound of a distant police siren.

41

CIERE

Everyone reacts, whether it's with a curse (that would be Devon), a sob (one of the passengers), or quiet resignation (Aditi Sen). Two of the passengers link hands, eyes on each other. Daniel just looks pissed.

Alan is somewhere behind Ciere; she senses the hum of the illusion. Either Maya doesn't sense it or she hasn't seen a need to dispel Ciere's work. Or maybe she hasn't spent months being bombarded with nightmares. Whatever the reason, Alan remains invisible and Ciere couldn't be more grateful. She should illusion them all, except the feds will have heat sensors and night vision—especially at this hour. But maybe her immunity can help protect these people.

The siren wail sharpens, and the sound pierces Ciere. It's

horrible in its familiarity; every criminal knows and dreads the rise and fall of the police siren.

The FBI agent, Gervais, glances toward the windows. His shoulders stoop, as if relaxing slightly. The sound is also familiar to him, but it's obvious that the noise is welcome rather than frightening. It reminds Ciere of a nature show she once saw, of how wolves howl to one another. Predators don't fear one another's calls; it's all just noise to them. As he relaxes, his gun droops the smallest inch.

It's a crucial mistake.

Maya darts forward, with the kind of speed that is fueled by panic. She lashes out, her foot connecting with Gervais's hand. He cries out in pain and the gun clatters to the concrete floor. Before anyone can react, the gun is in Maya's grip. She aims at Gervais's legs. "Get back."

Shock makes the FBI agent's face go slack. He recoils a few steps, and his confidence falters. "You don't want to do this."

"Of course I don't," snaps Maya. "But you forced this." She glances at the passengers.

"If we illusion all of you," Ciere says, stepping forward, "we might be able to slip away before the feds find us."

Maya Cooper never lowers the gun, but her attention snaps to Ciere. "What?"

"I can't illusion everyone here," says Ciere. The words

come out slowly; it's an effort to speak them at all. But if she can help these people, she won't hide what she is. Not anymore. "Neither can you. But together, we might manage it. If we go out on foot—"

"Bugger that," says Devon, and an outright grin breaks across his face. "We've got a car."

Ciere rounds on him. "We?"

Sen looks to him. "Mr. Lyre, I thought—"

"That I'm a spoiled rich kid?" Devon says baldly. "Yeah. I'm also an eidos who fled his home country after being found out. Trust me—if there's anyone who knows what these people are going through, it's me."

Sen looks at him, her expression softening with a fond sort of amusement. "Mr. Lyre. I do believe I like you more than your father."

He wrinkles his nose. "Yeah. Not much of a compliment, that."

"HEY!" a loud voice cracks out. Ciere winces, turning to see the FBI agent. He has his hands balled into fists. "I can't let you go," he says.

"We don't have time for this." Maya Cooper raises the gun, one-handedly keeping it on him. "Everybody, follow the British kid. Got it?"

The five passengers hasten away from the van, most of them edging panicked looks at Gervais.

"Put your hands on your head, turn around, and face the wall," says Maya. She jerks her chin at Daniel. "You, too. I saw you with him—I know you're a fed."

Ciere glances at Daniel, expecting him to reply with a quip. What she sees makes her heart stutter.

All the light is gone from his face, his lips a thin line, and the lines of his face are heavy and stiff. He doesn't protest. His eyes drop to the floor and he turns, hands on his head, twisting to face the wall.

"Daniel," she says.

He leans his head against the concrete, all the tension drained away. But it doesn't look as if he's relaxed—it's more like all the life leaving a dead body. "I can't go with you," he says dully. "I'm a danger. Aristeus knows too much. I can't— you should go."

Maya's gaze is still locked with Gervais. Her aim shifts slightly, the barrel of the gun edging toward Daniel. "Hands behind your head. Face the wall," she says coolly, and this time he does as she says.

"Daniel," repeats Ciere.

"Just go," says Daniel.

Maya's hand comes down on Ciere's shoulder, giving her a firm tug. She staggers back, and finds herself drawn toward the others. Her feet catch on before the rest of her does; she's running toward a different stairwell, one on the opposite side of the building. The sirens are getting louder, sending little jitters through Ciere. She half runs, half barrels down the stairs, keenly aware of how easily she could slip. When she makes it to the first floor safely, she lets out a breath. The others are ahead, vanishing through one of the exits.

They come out on another derelict street. Predawn light spills over the horizon, giving the snow a bluish cast.

A large black SUV is parked next to the curb, a stark contrast to the snow. So much for camouflage. At least it looks powerful, like the kind of cars that feds drive.

"There aren't enough seats in that car. I'll find a different building," says Sen. "I'll lie low. They won't find me."

Maya Cooper shakes her head. "Aditi—"

"Just get them out," says Sen firmly. She reaches out, takes one of Ciere's hands. Ciere is so startled, she doesn't draw back.

"Thank you," says Sen. Then she calls over Ciere's shoulder. "Same goes for you, Boulder!"

Devon is already unlocking the car, ushering everyone inside. Four of the passengers cram themselves into the open trunk, while Maya and the last passenger scoot into the backseat.

When Ciere looks back, Sen is gone. A shadow moves along the side of one building, then vanishes from sight.

Ciere closes her eyes and listens. The sirens are coming from the opposite direction—it looks like they got lucky. They might be able to slip away before anyone notices. But as she settles her mind, a familiar hum breaks into her consciousness.

Oh, crap.

"Devon," calls Ciere, hurrying to his side. "There's something you should know."

Devon, ready to climb into the driver's seat, barely looks at her. "What?"

Ciere sucks in a breath, then relaxes the hold on her immunity.

Alan winks into existence.

Devon jumps a foot into the air and utters a loud curse.

Alan smiles at him. "Good to see you, too."

Devon presses a hand to his forehead, rubbing hard. "Jesus. I should've guessed you'd be lurking around—"

"Don't say his name," warns Ciere, holding up a hand.

"Never planned to," says Devon. He gives Alan a curt nod. "Anastasia."

If the nickname bothers Alan, he doesn't show it. "Lyre."

"Idiots," says Ciere.

The sirens are close now. Ciere's body recoils from the noise—she feels her muscles draw tight and stomach turn over. Every inch of her needs to move.

Ciere hurries into the passenger's seat. Alan is already behind her, sitting beside a confused-looking Maya. "This time," Devon says, "you're not leaving me behind."

Ciere gives him a small smile. "I can't."

He beams at her.

Then she adds, because she can't help herself, "You're driving."

42

DANIEL

Daniel has always believed in doing things. So long as he's moving, planning, acting, he's fine. When he realized the feds might come after his sister, he drew all the attention to himself and then ran away. When he found himself on the streets, he became a pickpocket. When that wasn't enough, he joined up with a white-collar thieving crew. And when the feds caught him, he almost managed to escape.

The key word being *almost*.

Since that night, since Aristeus sat him down and poured his words into Daniel's mind like a poison, Daniel hasn't been doing anything. He hasn't been acting, he's been reacting. Taking orders. Going places people tell him to. Following criminals other people want caught. All of the movement, the planning, even most of the action, falls to someone else.

It feels like being immersed in water—so long as he's kicking, he stays afloat. Even with his newfound stagnation, he's managed to keep his head up. But now, the moment he sees Ciere go, he knows he has lost every secret about her, about Kit, about his whole criminal life, and he feels himself go under.

He's done.

Daniel doesn't bother following. There's no point. He can't be trusted; he can't go with them.

He is tied to the feds, to Aristeus. He belongs here.

Gervais darts into the shadows, retrieving the gun that Maya possessed. Gervais kicked it away from the chaos, and now that Maya has taken his Glock, it's all he has left. He picks up the small handgun, checks it over, and rushes to one of the garage's walls. Like most parking garages, there are simply huge slabs cut out of the walls—no glass, just open air. Some of the fresh snow floats inside, settling on the concrete. Gervais leans heavily on the railing, peering down as if trying to find his prey.

"What are you going to do?" asks Daniel. *Just let them go,* he silently pleads. *Just let them go.*

Gervais grates out the words. "They're criminals."

"She isn't kidnapping people." Daniel takes a step toward him. "I mean, you saw them. They could take her down, if they needed to. And they weren't scared of her..."

They were scared of you.

Gervais's shoulders bunch together, the muscles working beneath his coat. "They're criminals."

"They're just vaccinated people," says Daniel. "Please, please. Just stay here. Don't go after them, don't follow. They'll slip away and you can say—"

"That I failed again?" Gervais leans a little farther out of the window, as if following something with his eyes. "You know how it'll look to the Bureau. They'll think I let them go. They already think I let others go. I joined up to protect people from immune criminals; I didn't join to let them walk."

Daniel's words burst out of him. "You hate this job. You've hated it for months. You could leave, do something else."

Not like me.

"This job," murmurs Gervais. He shakes himself. "I have to go after them," he repeats. His voice is oddly inflected, the way Daniel once spoke after having his mouth shot up with Novocain, tongue almost refusing to respond. He looks down, at something Daniel can't see, and raises Maya Cooper's gun. He's not aiming—not yet—just bringing the weapon up so that he can use it if he needs to. Maybe he's just desperate for something to do, to prove he's not a failure.

"They're not criminals," says Daniel.

Gervais doesn't lower the gun. His eyes narrow.

"If he betrays us, don't hesitate to do what you have to."

Aristeus's words. Spoken in a moment of panic and anger. Far too open-ended. A dominus should have known better.

"Even if everything that Sen said is true, then they're still illegally leaving the country." Gervais's eyes flicker over the city below, and his white knuckles grip the railing.

"Because they're afraid," cries Daniel. His voice breaks on the last word. Exhaustion and helplessness burn within him. His hands ball into fists. "They're afraid of people like you!"

Gervais winces.

"You said you did this job to protect people." Daniel's voice shakes. He can't say the words the way he wants to— calmly and logically. "Who's protecting *them*?"

"They're dangerous," says Gervais woodenly. "I've seen what immune criminals can do. If there's even a chance...I have to stop them."

Gervais begins to turn. Daniel hears the movement, senses the way his breath speeds up, his heartbeat throbbing. He'll go after them. He'll arrest Maya Cooper, Devon Lyre, and Ciere. All those people will be taken into government custody and the immune ones will end up just like Daniel.

He can't let it happen. Cold fury kindles to life in Daniel's chest.

"I have to," repeats Gervais, his words nearly drowned out by the sirens. The sound of cars seems to bring him back to life; he shakes himself, preparing to move. He'll join the chase. He'll find Daniel's friends.

"If he betrays us—"

The problem with a dominus giving orders is that they need to be specific. Certain words need to be defined. Words like "us" and "them." They could mean anything, be anyone, all depending on a person's point of view.

"—don't hesitate…"

And Daniel doesn't.

Daniel runs at Gervais, at the man who treated him far more fairly than Daniel has ever deserved. It doesn't matter, none of this does. Daniel only knows one thing: he will not betray his friends again.

Gervais never has time to react. Daniel hurtles into him, his whole weight slamming into the unsuspecting FBI agent.

He judges the angle just right.

Gervais topples over the railing and Daniel falls with him.

43

CIERE

It occurs to Ciere that the only reason they haven't been caught yet is the garage's remote location. This area is so cut off, so dilapidated, that the city doesn't take any notice of it. Which means that there are weeks and weeks' worth of snow packed onto the pavement, making driving nearly impossible.

Unfortunately, the snow also hampers their escape.

Devon grips the steering wheel hard, pressing on the gas until Ciere clutches at her seat belt. The SUV barrels down the deserted street, bouncing as it hits snowdrifts. "If we get stuck…" she warns him.

"I know, I know," mutters Devon. He hasn't turned on the headlights, choosing to navigate by the dim dawn. "But—oh, shit."

She sees it in the rearview mirror: a black car, red and blue lights whirling atop its roof. Devon wrenches on the steering wheel, executing a clumsy right turn. The fed vanishes around the corner.

"We can't outrun them," says Alan tightly.

"Well, we can't disappear, either," snaps Devon.

That's what he thinks. The last time they worked together, Ciere wasn't the best illusionist. She could only cast over her own body; extending it into the world was physically painful.

That was before Guntram took it upon himself to train her.

Ciere twists back in her seat to look at Maya. The woman has the Glock in her lap, eyes glancing in every direction. "Hey," says Ciere, then wobbles as Devon takes another turn too quickly. The tires spin out, the snow kicking up in white clouds behind them. Ciere's stomach swoops, her middle gone weightless. She hates facing backward in a car.

"We'll need two for this," says Ciere. "I'll vanish the car. Can you take the snow?"

Maya understands immediately. "Yes." She leans back in her seat, fingers gripping the gun hard. She inhales, slow and measured, then releases the breath. At once, the snow behind them becomes smooth and pristine. Like no one has passed through it.

My turn, Ciere thinks, turning around. Once she's firmly

seated, she settles her own breathing. Her fingers go around the armrest and she pushes outward. Her immunity comes to life, stretching around the SUV. They're not invisible—it's too difficult to completely vanish the car. But she creates a mirrored effect, all the light and their surroundings reflecting back at anyone who cares to look. They're as close to invisible as she can manage.

Devon takes another turn, this time down an alley. There are taller buildings in the distance; he's heading for civilization, probably hoping to lose any pursuers in—

A heavy white car swerves out of another alley, appearing directly in front of them. Someone screams and Devon lets out a curse. "They can't see us," says Ciere. "They can't see us, they can't—"

The fed car is headed the same direction they are, only a few feet ahead. It slows, the brakes a flash of crimson in the dim light, and suddenly the SUV is nearly on top of the fed car. Devon slams on the brakes and Ciere is flung forward, her seat belt a tight band against her weight. She'll have bruises, if she survives this.

Ahead, a passenger-side window is rolled down and a man appears, holding a gun.

"PRETTY SURE THEY CAN SEE US!" Devon shouts.

Her eyes scan the fed car and then she sees it—the goggles. Night vision. They can see through her illusions.

"All right," says Devon, "everybody hold on." He throws his whole weight on the steering wheel and turns.

The car nearly flips. She can feel it as the tires lift on the left side, hears the screaming protest of the vehicle as Devon spins it around. There's a horrible screeching noise as they scrape one of the alley walls. When the car rights itself, Ciere sees they're pointing in the opposite direction. Devon slams on the gas and they jerk forward, heading back toward the parking garage.

"What the hell was that?" gasps Maya.

"Something I saw in a movie once," says Devon, sounding breathless. "Never thought I'd get to try it."

Ciere ducks around. Sure enough, the fed car is still barreling ahead—away from them. The feds aren't reckless enough to try a hairpin turn. Ciere presses a hand to her forehead, feels the sweat collecting around her hairline. She imagines trying to tell Kit about this, and a hysterical laugh bubbles up her throat.

"There's a cargo train leaving in thirty minutes," says Maya, checking her watch. "The station is twenty minutes from here—that's the next drop-off point. We need to get out of here, now."

Devon mutters a curse. "Couldn't have mentioned that earlier?" He turns right hard, this time bringing them into a loading dock. A gravel space opens up in front of them—probably some employees' smoking area—and Devon drives through it. The tall buildings make Ciere feel claustrophobic; she clutches at her seat belt and holds tightly to the illusion. Devon hits the gas again and drives over what is probably a traffic divider—with the snow packed over it, she can't tell.

"There's another one!" says Alan, and Ciere turns. Sure enough, a smaller cop car rushes toward the parking garage. When its driver sees them, there's no place to run.

"Oh, hell," says Devon desperately. He glances behind them, at the lights dancing in his rearview mirror. "Ciere, get my wallet."

She gapes at him. "What?"

"Back pocket—now!" A tremble runs through his whole body. "If they're just street cops, this might work."

Ciere doesn't ask again; she simply delves into one of his pockets and comes up with a new leather wallet. "Take down the illusions and pull out the name tag with the lanyard!"

This time Maya speaks up. "The illusions are the only thing protecting us!"

"JUST DO IT!"

With shaking fingers, Ciere manages to pry the wallet open and fumble inside. There's only one card attached to a lanyard and she pulls it free. Devon snatches it up, then swerves the car to the right, opening up space on that side of the road. He hits the dashboard, and his window begins to scroll downward; the cops can't see through the

SUV's tinted windows, Ciere realizes, and can't help but feel relieved. They haven't seen her face—not yet. "Take the wheel!" Devon says.

Ciere grabs at the steering wheel, holding it steady. It jerks beneath her hands, twitching every time they hit a patch of snow.

Devon leans through the open window, blocking most of Ciere's view, and holds up the card. They're slowing now, so that the cop car is nearly level with them.

"What the hell are you doing?" Devon screams. Not at Ciere, or anyone in the car, but at the cops.

He holds up his card and the cop's window rolls down. Devon repeats the question and then shouts, "I'm with the UAI, you asshole! You're interfering with an Adverse Effects investigation!"

The cop is a woman, with dark hair and wide eyes. "What?" she shouts back, her voice nearly lost on the wind.

Devon holds the ID steady. "You are interfering with the UAI! Look at our plates, you idiots! We're on your side! Tell your friends to stop chasing us or I swear to god I will have you working a strip mall for the rest of your life!"

The cop's jaw drops. The car slows, just enough to get a look at the plates. Then the car drops away, slowing until it's nearly at a crawl. Ciere turns around, watches the car pull to a stop. She waits for them to resume the chase, to see through Devon's bluff. One lanyard does not an alibi make.

But the cop car doesn't follow; it spins around and flies back toward the parking garage.

"What the hell just happened?" says Ciere as Devon takes back the steering wheel.

Devon laughs wildly, and the sound barely registers in the rushing wind. Chill air sweeps through the car. "The best lies aren't lies at all," he says cheerily. But his hands tremble, and his pupils are the size of pinpricks. He hits the window controls, and it glides upward. The scream of the wind dies away.

"He's with the UAI?" snaps Maya, and her gun comes up. Alan grabs her wrist.

"I was an intern," says Devon, the smile frozen on his lips. "And I, uh, borrowed this car from my boss. Trust me, if I really was working for the UAI, you'd all be in custody now. So don't be an idiot and shoot the driver."

Maya makes a choking noise. "You stole a *UAI* car?"

"Stole, borrowed, semantics," says Devon, winking at Ciere. She shakes her head.

Maya lowers the weapon, but her expression remains hard.

"Vanish us again," says Devon. "They'll disprove our story, but by then we'll be in actual traffic. I don't want anyone following us."

Ciere draws her immunity together and she knows Maya

has done the same. No one speaks for a few minutes; the only sounds are muttered curses from Devon.

And the amazing thing is, Devon's plan works; no other cars try to follow or cut them off. They pull out of an alley, finding a road leading back to civilization. Ciere holds on to her illusion, hiding the car from sight.

The morning commuter traffic is beginning to clog the roads. Devon somehow manages to dodge cars without so much as hitting the brakes. Ciere closes her eyes.

She has a hard time slowing her breathing. She can still feel the itch of pursuit and her legs ache with the need to run. Just sitting here, fingers digging into her seat belt, is too much stillness. Who knows if the feds are tracking them with traffic cams or maybe have set a tail on them—and if that tail has those night vision goggles, then all the illusions in the world won't matter.

"Take the overpass onto the freeway," comes Maya's clipped voice. Devon murmurs a response and Ciere feels the car ascend a ramp. Then she hears the ticking sounds of Devon hitting a blinker.

"I'm sorry," says Alan, "but did you just signal a left turn in an *invisible car*?"

Devon grumbles to himself. "Force of bleeding habit—"

He barely gets the sentence out before something slams

into them. Ciere jerks sideways, crashing into her door. Her eyes fly open and she scrambles to sit upright. Out of the corner of her eye she sees a red sedan attempting to merge into the overpass lane.

The impact registers in Ciere's mind as a spike of pain. She lets out a groan and the illusion shatters. Even without her immunity, she would know that everyone can see them. Because everyone starts honking.

The crash nearly sends the SUV into a spin. Devon jerks the steering wheel into a straight line, the tires screaming in protest. Ciere presses a hand to the cold window, trying to steady herself.

"You know the problem with driving an invisible car?" yells Devon as the car shudders. "People can't see you!"

"Well, they can now," she snaps back. "Maya, you want to take over?"

"Not if we want to live!" says Devon loudly. "I, for one, don't fancy dying in a five-car pile-up!"

"Also, I'm pretty sure we just traumatized a student driver!" calls one of the passengers.

"Isn't someone going to call the cops on us?" says Alan tightly, gripping the back of Ciere's seat. "A car just literally appeared in the middle of a freeway."

"Please," says Devon, hitting the horn and swerving around another driver. "That's the wonderful thing about this car. The plates say something along the lines of, 'Property of the government, so please piss off.' "

"Even so," Alan begins to say, but is interrupted.

"Here, here!" Maya suddenly says. "Take the turnoff here!"

Devon grits his teeth and throws his foot onto the brake. Ciere's palms hit the dashboard, and she braces herself. The car shivers, probably catching on a patch of ice, before cutting off yet another commuter and shooting down an off-ramp. The ramp twists in a full circle, coming around and melding into a smaller street. Maya directs him through several streets, until the neighborhoods are bleeding away, and there's a gravel road up to their left. "Take that," says Maya.

"What happens if we miss this train?" asks Ciere, glancing back at Maya. The woman's face is grave and she doesn't answer.

44

CIERE

The train station is tucked away, out of sight from the city, placed where it won't bother anyone. A clump of snow-spattered trees have crept close to the road. It's as if nature is slowly trying to retake this area. The gravel road opens up and Ciere finds herself looking at a square block of concrete and glass. "No one wants cargo trains near their homes," mutters Devon. "Stick them on the edges of the city, and no one cares."

The station is protected by a chain-link fence and a guard. Maya tells them to drive right up. Devon does so, his fingers tight on the steering wheel.

Maya reaches into the front seat, a piece of construction paper tucked between her index and middle fingers. "Pass him this."

Devon takes the paper and Ciere sees the star scribbled on it.

The SUV rolls gently to a halt and Devon hits the window controls. A gust of cold wind makes Ciere shiver.

The guard ambles up to the car. He's armed with little more than a radio and a baton, but he still looks formidable. "Yeah?"

Wordlessly, Devon passes him the paper. The man accepts it, rubs his thumb over the star, and nods. "No one else inside. Everyone's taking a snow day." He snorts, as if the fresh snowfall is nothing. "Go on in."

Devon swallows, looks to Ciere, and then gently presses on the gas. Ciere can't believe getting in is this easy—she was expecting bribes or threats.

"His sister was one of the first people Sen helped get out," says Maya, as if guessing her thoughts.

Maya instructs Devon to park near one of the train cars, and Ciere is willing to admit that she's glad the bumpy, hair-raising ride is over. Nearly in unison, every single car door swings open. Someone opens the trunk. Ciere stumbles out of the car, ballet flats slipping on the icy ground. Alan follows her.

"Stay with the car," Maya tells Devon. "Yell if you see anyone."

Devon gives her a flat stare.

"Stay with the car, UAI intern," says Maya. She smiles, but it's a hard little expression. "I don't take chances. That's how we've managed to stay ahead of everyone."

Devon heaves a long-suffering sigh and leans against the SUV's side. He crosses his arms. "Fine. I'll just stay here and twiddle my thumbs."

"I'd prefer if you kept a lookout," replies Maya. "We'll be back soon. You—illusionist girl. Help the man with the duffel bags. You, pretty dark-haired boy—you get these bags."

Ciere finds herself being loaded up with two heavy duffel bags and it takes her a moment to realize she's carrying someone's whole life. Whatever these people want to take with them, they have to take now. There's no coming back, not for them. Ciere grips the bags tightly and follows Maya and the passengers.

The train station is just like the one in Newark: it's crisscrossed with tracks, abandoned train cars block out huge areas of space, and nearly every surface is coated with spray paint. Taggers must find ways in at night—the security isn't that great. One guard and a fence won't keep out anyone really determined. The ground is mostly train tracks, turned a rusty orange with age and use.

One train is already sitting on a track, waiting while a mechanized arm is attached somewhere behind the engine.

"Some still require fuel," says one of the passengers, seeing her stare. "Those are the ones we jump on."

Dawn has fully broken over the horizon, and the nearby trees cast dappled shadows over the ground. Maya moves through the tracks with practiced speed. "Some trains just blaze on through," she calls back, hurrying over a long track. "You need to be careful—with no drivers, these trains won't care if you're in the way."

Ciere picks up her pace.

"There," calls Maya, and she hurries around a rusty green car.

The train is a faded bronze, probably a passenger train that was converted at some point. Maya grabs a crate and hurries up to one of the cars. Something metal gleams in her hands—a lock pick set, Ciere realizes. That's how she'll get them to safety.

Ciere leans up against a stack of crates. There's no place to sit, but leaning takes some of the ache from her legs. She lets out a breath, and most of her fear goes with it. Her muscles go loose with relief; they're safe. With that certainty, something horrible drops into her stomach. A thought she wishes she could take back—but she can't.

Because as much as she's come to rely on him, Alan doesn't belong to her. And he has his own priorities.

"You should go," she says.

Alan doesn't glance at her. "What?"

Ciere tries to clear some of the rust from her throat. "With them, I mean."

That gets his attention. He doesn't make eye contact, but his head snaps in her direction and his lips part, a sharp inhalation hissing through his teeth.

"What?" The word remains the same, but the inflection is wholly different.

She swallows.

"You could leave the country," she says. She speaks quietly; while the others are loading into the train, she doesn't want them to overhear. "Even if the feds think you're dead, and I can clear your name with the Syndicate, it'll never be safe for you here. You could find a place in Canada. I don't know, go look for a cabin or something. Maya's contacts could help.

"I'm pretty sure Canada isn't as obsessed with re-creating the vaccine as the U.S.," she adds, when he doesn't say anything. "You could go to school or get a job. You could have a life."

Still he remains silent.

"You want the formula to be safe," she says, even though each word hurts. "I get it. Your aunt's dead and you don't have a home here. Conrad taught you how to protect yourself. Kit got you fake tags. You don't have anything tying you down."

"You want the formula to be safe," repeats Ciere, and finally, she looks away. She can't say the words if she's looking at him. "I just—you've risked enough for me. And I—"

Because she's looking away, she doesn't see him move. Not until he's touching her, hand on her arm, angling himself so that he's before her. She opens her mouth to say something along the lines of, *What the hell*, when he kisses her.

Her perception fragments. All she knows is that Alan is kissing her. Fisting his hands in her jacket. Drawing her closer to him. It is the kind of kiss that takes no prisoners—raw heat and sharp angles, so good, it almost hurts. Touching him feels like sinking into a bath that's a few degrees too hot—all her muscles contract and her lungs seize up.

Her fingers are digging into the front of his jacket. She feels a button go, slip away, but she doesn't release her hold.

Alan pulls back with a gasp. For a moment, neither of them moves. His forehead rests against hers, fingers still tangled in her hair, and she hasn't released his jacket.

"Ciere," he says, the word a whisper against her lips, but then the cargo container next to him explodes.

Ciere falls to her knees, ducking out of the way. The roar of a gun makes her wince. She sees him in the moment before she hits the ground.

The pale-haired hit man stands not twenty feet away, a shotgun in one hand.

45

CIERE

Ciere drops to the ground, behind a pile of wooden crates. Her mind reels. The hit man. He's alive—she didn't kill him. Part of her is almost relieved at the thought. She's not a murderer.

The relief lasts only a moment, followed by a swell of panic. Ciere's conscience is safe, but the rest of her isn't.

Ciere hears the passengers cry out. Maya shouts, "Come on!" Ciere glances back and sees the last of the passengers scramble into a train. Maya slams the door shut behind them, the metal reverberating as the lock clicks into place. Already, the train is creaking, the engine heating up. It'll be leaving in a minute or two—but that might not be enough time.

The hit man's white-blond hair is streaked with dried blood, and there's a fury on his face she's never seen before.

His expression was always steady and implacable, but now his teeth are bared and fingers tight on his gun.

But how, she thinks. He shouldn't have been able to find them—they managed to outrun the feds, there's no way...

The tracker.

They never ditched the tracker. Getting away from the feds was so chaotic that the broken bracelet slipped her mind, but it must still be in Maya's bag.

Maya herself crouches behind a snowbank, her eyes squeezed shut. She looks like a person readying herself for a leap into freezing water. Her lips press together and she pulls Gervais's Glock out of her jacket. Ciere watches her lips silently count to three. Then Maya herself blurs, becoming little more than a pale outline. If Ciere hadn't been looking for her, she never would have seen the woman rise to her feet and fire two rounds at the Alberani hit man.

The man lunges to one side, turning his fall into a practiced roll. Still keeping low to the ground, he returns fire.

The moment he pulls the trigger, a wave of dread washes over Ciere. Maya may have managed to kill Pruitt, but that was a fluke. This woman isn't a professional assassin—she's an illusionist who has been relying on her immunity to get by. She didn't anticipate that the hit man wouldn't need to see his target. He could judge where his attacker was based on the bullets' trajectory.

All of these thoughts rush through Ciere in half a second. She screams, "GET DOWN!"

The pale-haired hit man pulls the trigger before Maya can react.

The distant rumble of an oncoming train swallows up the shot. Ciere never hears the crack of the gun, but she does see its result.

Maya Cooper flickers into sight, a startled look on her face. She falls to one knee, manages to stay upright for a moment, before sinking into the snow.

She doesn't get up.

Alan recovers first. He moves before Ciere, rushing toward the fallen Maya. A cry lodges in Ciere's throat—she wants to tell him not to bother—but it's not the woman he's after. He snatches up her fallen weapon, then scurries back behind a wooden pallet. He glances toward Ciere, who remains crouched on the ground, frozen with shock. Alan checks the gun over with a nearly professional eye, then raises it and fires.

A bullet embeds itself in a crate an inch from the hit man's nose. He jerks back, bringing the shotgun up, aiming toward where Alan's shot came from.

Terror courses through Ciere. She's not armed; she can't fight back.

"You might need a weapon."

Guntram's voice comes back to her, steady and cold, and she grabs hold of it like a lifeline.

Blinking several times, she tries to settle the panic in her mind. She draws up an illusion of Alan, pushes it into the real world, and manipulates it the way she might a hand puppet. Illusion-Alan rises to his feet, darting through the crates, in the opposite direction of the real Alan.

The hit man may be an eludere, but even Daniel admitted his instincts could be wrong—especially when there was no time to really feel them. She's counting on the hit man's anger and his injury. She can see the bandage wrapped around his skull; she must have concussed him. And head injuries wreak havoc with immunities.

The hit man lets out a growl and shoots twice at the illusion. When his gaze sweeps over the area, Ciere ducks back behind her crate and breathes hard. Alan has gone behind the snowbank, still holding the gun between two hands. Conrad must have taught him firearms. Alan doesn't handle the weapon with the same ease as the hit man, but he doesn't cringe away from it, either.

The hit man stops shooting. The ringing silence swells, blocking out all other sounds. Ciere can't even hear herself panting for breath.

For the longest moment, neither moves. Ciere can't—her legs have locked up. She wants to stand, to peek and see if the hit man is following her illusion. She feels sick with adrenaline, shaking so hard, she can barely keep her teeth from chattering. It's all she can do to keep the illusion of Alan moving, hopefully drawing the hit man's attention. If he follows it around, Alan might have a clean shot.

As if summoned by her thoughts, Alan looks up and his gaze meets hers.

Then the shotgun blasts again, and something tears through Ciere's shelter.

None of the rounds hit her. She waits for an impact that never comes—and she's so focused on waiting for it that she doesn't see the crates begin to tip. The shotgun blast unsettles the crates, and one of them falls.

Ciere doesn't move fast enough.

Pain flashes across her legs and she stumbles. Her back hits something hard and her vision swims. There's a hard digging sensation behind her left ear, and when her fingers reach up to pry it away, she realizes it's the edge of another crate.

She lies on her back, crumpled beneath a half-shattered mass of wood.

The roar of the shotgun makes her jerk upward. She tries to pry off the crate, desperately pushing at it, but it presses down, implacable and heavy.

She looks up, sees the hit man's turned back. He's reloading, feeding fresh rounds into the shotgun.

With mounting horror, Ciere watches the hit man rack the shotgun and fire again. She has no time to think, no time to react—she only knows she can't stop this man by herself. She isn't physically powerful enough to take on this man and win; she already tried and failed.

The rumble of the oncoming cargo train makes the crates wobble. Ciere pulls one leg free, managing to twist around until she can see the scene unfold.

Only an empty track separates Alan and the hit man. The advancing train is on that track, but Ciere has no hope that it will provide any cover. It's still a good ten seconds away and the shotgun is already fitted to the man's shoulder, raised and aimed directly at Alan's retreating back.

He's going to kill Alan.

He's going to kill them all.

She can't move. She can't fight back. So she does the only thing she can think of. She reaches into herself, into the burning adrenaline and absolute panic, and finds an illusion.

A perfect copy of Ciere appears behind the hit man. The illusion must catch the man's eye, because he whirls around, prepared to fire on her.

The illusion balls up its fist and hits him.

Ciere feels the contact, a spike of pain through her own skull, senses the way her illusion's knuckles make contact. She expects the fist to go right through, but it doesn't. Illusion-Ciere hits the man hard enough that he staggers backward, stunned by the strike. It wouldn't work if he weren't exhausted, frenzied, and probably concussed, but the man stumbles and barely manages to right himself. His attention snaps to the illusory girl, so focused on her that he doesn't notice where he is standing.

In the middle of the train tracks.

The fury and frustration play out on his face and he raises the gun again, ready to fire on the girl. His whole being is trained on the girl he was hired to kill. His bleary, livid gaze snaps to the illusion of Ciere. All he sees is the girl.

Not the approaching train. Doesn't feel the shaking of the ground nor hear the roar of the engines. His world is silent, peaceful. He senses nothing.

Ciere makes sure of it.

46

DEVON

The moment he hears the gunshots, he knows everything is falling apart.

Devon goes still.

He needs to do something. He needs to stand up, to help, to react. But his whole body is frozen, indecision seeping into his muscles like a paralytic.

He looked this up once. Apparently, it's an eidos thing—people with perfect recall experience memories much more strongly than regular people, and it can inhibit present actions. It was why eidos make for horrible soldiers. They can't deal with the things they see. Apparently, all of the eidos involved in the Pacific War ended up with major PTSD.

The study concluded with the depressing statistic that

eidos were twice as likely to become addicts or victims of suicide.

It also means Devon's mind has a tendency to splinter in two different directions. Just like it's doing now.

He tries to shake off his indecision. His legs falter and then he's moving them, rushing toward the trains. He nearly trips over the tracks, his long legs carrying him forward. The sound comes again, impossibly loud, like thunder brought down to earth. Devon lurches around one of the train cars and sees the scene spread out before him.

Ciere is half-buried beneath a crate and barely managing to sit upright. Someone is on the ground and there is a white-haired man holding a shotgun, aiming at... Ciere. *An illusion*, Devon realizes. Conjured by the real Ciere, who is still on the ground.

Devon sees it then. Sees the train coming down the tracks, impossibly fast. The white-haired man stands before it, raising his gun to shoot at the illusion of Ciere.

He isn't moving, though, like any sane person would. He's not leaping away from the train.

Because he can't see it, Devon realizes, and his blood runs cold. And so the pale-haired man doesn't move, doesn't even flinch—

Devon closes his eyes.

There is a crunch, like a soda can being thrown under a

car tire, then it's swallowed up by the roar of the train. For a second, Devon feels a twist in his midsection—*the train operator is going to be traumatized*—then he realizes that the train is unmanned. There will be no driver to traumatize. The train will continue on, uncaring, until it reaches its destination and someone notices the blood staining its grill.

Devon waits another moment, until he's sure he won't see anything. When he blinks the world back into view, he sees what's left of the scene.

Ciere remains on the ground, one hand extended as if reaching for something. The expression on her face is something he's never seen before; it's utterly still and calm. There is no fear, no anger, no anything. Her eyes never leave the place where the man stood.

There's no sign of the man—just the train rattling on its tracks, a steady thrumming of metal and engines.

She killed that man. Killed him with an illusion as surely as if she'd picked up a gun and shot him.

Then Alan is there, pushing the crates off her, talking in a low voice. She doesn't answer. Alan's touching her, talking to her, pulling her against him. She goes willingly, folds into his arms, and he presses a kiss to her forehead.

Nausea rolls through his stomach, and he feels like he might throw up. He takes a step back, and hits a stack of wooden pallets. *Acute stress reaction*, part of his brain chirps, as if it can't remain silent. *Your body is being flooded with adrenaline and norepinephrine. You're starting to disassociate yourself from this event by remembering facts and figures.*

He's shaking, he realizes. Shaking so hard, it feels like his bones might fall apart. He grasps at a pallet, tries to steady himself. That man—that man is dead.

Ciere killed him. Hit him with an illusion and then made sure he didn't see an oncoming train.

His mind begins to regurgitate the definition of *overkill*, but he manages to quash it. There—there had to be another way. Maybe use the illusion to knock the gun from the man's hands. Or distract him until they could all get away.

This shouldn't be happening. Devon was supposed to help some criminals escape, help keep his thoughts away, give Aristeus the metaphorical finger, and everything was supposed to go…well, not smoothly. His life never went smoothly. But this—this—

It wasn't supposed to be like this.

Devon takes a step back and the movement draws Ciere's attention. Even at this distance, he feels it when Ciere meets his eyes.

She killed that man.

She doesn't let go of Alan, but she angles herself toward Devon. He sees a question in her face, almost a plea. She looks how he felt, months ago when he was clinging to a car window, begging her not to leave him. He remembers the cold desperation, sees it clearly in her face now.

"You don't belong with us."

He doesn't go to her. He walks back to the SUV on wooden legs. His body takes over and he lets it—picking up the keys from where he dropped them in the snow, unlocking the SUV, and sliding the seat belt around his waist. He puts the key in the ignition and turns it.

He drives away and he doesn't look back.

47

DANIEL

For the briefest moment, Daniel is suspended in midair. His momentum carries him out, away from the building, and he feels like he's flying. He can't see anything; his face is buried in the back of Gervais's coat, but he imagines the wide-open sky. The gray clouds, the snow trickling down. He can imagine drifting upward into that sky and never coming down.

Then gravity takes hold. His stomach swoops, suddenly weightless, and he grasps blindly at Gervais. He's not sure why he's holding on so hard, only that he doesn't want to die flailing and alone. If he's going, then he wants to be holding on to something solid.

He's supposed to see his life flash before his eyes. He's supposed to see his old regrets, his hopes, his dreams—but no. What Daniel sees, in the moments before his death, are the stained patches of Gervais's jacket.

And that's all he has time to think before his arms nearly wrench from their sockets.

The jerk whips through his body, like snapping a belt. He feels the sensation travel from his neck to his knees, and if he survives this, he is going to have horrible whiplash—

That's when he realizes something.

He's not dead. He's not even falling anymore.

The ground is ten feet below, snowy and pockmarked with footprints. Daniel clings to Gervais's jacket, and so far the thick wool has held.

It takes a moment for his mind to register the obvious. They're in midair. There is nothing below them but snow and the first cops on the scene. The men and women stand next to their cars, mouths agape, staring up at Daniel and Gervais. At the levitating man and the teenager clinging to his lapels.

It's only when the fall begins again, slower and more controlled, that the word comes to Daniel.

Levitas.

When his feet hit the ground, Daniel staggers away from Gervais. His shoulders scream with pain and a deep ache settles into his back. He shakes himself, glances up.

Several of the cops have guns raised.

"Stand down," yells Gervais. He already has his badge in hand, flipping it open for all to see.

One of the cops swallows audibly. Then he lowers his gun.

"The perps were going east when I last saw them," barks Gervais, and then says something else.

The words blur together because all Daniel can think is, *You're just like me. You liar—you're just like me—you're just like the rest of us.*

Only after the cops have vanished into the garage does Daniel round on him. "What the fuck?"

Gervais's craggy face is hard with anger. "I could say the same. You just—you tried to kill me—"

"Does anyone at the Bureau know?" interrupts Daniel.

Gervais hesitates, then shakes his head. "No one who works at the Adverse Effects Division can be immune," he snarls, still furious. "Supposedly it would present a conflict of interests."

Which means he's been lying for *years*. To his coworkers, to his friends, maybe even to himself. Daniel learned a long time ago that the best way to con someone, to lie to someone, is to repeat a lie so often that even the liar believes it.

"What the hell were you thinking?" Gervais snaps. "If I wasn't…if I wasn't…"

"A levitas," says Daniel numbly.

Gervais flinches, as if the mere sound of the word is painful. "Don't say it."

"Why not?" Daniel takes a wobbly step back, toward the cement wall. "It's true. You're a liar, you out-lied me of all people. I should've known. I should've sensed it."

"I never use it." Gervais grinds his jaw, biting off the words.

Daniel laughs, a little hysterical. "Not unless someone pushes you off a ledge."

Anger flashes across Gervais's face. "If I wasn't...what I was, you would be dead. So would I, as a matter of fact." He steps closer, until Daniel is nearly pressed up against the parking garage's wall. All the cops have gone inside, and he can hear the sounds of them raiding the interior. People are crying out, fearful and startled. He hears the whispers of intent to run, and he knows how they feel.

It's not that Daniel wanted to die. It's just, he can't live like this.

"I can't do this anymore," says Daniel hollowly. "I've betrayed every person I've ever cared about. My mind isn't my own anymore and I'm just—I'm just this tool..."

Gervais looks at Daniel with wide eyes, staring at him the way Daniel imagines sailors used to look for stars in the sky— fixed points in a constantly moving world.

"You're a criminal," says Gervais.

"Don't you think I know that?" The words rip themselves through Daniel's throat. "But I can't—I'm not—not anymore—"

Gervais's hand hits Daniel in the breastbone. It's not a blow, more like a steady touch, and it snaps Daniel back to himself. Gervais is shaking his head.

"You're a criminal," he says again, voice like gravel.

Daniel stares at him. Tries to understand and fails. "He can control me," he says, and doesn't need to explain. "I can't fight back."

Fresh fire blazes in Gervais's eyes. "Then be a better criminal."

He steps back, scrubs a hand through his hair, and looks at the oncoming FBI cars. He'll have coworkers here soon. Coworkers who will learn what he is and what he can do.

"Did you let that family go?" asks Daniel. "The one you told me about—that immune family. Did you really take a wrong turn?"

Gervais doesn't answer. He takes a breath, then strides away. The last Daniel sees of him is Gervais clenching his fist, jaw tight with determination, and he vanishes around the corner. Maybe to help with the raid. Or ... maybe not.

Daniel leans against the wall, sinks down it, into the snow, and remains there. Shock settles into his limbs; he should be dead but he isn't, and he's still acclimating to that fact. As he sits, he notices a gleam of gold.

Gervais's FBI badge rests in the snow.

Daniel reaches down and picks up the badge, rubs his thumb over the embossed shield.

It warms at his touch.

48

CIERE

She doesn't remember exactly what happens after she kills the man.

The world narrows, goes fuzzy at the edges, until all that's left are flashes of memory.

—Devon looking at her with shock. Looking at her in a way she's only ever had cops look at her. Like she's something to be feared and distrusted. He turns away, and doesn't come back—

—The sight of Maya's body, prone on the ground—

—The train with the refugees, slowly gaining speed, a whirl of graffiti and icy metal as it vanishes around a turn—

Safe. The passengers are safe. We did it.

—Alan's hand around her arm, towing her. She feels like a puppet in his hands, and she's willing to give the control over to him—

—The sensation of movement. She's walking, jogging even, and she's not sure why. Alan's hand is tight on her forearm and he's saying something—

We can't get caught. We have to move.

—A bus station bathroom. Cold, the same color and shape as a cement block. A wet paper towel working through her fingers—

—Someone tightly wrapping her injured wrist—

—A bus. The rhythmic rocking of the engine, the low murmur of other passengers, the familiar smells of body odor and stale seats.

Time passes. It slips by in swift leaps and bounds, almost like she has a fever. She can't hold on to a single moment; she opens her eyes and she's in the city. Then there are trees and frozen fields. They're leaving DC—no, they've left DC. They're getting off a bus and getting onto another one.

The only constant is Alan. She can sense him next to her, a steady presence between her and the rest of the world. His voice is low when he pays for another set of bus tickets, and she wonders vaguely if they're headed back to Philadelphia. She closes her eyes and lets the world drift by.

Sometime later, Alan is tugging on her arm, half dragging her off the bus. There's more walking and the cold bites into her skin, nearly enough to rouse her. She stumbles along, barely able to keep up. When they finally stop walking, a house comes into view.

She vaguely recognizes the building. It's different, covered in snow. A farmhouse.

They're in Gettysburg.

All at once there are other voices, familiar voices, but she barely hears them.

—*In shock. I need Guntram—maybe another illusionist can help—*

—*Alberanis—*

—*Dead. I didn't kill him—*

Then she's inside the house, her feet automatically moving as two pairs of hands help her up the stairs. The attic. The familiar attic with its cots. She finds herself sitting on her old cot, running her fingers over the worn duvet.

—*Get some sleep. We'll talk in the morning.*

She does.

49

DANIEL

D aniel has never spent much time at UAI headquarters. Even after his recruitment, he only stuck around long enough for the initial training and lectures. He avoids the building when he can, choosing to spend his time with the FBI agents instead. They may hate him, but at least they're honest about it.

Or Daniel thought they were honest.

Daniel went back to Gervais's office and found several of his colleagues scouring it. "No sign of where he went," one was saying. Daniel, not daring to get too close, only caught snatches of the conversation.

"I knew it," said another. "I knew something was wrong with him."

"Probably working for a crime family the whole time—"

"Sympathizer."

"Traitor."

"Freak."

Gervais's colleagues hadn't known. None of them knew. Of course, Daniel didn't know, either, but he wasn't exactly the person Gervais would confide in.

Once the office had been thoroughly searched and emptied, Daniel snuck back inside. He grabbed up Gervais's chair, the rolling one with the thick leather seat. It was worn and comfortable and Gervais wouldn't be needing it anymore. Daniel hauled it out of the building and ignored the looks of passersby when he hailed a cab.

Now he pushes the rolling chair down the hall of the UAI offices. That creepy receptionist, Tiresia, cocks her head at his approach. "What...?" she says slowly, probably hearing the squeaky roll of the chair's wheels.

"It's Daniel Burkhart," says Daniel curtly. "And my new chair."

Tiresia shakes her head and her dark hair sweeps across her shoulders. "I haven't learned your step yet," she says, almost regretfully. "You don't come here enough."

"Good," says Daniel, and pushes the chair past her.

He finds an empty office. Not a cubicle, because screw that. He wants walls, windows—he wants a damn office. He takes a permanent marker to the office's door. It's not a metal plaque, but it'll have to do.

DANIEL BURKHART

The empty office consists of a desk, a chair, and a bookshelf. Daniel shoves the chair into the hallway, replaces it with his own. Then he reaches into his pocket and withdraws a single item: a Hello Kitty bobblehead. He places it on the desk—a lone ornament.

He'll add more things later—plants, office supplies, maybe some books. It'll look like a real office when he's done.

He's sitting in the worn chair, Gervais's FBI badge clasped loosely in one hand, when Morana shows up.

"You vandalized the door," she says, but she sounds amused.

"My door," Daniel corrects. "My office now."

She gives him a flat look. "Why?"

"Because Gervais was a liar," says Daniel. "He pretended to be normal, but he wasn't. He lied to me for months and I believed him. And you know what? I'm fucking sick of it. I'm sick of trying to work with people who lie to me. Who claim to despise what I am, when all the while they're the same. And you people may terrify the shit out of me, but you're not liars. You're honest about what you do."

His words seem to convince her. Probably because there's a vein of truth in them. She smiles at him, an honest smile rather than her usual flash of canines. "Good," she says. "Good." She turns to leave. "You still can't have the office, though."

"Just try to take it from me," he says cheerily. She snorts and lets the door click shut behind her.

She believed him. She would believe him.

Daniel smiles. For the first time in months, things feel right. He holds Gervais's words close, tries to brand them into his mind. *"Then be a better criminal."*

Gervais is gone and he won't be coming back. Too many people saw what he is. It makes Daniel hurt a little, to think about it. He liked Gervais, despite himself. He'll miss him. He owes the man a debt.

He thinks he gets it, though. Gervais was a levitas, working for people who hated people like him. An agent on the inside, even if he probably was conflicted about it. Maybe Gervais did it out of a sense of honor; maybe he did it to protect people he knew. Maybe he did it to protect himself—whatever the reason, Gervais spent years amidst his enemies.

And if he can do it, so can Daniel.

The world realigns. Because Daniel may be trapped with the UAI, may be cut off from his former life, may have nothing left, but he remembers what he is.

Daniel Burkhart is a con man and a thief. And he's living at the heart of enemy territory.

It's time to go back to work.

50

CIERE

For hours, she doesn't move.

She doesn't sleep, doesn't eat, doesn't talk. Ciere remains on her cot, curled into a ball, unwilling to face the world.

She wraps fingers around the cot's frame. Without it beneath her, she feels like she might fold onto the floor. She feels wrong. As if she's been broken and someone put her back together with the wrong-size bones. Something inside her has shifted and she's unsure how to live with it.

She hears people moving past her door, but she's left alone. Not even Alan stops by, and she isn't sure if that's a relief or not.

Finally, the door opens and someone steps inside. She recognizes his scent first—gunpowder and aftershave.

Guntram.

She slowly sits up, swinging her legs over the side of the cot, her bare skin catching on the metal springs. She must've torn the sheets off at some point during the night, tossing and turning.

Guntram has a head wound. A white bandage wraps around his temple and there are deep shadows beneath his eyes. He shuts the door behind him, walking stiffly into the room and settling onto a cot across from Ciere.

"Alan brought you here," he says. "Even though he knew it would put him in danger. He thought your illusion might have damaged you somehow—he wanted another illusionist to take a look at you."

She doesn't reply.

Guntram leans forward. He takes Ciere by the chin, tilting her head back and forth in a clinical fashion. Out of nowhere, he pulls out a penlight and flashes it into her eyes. She pulls out of his grip, blinking as her pupils contract painfully. "What the hell?" The words are ragged, but she manages to say them. "What was that for?"

Guntram eases back, smiling a little. "No reason. Just thought it might snap you out of it."

She rubs at her stinging eyes.

"You're fine," says Guntram. "You need a shower, but you're fine."

She shakes her head, almost wishing she could sink back into her numb stupor. Things are coming back to her, things she doesn't want to think about. "Did—did he tell you...?"

"Ashbottom told us everything." Guntram steeples his fingers and rests them on his knees. "He won't be punished for Pruitt's death."

"You believe him now." Bitterness creeps back into her voice.

Guntram gives her a steady look. "Yes. But even if I didn't, the man you took out... well, let's just say he fits the description of a professional hitter. After he dealt with you, it's likely the Alberanis would have paid him to kill me, too." He smiled faintly. "He would've failed, but there would have been casualties. You solved that problem for us. I'm considering it payment in full for any remaining debts." He sighs. "Hitters charge about sixty thousand for each kill, so technically the Syndicate might owe you money."

Nausea creeps up the back of her throat. She swallows hard. "I—I didn't mean to." She lets out a breath, but chokes on it, and her words come out on a sob. "I didn't want to." She rubs her hands together, then digs her nails into her palms, half hoping the physical pain will distract her.

All the humor vanishes from Guntram's face. He scoots off his cot and goes to sit next to Ciere. "I know. I know." His voice is softer than she's ever heard. She tries to hold another sob in, and it shakes her whole frame. He reaches down and clasps her hands, stilling them. "Would you feel better if I told you a secret?"

She doesn't reply.

"I was a politician," he says.

"I know." Another little shiver works through her.

Guntram huffs out a breath. "No, I mean I was really a politician. I was working my way up—I could've been president someday. Well, except for being an illusionist, but I managed to keep that secret. I had the money and the connections and I was damn good at my job. I left when I was in my prime. I—I left.

"I left," he says, fresh steel in his voice, "because I couldn't do the job I wanted to do anymore. I believe in the government and the good it can do. I believe in order and society—but after the war, our government focused on only two things: the immune and the threats other countries might pose. They only care about how many immune soldiers they can recruit, and if their enemies are doing the same. They stopped caring about the organized crime, about how many people were dying in mob wars or how crime families were practically running certain cities. I realized I couldn't stand by and do nothing. So I contacted Conrad, and several others I trusted. My wife and I agreed to move to Nevada, where some of the worst fighting was. And then we founded the Gyr Syndicate."

Ciere jerks in surprise, drawing her hands back. All this time, she thought he was just an enforcer. Just one of the Syndicate's higher-ups. She never thought he started the whole thing.

"Which means—" she says, because she gets it now—why the others were so wary of her. Because she is a real thief and they were just playing at it. Why the Syndicate consists of ex-military and cops. Why she's never seen them conduct a drug deal or smuggle their own weapons into the states. Why they don't play by the rules.

"You're vigilantes," she says, stunned.

Guntram exhales, and there's a slight groan to it. "I hate that word. We're a militia. Formed by American citizens who were scared that organized crime was getting out of hand. Which makes us criminals. But we've stopped drug runners, gunrunners, violent crime lords. We've tried to do it without blood, but we've killed when we had to. We—*I've* played judge, jury, and executioner."

Ciere tries to form words and fails. Guntram understands.

"We've portrayed ourselves as a crime syndicate because— and here's the ironic part—that's the only way the government will ignore us. So long as we're criminals, we're fine. But the moment we appear to be a rebellion..."

Ciere stares at him. "Are you a rebellion?"

"Not yet," says Guntram. "Maybe someday. But my point is...I never wanted to be a killer. Just like you didn't. I made a choice. I'm not sure if it was right. I only know that I couldn't stand by and let one more person get hurt when I could stop it."

"And me...?" Ciere says.

"When I found out what you were, I knew I wanted you to work with me," he says. "I thought I could teach you to harness your power, to have control over it. Your crime was rather petty when you get right down to it, and completely nonviolent. I thought you were a cause worth investing in, a powerful ally if I could recruit you."

"Would you have really turned me over to the feds?" she asks.

He smiles, a wry little expression. "I'm glad I didn't have to."

After so many bus rides, it's a relief when Guntram announces Conrad will be driving them back to Philadelphia. Alan has gathered up what's left of their belongings—and it's not much. Ciere's Hello Kitty backpack is brown now and smells of smoke. Alan's own bag was lost in the raid; all he has left is a wallet and his false ID tags.

"I can't believe it," says Alan faintly. "The Honda survived?"

Sure enough, the Honda Pilot is parked in the gravel driveway. There are a few new nicks, but it still looks functional.

Guntram pats the car, and the gesture reminds Ciere of how dog owners greet their favorite pets. "She's been through worse," says Conrad dryly, taking Ciere's backpack and tossing it into the backseat. "Let's go, kiddies."

Guntram's farewell to Alan consists of a jerky nod and the words, "Sorry for handcuffing you to a propane tank."

406

Alan climbs into the car.

Guntram leans in and rests a hand on Ciere's shoulder.

She says, "If you say something about responsibility with my power, I'll hit you again."

Guntram turns his startled laugh into a cough. "I was just going to tell you not to rob any more banks. At least not in my territory."

"Right," she replies. She reaches into her pocket and is surprised to find a scrap of paper in there. It's one she took from Maya Cooper, and she's surprised to see it survived everything. She thinks for a moment, lets her thoughts wander to the group of runaways who are on their way to Canada. She hands the paper to Guntram and says, "I'd look up Aditi Sen, if I were you. You guys have some common interests."

Guntram glances down at it, at the star, and then tucks the paper into his breast pocket.

The drive isn't long—only a few hours.

Alan and Ciere haven't really talked since the incident at the train station. There were brief words, mostly consisting of "good morning" and "pass the cereal." Sitting beside him for the whole car ride feels a little awkward. A numb shell separates her from the rest of the world, and she feels things at a distance. The cold air, the seat beneath her, Alan's presence—none of it really registers.

Conrad drops them off at the Wynnewood elsec gate. His tags won't let him through—he's not a millionaire or a criminal with millionaire tags. "Been nice working with you, Kitty," he says. "Never boring. And you, student." He reaches down and punches Alan on the shoulder. He says something in German that makes Alan redden and Conrad chuckle. He waves a brawny hand at them, executing a highly illegal U-turn and zooming back down the street.

Ciere and Alan give their tags to the elsec guards, who seem surprised at two teenagers on foot. But they're allowed through and they trek the last mile and a half to the house on Bolsover. Evening creeps in around them, and porch lights flicker as they pass by.

The Bolsover house hasn't changed. The driveway has been shoveled and there's salt on the sidewalk. Someone put the trash cans out. Ciere lingers by the gate, unsure if she wants to go inside yet. The house looks so familiar, yet feels so far away.

She wonders what Daniel is doing, if that hit man had a family, if anyone's found Maya's body yet, if Sen knows, if those passengers have reached Canada. What Devon might be doing. He left—there was no sign of the SUV when they left the train station. He might be back with his family—she hopes he is. He could be safe, protected, and never have to work for the UAI or crooks.

Or maybe the UAI arrested him.

"Ciere," says Alan softly, and it's the first thing he's really said to her since the train station. She just knows he's going to say something soothing and untrue, so she speaks before he can.

"It's not all right," she says, and is flooded with memory. She remembers when Magnus said those same words months ago.

"No," Alan agrees, "but you will be."

She glares at him. She's not sure why his certainty annoys her, but it does. "I thought you wanted to leave. You could've gotten on that train and gone to Canada or something. Why'd you stay?"

Why'd you kiss me? is what she really wants to ask.

He smiles at her. "I was told all my life that nothing was more important than the formula. It had to endure—which meant I had to endure. But if it was about to fall into the wrong hands, then I had to destroy it—and me. All my life people kept me hidden, kept me safe, and at the same time, told me to die if the circumstances demanded it. I was never me—I was always the sum of my mind.

"But when you fought that man," he says, "you weren't protecting the formula. You were protecting me." He moves closer, standing only a few inches from her. His closeness hums through her, and she tries to shake it off.

"You're the one person in the world who has known what I am and not looked at me any differently," he says. "You're the one person who looked at me and didn't just see the formula."

His hands ghost over her neck, thumbs skating along her jaw, and she couldn't pull away if she wanted to—which she doesn't. The warmth of his hands leaks through her numb shell, until it almost feels like she's back in the world again.

Her breath catches, but she manages to say, "So you don't want to be just Praevenir?"

"You said I could be more," says Alan. "I want to try. And...you?" The expression on Alan's face is something she's never seen before: determined, with just a bit of hesitation.

For a moment, she wonders if she should pull away. This could be disastrous—the last Fiacre will bring danger with him wherever he goes. But he's also brave and stupidly self-sacrificing, and he *gets* her. He's seen all of her and hasn't pulled away.

So neither does she.

The kiss, when it comes, is slower than the first time. It's gentle, the lightest brush of sensation, a question rather than a statement. His hand moves along her arm, tracing muscles, stroking whatever skin they can reach. He's gentle, his touches feather-light, like he's trying to be careful. Like he's trying to cradle a wild animal, to comfort it—like he thinks *Ciere* is the breakable one—

She digs her fingers into his collar and pulls him closer.

And that's when the front door bangs open. Ciere and Alan spring apart so fast that Alan trips over one of the trash cans, sending its contents all over the sidewalk. Ciere takes a step back, holding up a hand to shield her eyes. A figure walks toward the gate, unhurried and graceful, with long hair and wearing a waistcoat.

"I thought there was another stray cat in the garbage," says Kit Copperfield. "But no. Just two necking teenagers."

Another figure appears framed in the doorway behind Kit. Magnus grabs the front door, keeping it from swinging shut. "You're all right?" he says.

"They're fine," says Kit. He yanks the gate open and jerks his head at the door. "Shoes off at the mat. No snow on the hardwood floors."

A swell of affection makes Ciere grin. "That's it?" she says, choking back a laugh. She glances at Alan, sees him hurriedly scooping trash back into the can. He sets it upright, smiling all the while. "We've been with mobsters since July, done things you can't even imagine, and all you have to say is 'Don't ruin the floors'?"

Kit smiles. "Welcome home."

51

DEVON

Once he realized he was an eidos, Devon spent a lot of time reading anything he could find. He wanted to know everything. He read nearly every day. Legal documents. Old newspapers. He even found a medical textbook. And from that particular book, one passage stood out amid all the others.

The deepest wounds don't hurt. There are only so many pain receptors in the body and most of them are clustered around the surface. The brain won't feel a blade, but the skull will. The heart can't feel a bullet, but the skin it penetrated can.

Even back then, Devon understood. It only hurts when the weapon pierces you. Once it's inside, you'll never feel a thing.

There's a pub not far from the UAI headquarters.

Devon finds a booth in a corner and takes up residence there. He doesn't drink. He accepts glasses of free water with sliced lemon. It tastes fresh and clean, and he tries to ignore the way his trembling hands make the ice cubes clink together.

The place is nearly deserted, although since it's only ten in the morning, he's not surprised.

The shelves of liquor catch the dim light, holding it so that the bottles seem to glow from the inside. He knows how easily he can lose himself in one of them. It would numb him, separate himself from the sharp memories. He closes his eyes, tries to push the night away, and fails miserably.

He stares at his glass of water and wonders how many nightmares he will have. If he'll hear that pale-haired man's death over and over, like a sound bite set to repeat.

It would be so easy to drink. The numbness will inoculate him against nightmares—for a few hours, anyway.

But he doesn't want to be numb. Not anymore. Even this pain, this shock and horror, is better than oblivion.

He stays in the pub well into the afternoon, ordering something every hour so as to appease the staff. He picks at the food, shredding a roll and sipping free coffee refills.

And he thinks. He can't stop thinking, and this time, he doesn't try. He lets his mind chase itself in circles, like a dog let off its leash. Embracing the noise feels strange; he's so used to silencing it through drink or action.

413

He thinks and he thinks hard, and he always comes back to the same conclusion.

Ciere is an illusionist. Both her immunity and her life depend on showing the world one thing and doing another. The skill has bled into all other facets of herself. When she was with Devon, she only showed him the best parts of her life—the successful cons, the scores, the small thefts and the big wins. Even when something went wrong, it seemed like an adventure. Even after he watched her crew take down and kill a federal agent, it was still part of what he expected—he was among crooks and robbers. The cops were their enemy; it wasn't fun, but Devon could accept it as the natural order of things.

But this—watching criminal kill criminal, seeing Ciere's calculation, knowing that she played a role in that man's death—it churns his stomach until he wants to double over and clutch at himself. There is no sense to it.

She killed that man. She illusioned away a train—*a train*—from a single man. He's never seen her do anything like that, never knew she *could* do something like that. Her illusions were clumsy and tentative, and they worked on everyone around her. But she vanished that train from that man—only that man. Devon could see the train coming, and everyone else could, too. But her single-minded focus…the implications send a chill through him.

She wanted that man dead. She made sure it happened. She may not have blood on her hands, but she's still responsible.

And Devon can't reconcile that. Not with his best friend, not with the thief who steals from rich tourists and adopts stray dogs.

He buries his face in his hands, grinds fingers into his eyes.

Only when darkness has begun to creep into the sky does he fish into his wallet, withdraw what's left of his cash, and leave it crumpled on the table.

His legs carry him away from the pub, down slushy sidewalks and through holiday shoppers. He left Aristeus's car at the curb this morning and there's a parking ticket slid beneath a windshield wiper.

The government lots are easy to get into—he simply flashes his ID at a guard and they let him through. This parking garage is warm, clean, and filled with expensive cars. It couldn't be more different from the place he met Maya Cooper. He parks and walks into the UAI offices. He's not sure what he looks like; he's probably dirty and wet, and he can't begin to fathom what expression he's wearing. The guard at the front desk does a double take, but lets him go through.

Sia hasn't gone home yet. She hears his footsteps echo down the hall and her head lifts. "Lyre?" she says, unsure.

He doesn't answer aloud; instead, when he walks past her, he lets his fingers touch the back of her hand.

Yes, he thinks. *Is Aristeus here?* He pulls his hand away, before his thoughts have time to wander.

Sia blinks once, her hand following him, as if she wants the touch to linger. Then she draws back, as if realizing comfort won't be welcome. "No." She bites down on her lip. "I'm glad you came back."

He strides past her desk, through the row of cubicles until he comes to Morgan Clarke's—*no*, he thinks—*Morana's* door.

He walks inside and says, "Where's Aristeus?"

Morana takes him to a lift and uses her keycard to unlock a floor simply labeled G. They head down, far deeper into the building than Devon has ever ventured. It must be a secure training facility of some sort, because when they step out, they're faced with bolted blast doors, the kind used for bomb shelters. Devon blinks once, then watches as Morana activates a scanner. Her hand moves too quickly for him to grasp what she does, but then the scanner blinks green. She nods at him. "You still have your ID?"

The card that he used to bluff the cops with is still crammed in his wallet, the lanyard crinkled and mashed. He digs it out and Morana takes it, passing it over the scanner. It blinks green and she hands it back.

The doors rumble open and Devon steps inside.

The ceiling is too close and their footsteps echo. It smells like damp concrete. If this were a movie, Devon decides, it's where the stupid teenagers would get flayed alive by whatever monster was stalking them.

Beyond another set of doors is a firing range. Morana pauses by a rack along the wall and yanks off two sets of ear-muffs. Wordlessly, she hands one pair to Devon and he slips them on. The world goes silent and all he can hear is the air in his lungs and the beat of his heart.

It isn't comforting.

Aron Macourek/Aristeus stands before a set of targets. He's aimed a small handgun at them and is shooting, pausing between each squeeze of the trigger, his eyes narrowed and mouth set. Only when the last shell hits the ground does he realize that he isn't alone. His shoulders roll and he stretches, setting the gun on a small table. He pulls off his own pair of earmuffs.

Morana offers him a small smile and then turns on her heel, striding back to the elevator without a backward glance.

"I assume you brought my car back in one piece?" says Aristeus, cocking an eyebrow. But he looks interested, not angry. "We got a call from the local PD asking why the UAI was involved in a raid this morning."

"Yeah." Devon almost doesn't recognize his own voice. He

sounds tired, each word carried out on a heavy exhalation. "That would be my doing. Sorry about that."

Aristeus points at a wall, where there are several benches. "Do you want to talk about it?"

He shouldn't, but he does. Every inch of him is weighed down by the last twenty-four hours. And it's not like he has anyone else to talk to.

Devon goes to sit down. He grasps the lip of the metal bench, lets the sharp edges bite into his skin. "I can't tell you everything. There are things—people—that I won't talk about."

"Tell me what you can," says Aristeus simply. "I won't ask for more."

Devon does.

He leaves out Alan Fiacre and Ciere and Aditi Sen, telling him only about meeting up with Daniel and Gervais. How he joined up with Maya Cooper and the refugees, and how he used his UAI ID to help them escape.

When he's finished, Aristeus closes his eyes. He tilts his head back, lips parting as he inhales deeply. Resignation seeps into his youthful features.

"This is exactly the kind of situation I'm trying to avoid," he says, pinching the bridge of his nose. "People so afraid of their own government, they'd risk everything to flee. If I'd known…" He shakes himself, as if trying to brush away a memory. "I'd have offered them protection," he says, his voice firmer. "Brought them into the ranks."

"They'd be safer in the UAI?" Devon retorts.

"Divided, we're powerless." Aristeus glances around the firing range. "Together, we're safer. If we united, gathered as many immune as we could, we might be able to change things." He gives Devon a significant glance. "You've been on both sides of the line. You've worked with the UAI and with criminals. You know what we both have to offer.

"You're going to have to decide where you feel most at home." There's a note of apology in Aristeus's voice.

Devon knew that already. The certainty has crept up on him, and it's only now that he realizes he's ready to make this choice.

Ciere is his best friend. She never judged him for being an eidos. She encouraged it, with words and admiring glances, smiling when he could recite the layout of a building or hack a security camera. She illuminated the best parts of him. He loved feeling like this was who he was, who he was supposed to be. She was often irrational, short-tempered, and selfish, but he loves that about her, too. He is flawed, too, and they could be imperfect together.

She is his best friend. He loves her.

He closes his eyes for a moment, remembers the flash of anger and desperation in Ciere's eyes, remembers the sound of gunfire and the train. He remembers another man, a knife in his throat, his dark eyes wide. He remembers a girl with pale blonde curls and deft hands. Remembers her shouting at him.

He's seen the chaos, the blood, and the aftermath. He's seen the toll it takes, how running and hiding wears a person down. He's seen the haunted look in Alan Fiacre's eyes, and Devon knows he'll never understand what it means to live like that—on the run, never pausing for breath or to glance behind. He's not sure he wants to.

"You don't belong with us."

And the worst part is, he believes her now.

Devon squares his shoulders, tries to inhale and fails. "I already have."

With shaking fingers, he picks up the ID card and slips the lanyard around his neck.

ACKNOWLEDGMENTS

After writing four-hundred-something pages, you'd think another few paragraphs wouldn't be so difficult. But this part of the book always seems the most daunting.

All right. Let's dive in.

To my original editor and constant source of support, my mother.

To s.e. smith, for rereading this book about a thousand times and making sure I occasionally left my house. To Mary Elizabeth Summer, for all the e-mails and the dead mice. To Brittney Vandervelden, for putting up with three years of me not telling you what's going to happen to these characters. To Nikki Krueger, for keeping me in constant supply of deliciously trashy television shows. To Becky Gissel, without whom we would still be lost in Rome. To Jennifer Rush, for your kind words. To various family members—you know you who are—for going out into the world and demanding that random strangers read my book.

To all of the OneFours—hey, look: It's 2015. We made it!

To my family at Gallery Bookshop. Thank you for all the support, the coffee, and the inside jokes.

To my agent, Josh Adams. Thank you for all your hard work and encouragement. And to Tracey Adams, Quinlan Lee, and Samantha Bagood. All of you are awesome.

To the Little, Brown crew: Joel Tippie, who I cannot thank enough for these gorgeous covers; Tracy Shaw, for putting it all together; Andy Ball and Regina Castillo for their excellent copyediting; my wonderful publicist, Hallie Patterson; and to a fantastic production team, Renee Gelman and Rebecca Westall. And, as always, to the people who have made this all possible: Megan Tingley, Andrew Smith, and Alvina Ling.

And to my awesome editor, Pam Gruber, for...well, everything. I'm so glad to be working with you.

To the online YA community—all the bloggers, the tweeters, those who have written reviews. Those who have reblogged, pinned, liked, favorited, posted a quote or a picture. I adore each and every one of you.

To all the booksellers who have supported *Illusive*'s release. You are a fantastic bunch of people and I count myself lucky to be working among you.

And, again, I must finish by thanking you. Yes, you. The reader. Without you, I wouldn't be able to do this. I may be the one writing these words, but you're the one who brings them to life.

Thank you.